THE LONG HURT

RANDALL DENLEY

THE LONG HURT

A Kris Redner Mystery

OTTAWA
PRESS AND
PUBLISHING

Ottawa Press and Publishing

Copyright © Randall Denley 2022

ISBN 978-1-988437-81-1 (softcover)
ISBN 978-1-988437-83-5 (ePub)

Cover, design, composition: Magdalene Carson RGD / New Leaf Publication Design

Printed in Canada

Library and Archives Canada Cataloguing in Publication

Title: The Long Hurt : a Kris Redner mystery / Randall Denley.
Names: Denley, Randall, 1951- author.
Identifiers: Canadiana (print) 20220207577 | Canadiana (ebook) 20220207593 | ISBN 9781988437811
    (softcover) | ISBN 9781988437835 (EPUB)
Classification: LCC PS8607.E637 L66 2022 | DDC C813/.6—dc23

AUTHOR'S NOTE

Thanks to editor Deborah Richmond and book designer Magdalene Carson RGD for their fastidious work. Brian Shore provided useful background on the work of a private investigator. As always, the members of my readers' group helped make the book better. Thanks to my wife Linda, my brother Roger, and to Cathy Curry, Ray and Susan Foote, Marilyn MacIvor and Jeff and Angela Polowin.

THE LONG HURT

One
June 10, 1995

Ashley Tarrant woke up with that good feeling she always had on Saturday mornings. It was her favourite day of the week. She didn't have to get up early to catch the yellow school bus and on Saturdays, her parents took her down to the ByWard Market in downtown Ottawa where they had breakfast at a place called a diner. She always had two eggs with brown toast and bacon, plus real orange juice. Then the three of them would go for a walk in the market, looking at the flowers and all the farm stuff that was for sale.

It was the beginning of June, so Mama and Daddy always left her window open a little bit at night. She could smell the fresh breeze and hear birds singing in the maple tree that shaded her bedroom. It was already warm and she thought this would be the day that she got to wear the new pink dress her mother had bought for her two weeks ago. It was hanging in her closet, ready to go.

Mama and Daddy were already up and they would call her, like always, when it was time to get up. She could hear them talking downstairs and she could smell their coffee. It was gross. She rolled over and snuggled up with her Wrinkles stuffed dog. She'd had it since she was little, and she was eight years old now. It was her oldest friend.

Then Ashley heard the crunching sound of a car coming up their gravel driveway. That didn't happen too often because they lived in the woods, far from other houses. No matter what window you looked out, you couldn't see any neighbours. She wondered if it was Uncle Alex, Mama's brother. Sometimes he just dropped around. Mama said it was only because he wanted a free drink.

Ashley heard the doorbell ring, then the sound of heavy footsteps as Daddy went down the hall to answer it. She could hear him speaking to the person at the door but she couldn't tell what he was saying because she was at the back of the house, on the second floor.

Then Daddy's voice got louder and she heard him shout, "Get the hell out of my house." Right after that, Ashley heard the door slam back against the inside wall like it did sometimes when it was really windy. Then she heard the sound of glass breaking and something heavy falling over.

Ashley got quickly out of bed, but she didn't know what to do next. What was happening downstairs?

She heard Mama say "John, what's going on?" in a scared kind of voice. Then there was a loud, ringing bang. It was the sound they made on television when someone shot a gun, but she didn't think her Daddy had a gun. Ashley clutched Wrinkles to her and held him tight.

Then she heard Mama scream, "No! Please, no!" Then there was another loud bang. Something bad was happening to her parents, something really bad.

Then everything was silent and she held her breath so the man with the gun wouldn't hear her. She thought it was a man, and a big one. He'd have to be to overpower Daddy.

Then she heard heavy footsteps, coming up the stairs. It didn't sound like Daddy.

Ashley looked around desperately. She could hide in the closet, but wasn't that the first place he'd look? Then she thought of under the bed. Was that any better? She had to do something quick, so she scooted under the bed and squeezed up tight to the far wall. She tried to stay calm and quiet, but her heart was pounding. Were Mama and Daddy just hurt, or were they dead?

The footsteps stopped. Ashley figured the man had to be looking around, to see if he could see anyone else home. She scrunched down as small as she could.

Then she heard footsteps again. He was moving. The sound stopped right outside her door. The door creaked slowly open. Mama was always asking Daddy to oil it, but he kept forgetting.

She flattened her face to the floor and then she could see two black shiny boots and the bottoms of black pants. She started to pray, like Mama had taught her to do, but in her head, so the man couldn't hear.

He walked to the middle of the room, then she could see his boots moving as he turned around. He went to the closet and yanked open the door. She was glad she hadn't chosen that hiding place.

Then he was moving again and the next thing she knew, he was lying on the floor, staring at her. He wore a dark baseball hat and he had whiskers like Daddy got when he hadn't shaved for a few days. The man's breath smelled like cigarettes and his eyes were bloodshot.

"Come on out now. I won't hurt you," he said.

Ashley knew that was a lie, after what he'd done to her parents.

"No!" she screamed, and pressed herself against the wall.

"All right then," he said, his voice calm.

Then he snaked a big arm under her narrow bed, gripped her ankle and dragged her across the floor. Ashley grabbed the frame of the bed, but her little hands weren't strong enough to hold on.

The room seemed bright after being under the bed. She curled up on the floor like a baby, but when she peeked up, she could see that the man had a big black gun in his hand. It made a weird kind of stink. She looked higher, at his face, and was surprised to see that it didn't look mean, just kind of sad.

"What did you do to my parents?" she asked, trying to sound fierce.

He didn't answer, just looked at his gun, then at Ashley.

"Get on your feet," he said.

Ashley got up slowly. She could feel pee running down her leg.

Then he said one word: "Run."

Two

May 2021

Jenna Martin knocked on the open door of Vic Walker's office and said, "Sir?" in the most deferential tone she could muster. Walker held up his index finger, signalling her to wait a minute, finished reading whatever was on his computer screen, then closed it.

Before looking at her, he glanced at his watch, double checking that it was 9 a.m. precisely. Walker expected his coffee at 9, not at 8:59 or 9:01. It had to be a Starbucks grande, two shots of cream, darkest roast available.

Apparently pleased with her performance, Walker waved Jenna toward the desk and said, "Come," as if she were a dog, not an executive assistant. Jenna gritted her teeth and smiled, just like she had been doing all week. She stepped up to his desk and made eye contact. She knew Walker liked that, because he'd told her so.

His eyes were so startlingly blue that Jenna suspected coloured contacts. Why wouldn't his eye colour be fake? Everything else about the guy was. Walker was the head of a major national charity, but he still wanted you to think he was young and cool, even though he was 52. That's why he came to work in jeans and a blue Oxford-cloth shirt, tails hanging out, and wore leather deck shoes without socks. His hair was kind of long, but not rock star long, just enough to show you that he wasn't some suit.

Walker was also one of those guys who called himself a feminist and thought he knew more about women than women did themselves. The big thing he didn't know was that Jenna was a private investigator, not an office temp there on a five-day contract.

Walker took the lid off his coffee, inhaled the aroma, then said, "Am I right in thinking it's your last day?"

"It is. I guess it will be some other gig next week. Well, I hope so, anyway. Nothing lined up yet."

"Let's talk about that," Walker said. "Have a seat, Jas. You don't mind if I call you Jas do you?"

To Walker, Jenna was Jasmine Hamilton, the cute office temp, not Jenna Martin the PI. "Sure," she said. "All my friends do."

Walker smiled at the idea that he might be included among her friends. His teeth were remarkably white and looked exceptionally numerous.

'Oh," he said, like it had just occurred to him, "Why don't you close the office door, Jas. I like privacy when I'm conducting personnel matters."

Jenna felt the first flicker of hope that her five days of fetch and carry wouldn't be in vain. The other thing that Walker didn't know was that his boss, board chair Pamela Chambers, was out to nail his hide to the wall. Two female former employees had come to Chambers with sexual harassment complaints and it wasn't the usual bum-patting or tit-grabbing. One incident had been a hand up the skirt and in the other, Walker had asked for a blow job.

Problem was, neither of the women wanted to make their complaints official and there was no corroboration. Chambers wanted Walker out the door without having to write him a big cheque and she wanted it done discreetly. The charity Empowering Women Everywhere was largely dependent on handouts from the federal government. Any hint of a #MeToo scandal could cripple it.

The board needed an investigator, but not one that would gossip. Who better than a young, desperate PI without many community connections? It certainly didn't hurt that Jenna had spent five years with the Ontario Provincial Police, either.

It was the kind of case Jenna liked to take, doubly so because Chambers was an influential tech entrepreneur with a lot of contacts. Jenna had only been a private investigator for three months and so far her main business, what little there was of it, was from women who wanted to get the goods on cheating husbands. She hated to take their money.

Pamela had stumbled across Jenna in a social media scan. She had been blogging under the name The Female Detective and it had caught Pamela's eye.

Jenna closed the office door and pulled out the uncomfortable-looking chair in front of Walker's desk.

"No, no," he said. "I'm not a behind-a-desk kind of guy. Come over and sit on the couch with me."

That was promising. She was sure Walker had been mentally undressing her since she walked through his door as an emergency replacement for the last EA he had scared off. After working for years in a mostly-male environment, she was familiar with the lip-licking look. Walker hadn't stepped into dangerous territory yet, but he'd set his GPS. Jenna had her phone in the inside breast pocket of her jacket, with the recording app running, just in case. She didn't want a "he said, she said" situation.

The white leather couch was really more the size of a loveseat. When Jenna sat down, Walker was only inches away.

"So, have you enjoyed working here, Jas?" he asked, sweeping his arm expansively like where she worked was a lot like his big office with a view of Parliament Hill and the Gatineau Park beyond. In fact, her work station was a desk sitting just outside the office, so she'd be handy to come when he whistled.

"Absolutely," Jenna said with fake enthusiasm. "The work you do here is just *so* important, Vic. Sorry, can I call you Vic?"

"Of course. We're all on a first-name basis here. This isn't a corporate culture."

No, just the kind of place where women did all the coffee fetching and scut work, while the guy who ran the show enjoyed the big office, she thought.

"Tell me a little more about your background, Jas."

"Well, I'm from the area originally. I went to the University of Toronto where I studied sports psychology, then I played on the national soccer team."

In fact, all that was true. Walker wouldn't find any of it if he Googled Jasmine Hamilton, but by the time he got to that, her work would be done.

"Wow, national soccer team," he said, trying to act like he was impressed. Jenna figured he wasn't even interested. Most people weren't.

"So you've got a good education, good looks. Why are you still in the gig economy?"

"Well, you know what it's like. I guess I just need someone to give me my first big break."

"That's exactly the kind of thing I like to do, Jas. You probably know that I'm all about empowering and advancing women."

"Well, that's certainly what I hear."

"You look like someone who would fit in here, Jas, and the person you're filling in for, my EA, isn't coming back."

"Wow! That's interesting."

"The thing is, I need highly motivated people working here. Does that describe you?"

"Totally. Helping women and girls, that's just what I want to do. Plus, I'm a little bit desperate. You see, I've been looking after my mother. She's ill and not working. So, I really need a reliable job."

"Sorry to hear about your mom. Will she be OK?"

"I hope so."

"Me, too," Walker said. Jenna had to suppress a smile. At least the guy was consistent in his fake empathy.

"You seem like someone I'd want to see a lot more of, Jas. Would you like that, too?"

Jenna decided to sweeten the bait. She reached over and lightly touched Walker's knee, then said, "How much more of me would you like to see?"

Walker smiled and nodded, apparently pleased that his new EA Jas understood how the world worked.

"All of you, I would think," he said, moving along the couch so that the outside of their thighs touched. "What if I were to ask you to do something, like a little test?"

Jenna turned toward Walker, her face close to his, smiled, and said, "What, you mean like typing?"

"No, but close. It would involve your hand."

"Oh, and what would my hand be doing?" she asked, smiling and playing along.

"It would be stroking my cock. Would you be comfortable with that?"

And there we are, mission accomplished.

"I'm sorry, Vic. I'm afraid I'm going to have to disappoint you."

Walker reared back and said, "Really?" like he had never been disappointed before.

"Oh yeah," she said, "really." She reached into her jacket, pulled out her phone and showed him that it was recording.

Walker tried to grab the phone but Jenna pulled it back and said, "Don't even think about it, Vic. I was a cop for five years. Make that move and I'll have you face down and whimpering before you know what hit you."

Walker stood up, waving his arms like he hoped he might be able to fly away. "Who the hell are you, and what do you want?"

Jenna took a business card from her pocket and handed it to him. It was a nice card, gold-embossed, and it said Jenna Martin, Martin and Associates, Private Investigators. In fact, the only associate she had was her mom, Kris Redner, who looked after the office part-time, but it was always good to imply that you were at the head of an army.

"Who are you working for?" Walker demanded.

"Bad news there, Vic. My client is Pamela Chambers. You see, she's had complaints from a couple of your other victims, but Pamela is very fair. She wanted to make sure that you were as bad as they said. Now, I've got the proof."

"I'll give you money for that recording, a lot of money. How much do you want?"

"I'm afraid that's not how it works. I've already got a client."

Jenna was getting $4,000 for the week, plus she'd been able to expense three outfits. Having spent most of her working life in a uniform, she'd been a little light on office wear. She was sure that was a lot less than Vic was prepared to offer, but her integrity wasn't for sale.

"I can give you some free advice, though."

"What?" Walker said, his tone surly.

"You could resign by the end of the day. It would avoid a lot of unpleasantness for you. Play it off as a mid-life career change thing, looking for new opportunities to serve, that kind of bullshit. Or, you could talk about wanting to spend more time with your family. You've got a wife and two kids, right? I'm sure you don't want this to blow back on them."

Walked retreated behind his desk and collapsed into his plush executive chair. "You're ruining my life," he said.

"No, Vic. You already did that before I walked through your door. You're getting off easy, really. If the foundation wasn't so image sensitive, you'd be front page news."

"You bitch," Walker snarled. "Fuck you."

"Sorry Vic, you're not going to have that chance. But here, let me do one last thing for you."

Jenna picked up the still-hot coffee from Walker's desk and dumped it in his lap. He screamed. She felt like a fist pump, but maybe that would be unprofessional. In her short time in private investigation, she had learned that the work wasn't nearly as satisfying as arresting some perp, putting the cuffs on him and depositing him in the holding cells, but this had been a pretty close second.

 Three

I really shouldn't have been surprised by the way things had turned out. In 20 years as a journalist, I'd written countless columns about people whose lives had been changed as quickly as a snap of the fingers. I just never thought it would happen to me.

I had tried to face down a man with a shotgun, a man who had taken my daughter prisoner. Somehow, I didn't think he'd pull the trigger. Maybe it was because I'd had a long run of talking myself out of tricky situations. That came to a dramatic end when the blast from his shotgun slammed me in the shoulder like a hammer blow and dropped me into the snow in front of his remote cabin.

I had thought that was it for me, but here I was, on a Friday in the first week of May, looking out the window of my office on the second storey of the house I was renting on Frank Street in Ottawa's Golden Triangle, an old downtown neighbourhood that was no longer as golden as the name suggested. Once-fine houses were sandwiched between aging, mid-rise apartment buildings. Some of the houses had been renovated, but there was a feeling of genteel decay in the neighbourhood.

Across the street, pre-schoolers were playing on the climbing equipment in St. Luke's Park, which was really more of a sports activity place than what I'd call a park. I liked watching the kids and the young moms. Part of me envied them, but I knew I had never been cut out to be a mother. And yet, now I was. It was a disconcerting experience, partly because the baby I had last seen wrapped in a pink blanket had reappeared in my life as a 25-year-old in a police uniform. Jenna and I were still feeling out our adult relationship, but we had one, and for that I was glad.

My main reason for checking the street was to see if Jenna had turned off Elgin on to Frank. She had texted me, saying "mission accomplished," and now she was walking home from a job on Queen Street up near the Hill. I don't know why I worried about her. It was not a dangerous assignment, trying to get some lecher to do his thing so his employer could ease him out. Not like when she was with the OPP. The most agonizing part of my near-death experience in November had not been thinking that I would die, but knowing that she could be next.

I was sure that what Jenna had gone through had been nearly as traumatic as my own experience, but she didn't show it or want to talk about it. I got that. I was the same way, but it didn't make it healthy.

I had been surprised when she had resigned from the police shortly after the incident. Being a cop had been the focus of her life, but she just couldn't abide the way the real story of what happened to us in the woods had been covered up by the top brass. Jenna wanted ethics and integrity from the people she worked for. I wondered if that was genetic. I had always been driven by the same unlikely expectation. It certainly wasn't because of the way I had raised her, because I had abandoned her when she was a baby.

After my injury, I had been in no shape to write the story of the long-buried secret that left seven men dead, and the news moved on to other things while I was recuperating. Then I got a surprise, which seemed to be my new thing. Janet Sellick, a literary agent from Toronto, had called me out of the blue and asked how I would feel about writing a true crime book telling the inside story of what had happened in the little Ottawa Valley village of Madawaska Mills. The offer came with a solid advance and since I was on medical leave from my job at the newspaper anyway, there didn't seem to be a downside.

Seeing no sign of Jenna, I returned to my desk and stared at the computer screen. The work was proving more difficult than I had imagined. My brain was programmed to write 750-word newspaper columns on deadline, three or four times a week. Now, I faced the challenge of putting together a book that would be between 100,000 and 125,000 words. I was 17,000 words in and I already felt like I'd run a marathon when I'd barely made it around the first lap.

It was not just the length of the story that was daunting, but deciding how much of it to tell. The genre was true crime, but which parts of the truth was I prepared to share? Not all of it, I knew that much. The problem was that I was not just a passive observer of the story, or a writer who had come along later to reconstruct it. I had lived the horror Madawaska Mills experienced, and it was personal. The story involved my best friend from childhood, but more important, it was about rediscovering my lost daughter and the man who was her biological father. I knew I had to talk about Jenna. Janet had called that "a must-have detail." But how much did I want to talk about Jenna's father, Darcy Lamb? Back in November, when all of this happened, my relationship with Darcy could have been described as either high school crush or one-night stand, followed by years of resentment and anger. Then, he had saved Jenna and now it was all a lot more complicated.

I turned away from the accusing glare of the blank computer screen. What was the rush? I didn't have to turn in the manuscript until the end of January. I had been telling myself that a lot lately. I always thought I had real discipline when it came to writing, but now I was discovering that it was mostly deadline-driven and a deadline in January didn't mean that much on a nice day in May.

I got up again and shoved open one of the four double-hung windows across the front of the office. I could feel a twinge of pain in my shoulder. I was still getting physio once a week to combat the damage from the shotgun wound.

I could hear birds and children and the air smelled of the freshness of early spring with a strong undercurrent of cooking smells from the restaurant row on Elgin, a main commercial street that crosses Frank at the end of my block. The weather was in the low 20s, abnormally warm for so early in May but a relief after a winter that had buried the city in snow. The rapid spring melt had raised the Ottawa River to dangerous levels and the flooding was dominating the news.

My new place was just five minutes' walk from the apartment I used to sublet above a pub on Elgin. I had to move in a hurry when the owner came back from an overseas posting. I'd gotten a bit lucky. George Macklem was a property developer I'd met when I did a series of columns about the murder of his daughter. I gave him a call to ask if he knew of anything available to rent downtown and it turned out that he had an Edwardian house where the main floor had been turned into a photography studio and the second and third floors were apartments. George told me that he'd let me have it for a song, which turned out to be $3,000 a month. When it came to money, George's songbook was obviously different from mine, but Jenna was looking for a place, too, so we decided to go in together. Now, I lived on the second floor, she was on the third, and Martin Investigations had its office on the main floor.

George had made it clear that we shouldn't get too comfortable, because his ultimate plan was to tear down the house. He already owned a couple of four-storey apartment buildings down the street, and when the house next door came on the market, he intended to buy it and then clear all the lots for one big building that would be far more lucrative. The only hold up was Bill Ferguson, an 85-year-old who lived next door and refused to sell. Bill was a grouchy old bastard, but I wished him long good health.

The house we were renting had been fairly grand once, and I could still see it in the carefully detailed oak staircase that led from the main floor to the second, in the tall ceilings and the bow window in the office reception area. They didn't overcome the general air of shabbiness and disrepair. George had owned the house for a decade and proudly boasted that he hadn't spent a dime on maintenance. The last update had been sometime in the 1950s. Jenna's bathroom had pink tiles and mine had baby blue. I'd seen better kitchens in trailers, but neither one of us was the type to worry much about that.

For me, my office was what made the house. I think it had originally been a sunroom and it perched on top of the narrow verandah that framed the house's central door. It was a red brick place with one of those barn-style roofs. A gambrel roof, it was called. I had learned quite a bit about old houses since I'd moved in.

My office was a jumble of stuff that Jenna and I had picked up at flea markets and garage sales. Neither of us had owned any furniture. My desk was a big oak thing that took two strong men to carry upstairs, cursing the whole way. The drawers all stuck and the top was scarred by cigarette burns, but it had cost me only $25. My desk chair was oak, too, and from the same era. Hard as a rock to sit on. I bought a fake Persian rug from IKEA and that was about it. The room was all windows, so there was no place for art, even if I had been interested in it.

In theory, I kept an eye on Jenna's office when she was out, in my capacity as unofficial office manager and receptionist. I was the associate in Martin and Associates. It was a title that came with no pay and little work, but I was happy to help Jenna in any way I could. In the three months since the office opened, two customers had walked up to the door, both abused wives who were afraid to use a phone or computer to communicate.

Frank was a popular place to park for people visiting the shops and restaurants on Elgin, so I didn't think much of it when a shiny black Cadillac Escalade pulled up in front of the house. A woman with long red hair, a black business suit and large sunglasses got out, removed the glasses and then looked at her phone, checking something. To my surprise, she didn't head back towards Elgin but started towards my house.

Shit, I was wearing a pair of jeans with holes in the knees and a Tragically Hip T-shirt. I heard the doorbell ring. Maybe I could tell her I was the cleaner. I knew I had to answer it because this woman looked like a client, and one with money. Younger than average though, probably mid-30s. There was no warranty on a marriage.

I hustled downstairs and swung open the door. Up close, the woman looked intelligent and self-assured, but agitated and struggling not to show it. Her green eyes were hard and seemed to glitter in the sunlight. She gave me a forced smile, showing a slight gap between her front teeth. It appeared to be the only imperfection she allowed herself. In all, she was certainly not the classic abused spouse, but they came in all types and income brackets.

"I'm looking for Jenna Martin," she said, her voice terse and impatient. "I'm a previous client."

That was an encouraging first. "Kris Redner," I said. "I'm Jenna's assistant. Excuse the way I'm dressed. Just doing a few chores."

It was clear from her expression that the woman didn't care about me or my clothes. "Is she in? It's urgent."

"I'm expecting her momentarily. Please, come in. Have a seat in the waiting room and I'll contact Jenna."

I showed the woman into the front room of the house, what we called the waiting room now. There were three matching grey chairs, fake leather. They didn't look bad until you sat on them.

"All right then," the woman said, looking at her watch. She was clearly someone who wasn't using to waiting for anything.

"Tell her Alicia is here."

 Four

Jenna Martin was only three blocks from home when she got a message from Kris saying, "Client here. When u back?"

Jenna thumbed "There in 5" and picked up her pace. Back-to-back jobs? Maybe a good day was about to get better. When Jenna turned off Elgin and on to Frank Street, she noticed a hulking, black Cadillac SUV parked in front of her house. As she got closer, she saw that the vanity plate on the Cadillac said TECHGAL. It wasn't one she would easily forget. Alicia Jameson had been her first client, back in March.

Maybe it wasn't technically correct to call Alicia a client, not a private investigation client anyway. After a few glasses of wine one night, Jenna had been scrolling through web pages when she saw an ad for a woman seeking a maid of honour. The person who placed the ad had offered a "generous honorarium" for what sounded like a day of work.

Her first thought had been what kind of loser has to advertise for a maid of honour, but her second had been that the job would be easy money and a bit of an adventure. She hadn't expected some-one like Alicia. Not only was she gorgeous, she said she was going to marry the tech millionaire Simon Cousens in just three weeks. It was one of those whirlwind courtships, Alicia had said.

It soon became apparent that the job was not a one-day gig, or at least it turned out that way once Jenna mentioned that her main work was private investigation. Alicia wanted someone to help her figure out what she was getting into. She wasn't concerned about money, which Simon had bags of, or their age differential, which was significant. Simon was 62, Alicia only 35. What bothered her was Simon's marital track record. He had four previous wives. Was he just unlucky in love, or was he a serial philanderer? Alicia had said, "I don't want to become the next former Mrs. Cousens."

Jenna knew immediately that Alicia was asking for the

impossible. While reluctant to reject what would have been her first private investigation job, Jenna had gently suggested that she couldn't predict Simon's future fidelity. Alicia disagreed. She explained that she was an engineer and that she made decisions every day based on data and probabilities. Her problem was how to gather the data. She couldn't very well go poking around in Simon's past and quizzing his friends without creating the impression that she was getting cold feet, but if her best friend and future bridesmaid was doing the asking, it would seem more natural.

"Simon is my dream man," Alicia had said, "but I just want to make sure it isn't *just* a dream."

It wasn't a crazy idea, but it quickly hit a wall when Alicia herself got cold feet and wouldn't supply the names of any of Simon's friends and also put the former wives off limits. It made Jenna wonder what Alicia was really up to. Instead, Alicia decided to act like Jenna really was her BFF and called frequently to talk about wedding preparations. It had been weird, to say the least.

Out of curiosity, Jenna did a media scan on Simon. As she soon discovered, the phrase "flamboyant tech playboy" was frequently used when journalists wrote about him, which they used to do a lot. About six years ago, the stories petered out. Either all of that was behind him or the media had lost interest and moved on.

Jenna only got to meet Simon briefly, at the wedding. He was soft-spoken and gentlemanly, with a kind of aged George Clooney look. Not to mention the bags of money. It wasn't hard to see why Alicia was marrying him.

It was a little more difficult to figure out what Simon saw in Alicia, besides her relative youth. Not that Jenna thought 35 was young, but it was if you were 62. Alicia was a cold piece of work. That wasn't Jenna's problem, though. Alicia paid promptly for the maid of honour work, even giving Jenna her full private investigation fee for the wedding day, and an invitation to the fancy wedding dinner at the Brookstreet Hotel in the tech suburb of Kanata, plus a baby-blue dress that she'd never wear again in a million years.

As Jenna headed up the front steps towards her office, she wondered what Alicia wanted now. Surely Simon hadn't strayed already. Jenna paused before entering the old house she shared with Kris and looked at her reflection in the glass of the door. She was working up a new facial expression for private investigation work. As a cop, she had gone with cool and unflappable, but she had softened that by adding empathetic and concerned. It seemed to be working. Besides, she did want to help people. That's why she was doing the work. It sure wasn't for the money. She had left behind $100K a year, full benefits and a pension.

Jenna swung open the door and was immediately hit with that closed-up, old house smell that always seemed to linger, no matter how many windows she opened. Then she looked through the French doors that separated the office from the hallway and saw Kris and Alicia sitting on those rock-hard grey chairs, chatting like they were old buddies.

That didn't surprise her. Kris was good at gaining people's trust to get information from them. The best cops had that gift, too, but Jenna knew she had a ways to go. When she was with the OPP, she had leaned a little too much on the persuasive powers of a badge and possible criminal charges.

Jenna just wished Kris wasn't wearing torn jeans and a T-shirt. It was unprofessional, but she couldn't very well expect Kris to sit around home in office wear in the off chance that a client would walk in the door. It's not like Jenna was paying her. Their professional relationship was a work in progress but the personal one was even more challenging. Really, how do you relate to a mother who abandoned you as an infant, then popped back into your life 25 years later?

Alicia, by contrast, wore an expensive-looking black business suit and a single strand of pearls that were no doubt real. Her makeup was perfect, maybe a little too perfect. With Alicia, it was always hard to tell what was authentic and what wasn't.

Jenna reminded herself that the main point was that Alicia's money was certainly real. She didn't have to like every client. Putting on what she hoped was a glad-to-see-you expression, Jenna swung open the glass door and walked confidently into the outer office, just like she owned the place, or at least rented it.

She stuck out her hand and said, "Alicia, I'm surprised to see you again so soon."

Alicia's grip was firm. Jenna knew she was a gym rat. "There's been a complication, an extremely troubling complication," Alicia said. "I could use your help."

"Of course. Come into my private office."

Kris gave her a questioning look. Did she want her to sit in?

Jenna knew that could be useful, but she also knew that her mother could be a little bit intimidating and tended to take over a conversation. Alicia was *her* client, someone she knew already. Kris had spent a few minutes with her. They'd compare notes later, but first Jenna had to assess the situation herself.

"Thanks so much Kris," she said. "I'll let you get back to it."

Turning to Alicia, Jenna said, "Come on in. Can I get you anything?"

"No, I'm good."

Was she good, Jenna wondered? She had spent three weeks with the woman and had found out quite a lot about her, but she couldn't answer that question.

 # Five

I went back up to my second-floor office, not sure whether to be proud that Jenna was adapting so well to her new job or miffed because she didn't want my help. We'd had a few frank discussions about "boundary issues," as Jenna called them. From what little I knew of families, it wasn't unusual between a mother and a daughter, but not many mothers and daughters had the kind of situation that Jenna and I did. The years between her birth and now were a hazy outline that Jenna was slowly filling in. I knew that I had to let her proceed at her own pace, but I had an unexpected, pent-up desire to mother her. It sometimes got in the way.

Naturally, I wanted to know what was happening with this repeat client. Part of that was just my normal nosiness, I had to admit, but my long-honed journalistic instincts told me that there was a story in this Alicia Jameson, and it wasn't a good one. There was something off about her. Maybe it was the look in her eyes. It was one I recognized; the long hurt that that comes from a childhood trauma and never really goes away. I saw it in myself.

I had never met Alicia before today, but I remembered her story, of course. Jenna and I had talked about it quite a bit at the time. My impression was that Alicia was an over-thinker. She was an attractive younger woman about to marry a far older, rich man. It looked like a straight exchange of sex and youth for money and security, the oldest deal in the book.

The situation had proven to be more complicated, as it often did. Alicia was an engineer working on green technologies. Working, in fact, for the guy she was about to marry. It wasn't the usual employment relationship. This Simon Cousens ran what Alicia called an "incubator," which I gathered was a setup where rich guys gave office space and connections to a lot of young tech people, hoping that some of them would come up with products that the rich guys could take to market and make a killing on. The person with the idea got a slice.

Alicia was intensely involved with her work, she had told Jenna back in March, and she'd never taken the time for romance. To her, sex was just a physical activity, sort of like a gym workout. Then Simon had come along and Alicia's whole life had turned upside down, or so she had told Jenna. Alicia kept going on about how fascinating Simon was, the most complex man she'd ever known. Maybe it was because she'd known him for longer than one night, I had suggested. Jenna didn't like that. She was more idealistic than me, and that was a good thing. She hadn't stayed in policing long enough to become skeptical about everyone and everything, like most veteran cops.

I had to admit that Simon did sound interesting. I did a bit of online digging on my own and quickly learned that Simon wasn't the prototypical tech nerd, although he had a PhD in electrical engineering. He'd spent his 20s in England, but the stories were always a bit vague on where he was actually born. Simon had worked for the now-dead tech giant Nortel, then spun off a series of companies with his partner, Brendan Connor. Ottawa's original tech heyday was way before my time, but I'd heard of the two of them.

Simon had an extensive collection of vintage cars. He was a world traveller and had been just about everywhere. He didn't hesitate to spend lavish sums on his own pleasures, but he gave a lot of money away to worthy causes, mostly in the Third World. He seemed to like being married, having tried it four times. And yet, none of them had worked out. The guy was a bit of a conundrum.

I could see why Alicia would be intimidated by him. I would have been, too. With Simon's track record, her caution was understandable. Alicia had her own backstory, too, and from what Jenna told me, it was a lot murkier than Simon's. For example, she mentioned that she had been orphaned as a child, but Alicia never wanted to talk about that.

Had I been approaching the story of Simon and Alicia as a journalist, I'd have spent as much time on her as I did on him. That wasn't how it worked for a private investigator, though. Alicia was the client. Her own story and motivation were none of my business, as I had to keep reminding myself at the time.

I tried to stop thinking about Alicia, willing myself to concentrate on the story that I was turning into a book. It was proving tougher than I expected, because I was forcing myself back to a scary place, and if I were going to tell the story properly, I'd have to reveal a lot more about myself than I was comfortable with.

I stared at the computer screen and tried to imagine what Jenna was being told in the office below. I could hear the indistinct sound of voices, but not make out actual words. The most likely thing was that Alicia's new husband had strayed already and Alicia wanted Jenna to get the goods on him. I hoped it was something that mundane, a case that would provide her with a good paycheque and no real risk.

I feared that I was being uncharacteristically optimistic. My own experience had told me that rich people were dangerous. I knew trouble when I saw it, and this woman was trouble in high heels.

 Six

As Alicia settled into the visitor's chair on the other side of Jenna's desk, she looked around like she was inspecting everything, then said, "Nice office."

It was Alicia's first visit to the house on Frank. When they'd met for business before, it had been at Zoe's, an expensive bar in the Chateau Laurier downtown. Jenna was surprised by Alicia's reaction. In her limited experience with Alicia, the woman had been stinting with compliments, and the office wasn't really all that great. Jenna's desk was chipboard covered in a laminate that was supposed to look like walnut and the chair was a low-end model from Staples. The room was painted a sombre grey and the only adornments on the walls were three framed documents: Jenna's degree from the University of Toronto, her graduation diploma from the Ontario Police College and a certificate from the online company where she'd taken a course to get her Ontario private investigator's licence. She hoped that they would somehow cluster together and make up for her obvious lack of experience as a PI.

"Well, I don't use it much. I'm out on the job most of the time." Jenna took a yellow legal pad from her desk drawer and said, "How can I help you, Alicia?"

Alicia gave a curt nod. Jenna had been right to think the other woman would want to get right down to it rather than exchange pleasantries.

"There's a problem. Simon is gone and so is $10 million."

Jenna tried not to look surprised. That was a hell of a big sum. Was the problem that Simon was gone, or the money?

"All right. Let's start with Simon, then. How long has he been missing?"

"I haven't seen him since Monday."

Jenna made a note, careful to keep her professional mask on. Most wives might have been interested in the whereabouts of their husbands before four days had passed. But then, Alicia and Simon certainly weren't most people.

"And what was happening the last time you saw him?"

"He was in his office, working on his computer. I had to leave to go to work."

"Did you talk to him?"

"Not really. I brought him a cup of coffee, like I usually do. Said I hoped he had a good day. I was in a rush."

"And you got home from work when?"

"Around 5:30. He wasn't home, but that wasn't unusual. He walks the dog about that time, out in the bush at the back of our property. The dog wasn't there, either, so I assumed that was what he was doing. Rex, the dog, is a Bernese. I worry about him getting ticks under all that fur, but Simon isn't concerned."

"So Simon is out walking the dog, but then he doesn't come home for dinner, right?"

"Yes. I'd gotten Thai from a place in Kanata. I don't cook. I waited for him until about 7:30, then I went ahead and ate. Of course, I called his cell and texted him, but there wasn't any response."

"That must have made you worried."

"Not at the time. Simon goes where he likes and he doesn't feel the need to tell me the details. Sometimes he likes to hop in one of those vintage cars of his and just hit the road. He often takes the dog with him."

Jenna was picking up little shards of resentment. Simon wasn't interested in his new wife's concerns about the dog. He didn't bother to tell her where he was going. It seemed at odds with the gentlemanly fellow she'd met, but anyone could put on a good front for a short time.

"So what did you do next?"

"I was pissed off, frankly. I finished a bottle of Riesling and went to bed."

Jenna looked up at Alicia. Her face was impassive, unemotional, like she was describing a story she had read, not something she had experienced.

"So you were angry at him?"

"Of course I was. We're in the middle of a sensitive business negotiation and he just takes off without telling me? That's unacceptable."

"Let's circle back to the business negotiation and stay focused on Simon for now. So you wake up Tuesday morning and he's not home. What did you do?"

"I started calling around to his cousin and people at work, to see if they knew anything. I felt like a bloody fool, but I did it. No one had heard a thing. Simon still wasn't home and neither was the dog.

"Then, around 11 a.m., Rex turns up, his coat just full of burrs. I checked in the garage, thinking Simon must have come home. One of his cars was still gone. It's a white Mercedes roadster from the early 1960s, cute little thing with a red leather interior. I'm sorry, I don't know the model or plate number. I could look those up."

"Sure, the more information I have, the better," Jenna said, wishing she had the ability to put out a BOLO on a vehicle. She still needed the information, because this sounded like something that could end up in the hands of the police.

"Then I tried his cell phone again, but this time I was standing close to his office. I could hear it ringing. I rushed in and found it in his desk drawer. There is no way Simon would go anywhere without that phone. It's like part of his body. That's when I started to get worried."

"So that was Tuesday morning. Did you call the police at that point?"

"I didn't. Don't you have to wait 48 hours or something?"

"No, that's a myth. You can report a missing person right away. Look, I appreciate you bringing this to me, but I think you'd be better off with the police, if you really think something has happened to Simon. They've got a lot more resources than I have."

"I can't take this to the police."

"OK. We're back to the business arrangement and the $10 million, right?"

Alicia looked down, twisting her wedding ring as she formulated her answer. It was a wide gold band made up of a complex nest of strands and topped by a diamond that looked like one of the crown jewels.

"I can't say too much about the business deal, but here's the essence of it. While I was doing research at Simon's incubator, I developed a process for scrubbing greenhouse gases from industrial smoke stacks. It's far more efficient than anything on the market and every manufacturing company is going to need it as environmental regulations get tighter. As part of the incubator deal, Simon owns the rights to it and I get 10 per cent.

"It will take a substantial amount of money to get it into production, though. Simon turned to his old partner, Brendan Connor, who agreed to put the $10 million into the corporation Simon was forming. Simon was to match the money, then Brendan was going to use Simon's reputation and technical credibility to draw in serious additional private investment.

"When Simon still hadn't made contact on Wednesday, I started to go through his credit cards and financials, looking for a spending trail. While I was at it, I checked the status of the new corporate account. Last week, it contained Brendan Connor's $10 million. Now, there isn't a dime."

"Wow. You think Simon stole the money?"

"Why would he steal money that was going to benefit him? It doesn't make sense. No, something else is going on. I'm worried that something has happened to him. Maybe he's been kidnapped or extorted."

"Obviously no kidnapper has contacted you."

"No, but maybe they've already gotten what they want from Simon. He could be dead in a ditch somewhere."

Alicia paused and looked straight at Jenna. There was fire in her eyes now, but Jenna wasn't sure of the source.

"Jenna, I need you to find him, or at least find out what happened to him. No one else can know. If word gets out that he's missing, Brendan is going to come looking for his cash and I don't have it. Brendan is not a very pleasant man, especially when it comes to money. And it's not just that. It would kill the company, the deal, and my invention. If Simon doesn't turn up, it puts everything into limbo. Worst case, he never returns and he won't be declared dead for seven years. The technology will be obsolete by then."

So which was she more worried about, her new husband or the money? Jenna wondered. Then she reminded herself that it didn't matter. Alicia was the client. It wasn't up to Jenna to judge her.

"I'll do what I can," Jenna said. "Approaching people about Simon without telling them that he's missing is going to be tricky, though."

"Yes, but I'm prepared to double your usual fee. You'll think of something. "

It was a tricky problem, but Jenna saw a possible solution. A certain journalist she knew might be just the person to ask a bunch of questions without setting off the same alarms that a private investigator would.

Alicia took a file folder from her large, black leather purse and placed it on Jenna's desk. "Everything I know is here, contacts information and company financials. I'll send you the specs on his car. Leave the credit cards with me. I'll monitor those.

"I have to have answers by next Friday afternoon. Simon is scheduled to meet with Brendan to talk about the fine points of the deal. Brendan can't know that Simon and the money are gone. Whatever you do, don't approach him directly.

"You've got seven days."

 Seven

Darcy Lamb and I had only one rule when it came to the kitchens we shared at my place in town and his log house up at Round Lake: He cooked and I watched. It wasn't that I was too lazy to cook, I just had no aptitude for it, something I had proven in the few disastrous meals that I had prepared for him and Jenna. The lasagna that required a steak knife to cut stood out.

So I watched as Darcy chopped carrots, red peppers, snow peas and onions on a large white plastic cutting board. His powerful forearms flexed as he levered the knife up and down, cutting the vegetables in the same, machine-like way that people did in those TV cooking shows he liked to watch. Darcy was a big man and his tight-fitting navy golf shirt emphasized his upper body. Although he was 46 and eight years out of the NHL, he was proud that he was still at his playing weight of 212 pounds. I knew from personal inspection that there wasn't a visible ounce of fat on him.

"The thing is to keep all the vegetables a similar size, so that they will cook at the same rate. You want to keep the pasta small, too. That's why I'm using fusilli," he said.

"Right, got it," I said, taking another sip from my oversized glass of pinot grigio. I was charmed by Darcy's attempts to teach me how to cook, so much so that I pretended I was taking in his instructions for future use. I think we both knew that I was never going to make pasta primavera, or anything else, if Darcy and Jenna were lucky. I had managed to live all my adult life on restaurant take-out and micro-waved food. I liked to put that down to the irregular schedule of a journalist, but truthfully, I just couldn't be bothered to cook for myself, so I never learned.

Darcy turned to check the progress of two pots on the stove. I liked the view from that side, too. I preferred men with a solid ass, not those wimpy little flesh bags so many sedentary men had. In that way, Darcy reminded me of a young lover I had had down in the Adirondacks. I quickly put that thought from my mind. It hadn't ended well.

Darcy had made garlic butter to add to the sauce, and its aromatic smell filled the kitchen. The pasta was boiling, a cloud of steam rising from the pot. The kitchen in my place was so primitive that there wasn't even a fan above the ancient and dented electric-coil stove. I had opened a window to let in some fresh air. The kitchen was painted yellow, but not lately. The painter must have thought it would go with the red counter top, which predated the ability to bend Formica, or whatever it was. The edge was a chrome strip that reminded me of the old kitchen table my parents had. The floor had a black and white checkerboard pattern with vinyl tiles that were cracked and chipped in places. It was hard to look at, especially if you'd had a bit too much to drink.

If I was being kind, I'd have called the kitchen retro, but really it was almost totally useless. The cupboard doors didn't fit right and most of the drawers stuck. Luckily, I didn't have much to put in them.

"I appreciate you changing plans and coming down here tonight," I said. Normally, we rotated the location of our weekend dinner, and this was to be his night. After Jenna had finished with Alicia Jameson, she told me that it was a big case with a tight time line and that she needed my help. I had called Darcy to tell him that we couldn't make the two-hour drive up to the lake.

"What, you're not going to eat?" he had said, then offered to bring everything to us. I couldn't very well say no. Darcy called these dinners our date nights. It was a tradition we'd started at his place, when I was convalescing from the gunshot wound I'd received last November. Darcy insisted that he should look after me at his house. I'd resisted, but not too hard. The slow, quiet winter days had given us a chance to start to get to know each other and to catch up on the lives we'd led since we'd been teenagers in Madawaska Mills. Our encounter one night at a bush party had led to Jenna and changed my life forever. Darcy never knew he had a daughter, not until I needed his help to save her life. Eventually, inevitably, we'd become lovers. Like everything about my new family, I worried that it was too much, too fast, but I knew that Darcy made me feel safe, and after what I'd been through in the last couple of years, that was hugely important.

"It wasn't a problem to change plans," he said. "You know how I look forward to these date nights."

"Me too."

He smiled at that. Although I certainly wouldn't describe Darcy's ego as small, he liked it when I reassured him. I needed to remind myself that all this was new for him, too.

"So what's this big case that Jenna has?"

"I don't know too much about it yet. All I know is that involves the wife of a tech guy called Simon Cousens. Seems like Cousens is missing and so is $10 million."

Darcy gave a low whistle. "That's serious change."

"Yeah, the wife is pretty keen to get Simon and the money back, maybe not in that order."

"I know who Cousens is. He's been around forever, always seemed to be in the paper for starting a company, partying or getting divorced. He must be in his 60s now. How old is the wife?"

"Somewhere in her 30s, but she's wife number five."

'Jesus," Darcy said, shaking his head in disbelief. His full, brown hair was a bit curly and it bounced around when he did that. "I used to play with some guys who had a string of wives, but I don't think anyone got up to five. They'd have been younger, of course."

"It's not really an enviable record."

"No. Expensive, too."

I decided not to respond to that. Darcy's own love life, prior to me, had involved an endless string of puck bunnies. He changed them up about as often as he changed hockey sticks. I suspected it was always a different version of the same girl and the same age. When I met him again last November, he was dating a teenager. I wasn't sure what to make of his new fidelity and his sudden preference for a woman nearly his own age. Maybe he was finally starting to grow up.

I heard the sound of quick footsteps coming from upstairs, then the apartment door opened and Jenna walked into the kitchen. She wore jean shorts, a red tank top and flip-flops, her shoulder-length brown hair pulled back in a simple pony tail. Jenna was an athlete and I was always struck by her muscular, toned arms and legs, something I had never attained.

"Hey Darcy, what's for dinner?" she asked.

Our daughter called us Darcy and Kris. I suppose Mom and Dad would have been too much to expect, since I'd given her up for adoption at birth and Darcy had been playing the role of father for less than a year.

"Pasta primavera. I hope you're hungry."

"I am. I've had a hell of a day."

"So Kris was saying. Tell us about it."

Jenna poured herself a glass of the pinot and sat down at the kitchen table at the end closest to Darcy. "Well, it started pretty well. I've been doing sort of an undercover thing at a charity downtown. The board had heard that the CEO was a major-league lech, and they were right. I nailed him for it. The guy actually asked for a hand job, right in his office. Do you believe it?"

"I guess he doesn't follow the news these days," Darcy said.

"Unfortunately, he won't be in it. The goal was a quiet resignation, no embarrassment for the charity. Still, I took him out. So much better than following cheating spouses and looking into insurance cases. It's the kind of thing I hoped to do when I got into this work, make things happen, not just process people through the court system so they could be put back on the street.

"Anyway, I was coming home early, feeling pretty good, eager to get out of that skirt and jacket outfit I'd been wearing and thinking about the weekend. Then Kris texts me and says there's another client. So I'm happy until I get pretty close to the house and I recognize the big SUV with the TECHGAL vanity plate.

"You remember me talking about Alicia Jameson, my first client?"

"Yeah, of course. Kris tells me she's back, missing a husband and $10 million."

Jenna looked at me, disappointed. "I didn't tell your whole story, just the headline. I don't even know the whole story. Why don't you tell us?"

I listened with interest as Jenna recounted her conversation with this Alicia, and with every additional detail, I became more convinced that my initial intuition about her was correct. Her story didn't add up. Why did she wait so long to try to find her missing husband? Why hadn't she called the police? That behaviour didn't ring true. Jenna said it was all to avoid scuppering a huge business deal, one that would fall apart if people knew that Simon was unaccounted for. Alicia certainly seemed to be putting money over love. It didn't surprise me. Her relationship with her husband had struck me as a financial transaction from the beginning. The question now was what was Alicia's angle? Twenty years of covering criminals made me think that the most likely scenario was that Alicia had killed Simon Cousens and taken the money.

I refocused on the conversation when Jenna said, "So Kris, here's how you can help."

"Whatever you need."

"There's a wrinkle in all of this. Two, actually. Alicia is desperate to find out what happened to her husband, and the money, before a big meeting next Friday with Simon's former business partner, Brendan Connor. He's the guy who put up the $10 million. She wants me to track down Simon and I only have seven days to do it. That won't be easy, but Alicia also wants to make sure that my investigation doesn't tip anyone to the fact that he's missing, especially this guy Connor. Not only would that kill the deal, Connor would demand his money back and Alicia doesn't have it."

"OK, but how do we know she doesn't have it? Have you considered that Alicia might have disposed of the husband and transferred the money into an offshore account?"

"If I were still wearing a uniform that would be the first thing I'd look at, but that's not my job any more. My job is to find Simon, not investigate Alicia. She says that only Simon and Brendan Connor can remove funds from that corporate account. All she can do is look at the numbers on Simon's computer. Naturally, our suspicious minds wonder about Alicia but she stands to make a lot of money if this deal goes ahead. Killing Simon would be against her interests."

"Maybe she wanted the $10 million now, rather than wait and hope this business plan works out."

"Maybe. I'm not saying I trust Alicia, but the job is to chase down the contacts she provided me with and any leads they give us, in the hope of finding out where Simon is. The problem is that, if I show up saying I'm a private investigator, people are going to know that something is off and word could very well get back to Connor."

"All right. So where do I come in?"

"You're a writer. What if you told people you were writing a book about Simon, and the hook is that you hear he's going to be back on top again soon? That would give you a reason to ask a lot of questions. I could sit in as your research assistant."

It wasn't a terrible idea, but I saw one problem. "OK, but all someone has to do is Google me and they will find out I'm a newspaper crime writer. Why would a crime writer be asking about Simon?"

Jenna gave me a sympathetic look and said, "How can I say this, Kris? Not everyone reads the mainstream media any more. Maybe you're not as famous as you think. Besides, you've got a website now, right?"

It was true. I thought it was stupid, but my agent had insisted that I needed to start establishing a social media presence, heralding the arrival of the book I had not yet written.

"So?"

"So you tweak the site to call yourself a writer of non-fiction and biography. We'll run off a batch of quickie business cards, send people right to that site. Even if they do dig into you, you're not in the paper right now. I know it's not perfect, but it's the best I've got."

My first thought was about the book I was struggling with and how far behind I was already. But this would only take a week, maybe less, and I had to admit that I was attracted to the Simon and Alicia story. What was really going on?

Then I realized that I had to stop putting myself first. That wasn't the person I wanted to be. Jenna had asked for my help. Of course, I was going to give it to her.

 # Eight

By 8 p.m., Darcy was gone, wanting to make at least part of the drive back to the lake in the light. He hadn't been entirely thrilled when I told him that Jenna and I needed to get to work on the Simon Cousens case right away. Our normal routine consisted of sex, followed by a good night's sleep, than a leisurely morning walk down to the ByWard Market, where we'd buy coffee and some French pastries from Le Moulin de Provence, then sit on the patio and people watch.

I hated to give that up, but there would be plenty of weeks ahead. Saying that to myself made me wonder what I thought the goal was when it came to Darcy. We acted like we were married for a day or two, then we didn't see each other for days. Were we building up to a full-time relationship, or were we limiting our time together because we were both afraid what we had wouldn't sustain that much contact? And yet, it had when I was at his place in the winter. Maybe we were going backward.

I reluctantly put Darcy from my mind and turned back to the notes and contact information that Jenna had spread on the kitchen table. "OK, how are we going to divvy this up? You want in on everything?"

"Of course I do. It's my case, remember?"

"Sure, right. I'm just the writer with a fake interest in Simon."

"Is this going to be a problem, us working together?"

"Not at all," I said, although I wasn't too sure. Working with someone else on a story was something that I avoided at all costs. Then I reminded myself that there was no story. Not one that I was going to write, anyway.

"What I want you to do, Kris, is reach out to these four former wives, see if we can find at least one who is co-operative enough to talk to us."

"Let's say one of them does. What makes you think she'd have any idea of where Simon is?"

"I'm not expecting it, but we have to work through the steps. When people are in trouble or in danger, they often reach out to someone they know, someone they can trust. Simon must have loved each of these women at one time, or thought he did. Maybe there's still something there."

"Could be, but the guy is loaded. With his resources, he could be anywhere in the world. Maybe he's got his own private island in the Caribbean."

"Maybe. Let's ask about that. Or, is there some place from his past, somewhere he'd feel safe? That's the kind of thing we're looking for," Jenna said. "We need to be able to get inside his head, know how he thinks."

"Agreed. I'm going to make coffee. You want one?"

"Sure. We could be at this a while."

The Keurig was the kitchen's one 21st century feature, a gift from Darcy. I would make myself a Starbucks, but Jenna preferred Tim Horton's, a bad habit picked up from too many hours on the road with the OPP. As I fixed the coffee, I watched Jenna work. She had that legal pad she liked and was drawing up a page for each wife, with questions in point form. I thought I could have figured that out for myself, but I wasn't going to alter her style. She was methodical, like any good cop, or journalist, for that matter.

I returned to the table with the steaming coffee. We both took it black. "You know, the big question is why would Simon Cousens run? Who's he running from, and why now? He was on the verge of a substantial business deal and he'd only been married for a few months. I know he goes through wives, but from what you've told me his cycle is years, not months. An older guy, a younger wife, you'd think the sex alone would keep him around."

"I think the why is Alicia's problem. Our only concern is the where."

"Sure, but the why and the where could be connected. If he's hiding, who is he hiding from? In Simon's story, who are the good guys and who are the bad guys?"

Jenna nodded. "I agree with that. We need to know everything there is to know about Simon."

"And what about Alicia? What's your take on her?"

"She knows more than she was telling me. She's angry, that's obvious. I was picking up little things in our conversation, like Simon disregarding her concerns about their dog getting ticks. He also collects old cars and likes to take off on road trips without telling her where he's going or when he's coming back."

"You think he's on one now?"

"Maybe. Alicia says one of his favourite cars is gone, an old Mercedes. Hard to see him taking off with a big business deal in the works, though."

"It seems to me that we need to know more about Alicia and her relationship with Simon. Maybe it's her that he's running from," I said.

"It could be. I feel like there's something cold in her, maybe dangerous. Let's find out who Simon's divorce lawyer is, see if he or she will tell us anything."

"Good idea, but I still think we need a better read on Alicia, better than I've got from a short conversation. What if we're getting played?"

"Maybe we are, but stop thinking like a journalist. You don't need to write a story that tells people who's right and who's wrong. This is a good case and we need to deliver. Did I mention that Alicia is paying me double my usual fee for a quick turnaround?"

"You didn't. That doesn't mean we turn a blind eye if we find something criminal, right?"

"Of course not, but we don't have the resources to build a case against Alicia, and it's not my job."

"What if Simon's dead?"

"We take it to the police, but I doubt we're going to discover that. All we are doing is canvassing the names Alicia gave us to see if we can find a lead on where he is. I hear you about Alicia, but we can't make her the object of an investigation. Tell you what, let's try to get through half the names on the list, then we can offer to meet Alicia at her place for an update. That will give you a chance to assess her."

"All right, that sounds good. It's not just Alicia we need to understand better. Seeing how Simon lives might help us understand where he's gone."

"Maybe, but I want to be careful with Alicia. Let's start with the wives."

"You've got addresses for them, right?"

"Yes, full contact info."

"I suggest that we take them in order, start with the beginning. I also think we need to start early tomorrow and hit them in rapid order. Once we start asking questions, word might get from one to the next. If Simon is hiding out with one of the exes, we will spook him."

"So just show up at their doors?"

"Trust me, it's the best way to go. I've been doing this for years. It's a lot harder to say no to someone when you're looking them in the eye. Once we get in, we can charm them."

Jenna smiled. "So who do you have pegged as the charming one?"

"Both of us. Mother and daughter team working on a project. Women can relate to that."

"You really think there's a chance that one of the wives is going to reach out to another? I don't have a lot of experience with ex-wives, but seems like they'd hate each other, right?"

"Maybe, but for all we know they get together for bridge. There are enough of them."

"OK then, quick strike, see where this is going. Then we can branch out to the rest of the list. It's fairly short."

"Sounds like a plan. I'm going to my office to see what I can find out about these women online."

"All right. I'll go up to my place, finish up my questions for them. We'll compare notes in the morning."

Jenna picked up her coffee cup, rinsed it out, and then left the kitchen, stopping to wave and say "Good night."

I was pretty sure I wasn't going to like Alicia, but I was definitely going to like this opportunity to work with Jenna. I was looking for a new direction in my life. Maybe it would be writing books, or perhaps a mother-daughter detective agency. Could that work? I was willing to spend a few days finding out.

 # Nine

It was 8:30 Saturday morning when we rolled up outside the house of wife number one. Margaret Radmore's place was just a short drive from our house on Frank. Her house was a two-storey red brick with a verandah across the front and a huge maple that filled the whole lawn. The tree's massive limbs almost obscured the house and cast it in shadow despite the cloudless morning.

It was a neat place that didn't have the pretension to style that our rental had, but Aylmer was one of the best streets in Ottawa South, tucked away just a block from the Rideau Canal. I guessed that the house was about 100 years old. Back then, Ottawa South was just another suburb, before the city spread out east, west and south. Now, it was a pricey neighbourhood, partly because it was within walking distance of Carleton University, where Radmore taught physics.

I glanced across at Jenna, who had certainly gotten into her part. She wore the dark skirt and jacket she'd been wearing to her office gig, along with a white, button-down shirt. She'd even added a pair of black-rimmed glasses, which gave her a studious look. I wore khaki pants, a blue shirt and a navy blazer. It was kind of a unisex look that I found worked most anywhere.

"You ready to do this?" Jenna asked.

"Sure," I said, trying to radiate confidence. Knocking on strangers' doors and asking impertinent questions wasn't uncomfortable for me, but this time I would be flat out lying about my real intentions. That wasn't unique, but it wasn't my first choice, either. Usually I got past it by telling myself that my real goal was the truth. That wasn't quite the case here, but when was the truth ever simple?

We got out of the car and headed across the street, Jenna carrying a briefcase to support her role as my note-taking flunkie. I went up the steps and onto the verandah like I owned the place, then rapped loudly on the door. I really hoped that Margaret Radmore would be home. If not, it would be on to wife number two, but any story is best told from the beginning, and Simon and Margaret had married young, both in their early twenties.

As we stood on the verandah, waiting to see if Radmore would come to the door, Jenna peeked around the corner at the narrow driveway and said, "No Mercedes."

Not that we'd expected there to be. If Simon didn't want to be found, he'd hardly have parked his car in sight.

I was about to knock again when I heard footsteps inside, then the door swung open and I saw a trim, tall woman with white hair pulled back into bun, a few strands floating loose and framing a face that had the kind of bone structure that aged well. She wore jeans, a flowery, loose-fitting shirt and a pair of lime-green Crocs that didn't go with the outfit. She gave us a quick once-over, sniffed, then said "Yes?" in a tone so crisp it could have snapped.

"Hi, I'm Kris Redner and this is my daughter and research assistant, Jenna," I said, handing Radmore a business card. "I have a somewhat unusual request. I'm a writer working on a biography of Simon Cousens and I was hoping you might have a few minutes to give us some insight into him."

Radmore snorted, then said, "Simon Cousens. Now there's a name I haven't heard in years. Still alive is he?"

"Very much so," I said, although I thought it no better than a 50-50 proposition. "I know you were a hugely important part of Simon's early life, and I think one of the few good sources available about that part of his story. I really would appreciate your help."

Radmore examined my business card as if she'd picked up something rotten and said, "I've never heard of you."

That was good news. "Well, I'm somewhat less than famous, but I do think that Simon has an interesting story, one that deserves to be told. Wouldn't you agree?"

"You're on a first-name basis with him, are you?"

"Not yet, but we have spoken to his current wife, who assures us that he will give full co-operation. Of course, I've been around long enough to know that the story he tells about himself might be a little different than what others observed."

Radmore allowed herself a grim little smile and said, "No doubt. How many wives has he had now?"

"Five, actually."

She shook her head. "Quite remarkable, but then Simon was always a rather unusual man."

I nodded enthusiastically, as if I was already grateful for this banal scrap of information. "Would it be a terrible inconvenience to take up just a bit of your time now, as we're already here?"

"This is how you work, is it? Just show up at people's doors."

I decided to take a chance. "It reduces the likelihood that they will tell me to piss off."

Radmore smiled at that, showing her first flash of humanity.

"All right. Why not? I'll give you the lowdown on the Simon I knew back then, but you have to remember, we were married more than 40 years ago and were only together for a few years."

"Of course, but early experiences are formative."

Radmore nodded, then stepped back and said, "Come in, then. We will have tea."

We stepped inside and I saw a longish hallway, floors refinished to a high gloss and everything else painted white. A board with a row of coat hooks was affixed to the left-hand wall. Hanging on it were a short pink raincoat, an umbrella with a pattern of song birds, and a baggy brown cardigan with a pair of gardening gloves stuffed into the pocket. No sign of a man on the premises.

Radmore pointed us to a narrow living room, also white. The walls were covered with pictures of waterfalls, a rushing stream, a forest in fall, the same forest in winter. Most were acrylics, some were watercolours. The subjects were conventional, but the artist wasn't without talent. I wondered if it was Radmore herself.

"Have a seat," she said, pointing us towards a stiff white couch. Then she disappeared toward the back of the house and we could hear water running into a kettle.

"What do you think?" Jenna whispered.

"Wary but interested. No love lost between the two of them after all of these years."

"Agreed. I think we are going to hear a lot of ancient history. Perhaps I prepared too many questions. Maybe we should keep it short."

"Let's play it by ear. The more we know about Simon, the better chance we have of figuring out where he'd seek refuge."

By the time Radmore came back with a tea tray that held a flower-patterned pot and three matching cups, Jenna had her notebook out and ready. We'd decided that I'd try to engage the wives in conversation, get them to focus on me and hope they'd ignore the fact that notes were being taken. People didn't speak as freely when they were worried that their words would form some kind of record.

I sipped the tea, Earl Grey, I thought, then said, "I know your time is valuable, so let's get started. You mentioned that you and Simon married quite young. Where did you first meet?"

"We were students at Cambridge, the Cavendish Laboratory. I'm sure you've heard of it. It's world famous."

What little I knew about physics came from watching The Big Bang Theory, but I nodded and said, "Of course."

"Simon was a bit of an exotic creature, coming as he did from the wilds of Canada."

She said that without any apparent irony. According to Wikipedia, Simon was born on a farm near Arnprior, just outside of Ottawa, hardly the wilds of anywhere.

"He was a scholarship student, exceptionally bright. Not that high intelligence was unusual at the Cavendish, but Simon had a kind of charisma, a self-confidence that was in stark contrast to the nerdy group of Brits who were our classmates.

"We met in a mathematics class, actually. It was Michaelmas term, first term as you'd call it here. I won't bore you with the details. I knew right away that I fancied him. He was exceptionally tall and had a movie star look about him." She paused, shrugged and said, "I suppose that sounds shallow, but I was young.

"I was confident that I would get him. As you can imagine, the number of women studying physics in the late 1970s was limited. As it turned out, I didn't have to work at it. Simon had noticed me, too. I was a handsome woman when I was younger. Not pretty, although at the time I didn't think that mattered to Simon. That very first day, he invited me for coffee. I didn't drink it back then. Strictly tea in my house growing up, but Simon had North American tastes, of course."

I wasn't sure this was going to lead anywhere useful, but I didn't want to interrupt her flow. At least I was getting a good idea of Simon, as he had been.

"By Lent term, we were sleeping together and a few months later, we moved in to a cramped little flat above a fish and chips shop. You could always smell the frying.

"I thought I had found my soul-mate. Both Simon and I were intensely interested in physics, of course. It was our life and I expected that it would be our life's work. We both came down from Cambridge with master's degrees.

"Then we faced a decision about where to do our PhDs. I was planning on either MIT or Harvard, but Simon wanted to come home to Canada. I compromised, or perhaps I should say I went along with his plan to attend the University of Toronto. We were accepted, naturally, but U of T is hardly Harvard or MIT. It was a decision that decidedly narrowed the scope of my career."

As fascinating as Margaret Radmore found herself, it was Simon I was interested in. "And what about Simon, was he happy there?"

"Oh, quite. Toronto is the centre of Canada's little universe, after all. He surprised me, though, by switching from physics to electronics engineering. It was a prescient move on his part. The technology revolution was just taking off. Physics, on the other hand, is more of a pure academic discipline. I'm interested in the big ideas, but Simon became fascinated by electronic gadgets."

Radmore refreshed her tea cup from the pot and continued. "After we finished our doctorates, Simon wanted to head to Ottawa and the National Research Council. Once again, I followed along, taking a position at Carleton. I had never envisioned myself at a mid-level provincial university, but there you are."

And I thought I had been reaching high by attending Ryerson for journalism. We hadn't gotten to what split up Radmore and Simon yet, but I was beginning to get some insight. What a snob she was.

Radmore put her tea cup back on the tray, as if her story was finished. I wanted to hear a couple more chapters. "So Simon was at the research council and you were at Carleton. Any kids?"

"Thankfully not. I didn't really have the time for them and I certainly didn't want to risk being left a single mother. By the time Simon and I arrived in Ottawa, I was already getting the feeling that our relationship might not last. Simon is an enthusiast, you see. He leaped into our marriage with very little thought or planning. At the time, I thought it was because he recognized me as the one he was meant to be with.

"One is easily deluded in one's youth, although I have observed from my students that the expectation of a long relationship isn't nearly what it was."

"There was another woman, then?" I said.

"Yes. Marie-France Latour. I introduced them, as it happens. I was just getting started with my own art at the time and I had met her through a class. Then I bumped into her at a gallery opening downtown. Simon was interested in her right away, I could see that."

"What was the attraction?"

"Sex, of course. It usually is, isn't it? It certainly wasn't her art, which was nothing but lazy swirls of colour, something that could be done by a child. She had that French way about her, though. Always touching, hugging. Apparently Simon craved that. He certainly didn't get it from me. Not the way I was brought up.

"She introduced him to a whole new, Bohemian world, quite different from my own. She had a place across the river in Old Chelsea. I suppose she still does. Quite a colony of artists and creative types there at the time. Not a scene in which I would have pictured Simon, but the man is a chameleon, always adapting to his environment. He actually grew a goatee. Quite ridiculous."

Margaret Radmore still had an ample store of venom, considering her relationship with Simon ended decades ago. I supposed it had been some time since she'd had the opportunity to vent about it.

"You will find Simon rather difficult to define in this book of yours," Radmore said. "He's a man who has had five different wives and five different lives, I expect. Not that I follow his exploits carefully. One can hardly have missed his playboy period, dancing in clubs until all hours, squandering his new millions. I was ancient history to him by then, of course."

"When did you actually divorce?"

"It was 1987. We'd been together for nearly 10 years. You will learn that 10 is Simon's magic number. He's not a philanderer, but rather, a serial monogamist. After 10 years, he gets bored and moves on. I suppose he might get bored earlier, but he acts around the 10-year mark."

"You think that's some kind of conscious plan?"

"Probably not, just how his brain is programmed."

"When was the last time you saw him?" Jenna asked.

"Simon? Let me think. Probably eight years ago? He was receiving an honorary degree at Carleton and I went to the ceremony, just to see how he looked now, in the way that one does. We didn't speak."

"This has certainly been helpful. I'm getting a better idea of Simon as a young man. Yours will be the primary view on that, but I wonder if there were any particular friends or relatives at that time, people who might give me additional insight."

What I really meant were people who might know where Simon would hide out. Old friends, the kind he had before becoming rich and somewhat famous, might be people he would trust now.

"By the time Simon and I came back here, it had been years since he'd been part of the little world he grew up in. We didn't talk about his past much. Frankly, I suspect it was rather uninteresting. The only name I do remember is his cousin, Rob. We called him the Cousens cousin. They were close growing up. Where he is now and whether he's even still alive, I have no idea.

"Now, if there is nothing else, I do have some rather pressing work to do."

"You've been generous with your time. I'll see that you get a copy of the book when it comes out."

Radmore looked as if she'd just been offered something extremely distasteful. "Don't bother. I've squandered enough of my time on Simon Cousens. I won't invest any more."

With that, Jenna and I thanked her again and headed back to the car. "Do you think we got anything useful out of that?" she asked.

"Maybe. We need to find out who Simon really is, how he thinks. We can certainly rule out Margaret Radmore as a source of refuge for him."

"I'll say. What a cold bitch."

"Asking about a former husband doesn't bring out the best in most people. She's a scientist who deals in facts and figures, not emotions."

"Sounds like wife number two filled that gap."

"We'll soon find out." Marie-France Latour's gallery was on our list for Sunday, but first, Jenna had arranged a special audience.

 Ten

Simon Cousens's fourth wife, Miranda Chambers-Addington, wasn't the sort of person one just dropped in on. Miranda, if I could be so audacious as to address her by her first name, was Ottawa's top divorce lawyer and a legend around the courthouse. I had never seen her in action, since I mostly covered the grubbier end of crime, but the short take on Miranda was that if your wife got her for a lawyer, the best course was to sign over everything, as it would be less painful than what Miranda would put you through.

As a result, Miranda was loaded, but she hadn't stopped there. Four years ago, she had married Frederick Addington, the founding partner of Addington, Schrenk and Barr, a big corporate law firm that siphoned money out of businessmen's pockets even faster than Miranda hoovered it up from unlucky husbands. Courthouse wags had called the marriage "the merger of the year."

Then it had gotten better. The septuagenarian Addington had died of a heart attack after only six months of wedded bliss, leaving Miranda with a big stake in the law firm and sole control of the Addington Foundation, her late husband's richly bankrolled philanthropic endeavour. As a result, Miranda had retired from the legal profession and now drifted through the upper levels of Ottawa society, bestowing gifts on charitable causes as it suited her.

Back when Miranda was a divorce lawyer, she was never difficult to get hold of because hard-to-reach lawyers were soon out-of-business lawyers. As a philanthropist and head of a major charitable foundation, she no longer needed to connect with the everyday world.

We'd gotten a break, though. Miranda was the sister of Pamela Chambers, the woman Jenna had just helped out at the women's charity. Jenna had clearly made a good impression there, because all it took was one phone call to set up a same-day appointment and on a Saturday, too. Although the plan had been to interview the wives in order, we had to take this chance while we had it.

The Addington Foundation had a suite of offices at 160 Elgin, a towering building right across the street from the courthouse. I knew it well from my job covering the courts as 160 was infested with lawyers, many of whom were my regular contacts.

Jenna and I were outside now, scarfing down sausages from a street vendor and waiting for our 1:30 appointment.

"Remember, we have to play this one differently," Jenna said. "Miranda knows I'm a private investigator, but our story is still that you're writing a book on Simon. The only difference is that I'll just be there as the person making the connection, not the girl taking notes."

"You're not going to take notes?"

"I might. I just won't be playing the mousey assistant."

'Mousey? I thought you looked fine."

"Of course I looked fine, but I don't like being anyone's assistant."

"And yet, you have asked me to be your assistant in this investigation."

"More like a front person or a kind of diversion."

"Thanks, you really know how to butter me up."

The expression on Jenna's face told me that he wasn't quite sure how to deal with my banter yet, although I would have thought she'd gotten a lot of experience with that when she was in the OPP. It was different with a newfound mother, I supposed.

"Look, I'm fine with this," I said. "It's a welcome relief from the book I'm supposed to be working on."

"So you've gone from pretending to work on one book to pretending to work on another?"

That was more like it. I smiled and gave her a little fist bump on the bicep.

"Does this Miranda know you, from the courthouse I mean?" Jenna asked.

"Maybe. We've never spoken but I know lawyers read my courthouse stuff faithfully. What could be more interesting than stories about their little world?"

"Exactly. Not a line of work where lack of ego is an issue."

"No, but it's understandable. To be good at the job, you have to out-think, out-argue and out-bullshit your opponent. Ego helps."

I looked at my watch and said, "Just about time. Shall we meet Miranda?"

Jenna tossed what was left of her sausage into a garbage can beside the food truck. We went through the tall, heavy glass doors and entered the lobby, headed for the elevators. Miranda's office was on the 20th floor. As we glided upward, I thought about how to play the interview with Miranda Chambers-Addington. She was Simon's most recent ex-wife, but they had been married only two years and had divorced six years ago. How much would she really know about him? On the other hand, she had married him and divorced him in short order. Perhaps she had found out something important.

The door to The Addington Foundation office was about eight feet tall and was made of a dark, heavy wood. It looked like it would withstand an assault from even the most determined charity seeker. Two sidelights flanked the door, their glass frosted to protect those within from the eyes of envious neighbours. A discreet brass plaque to the side of the door carried the foundation's name. The overall presentation didn't exactly shout "Come on in. We're here to help." I wondered how Chambers-Addington herself would compare to Margaret Radmore on the Celsius scale.

We stepped into the reception area, our footsteps muffled by a plush white carpet. The walls were covered in art of the explosion of colour school. I was sure it was expensive. I knew nothing about art and cared even less. Everything about the space was over sized, including the butter-coloured leather couches and the walls themselves, which had to be 12 feet high. I wondered how they managed that in an office building. If the goal was to make people feel small, it was a raging success.

In a far corner of the room, behind a shining glass desk, sat a young woman in a black skirt and jacket and white blouse. Her hair was short, dark and glossy, her features as sculpted as those of a statue. She had accessorized her funeral director's outfit with a triple strand of pearls and red high heels. She must be the receptionist, although no doubt she had a far grander job title.

The woman finished whatever she was doing on her computer, then finally looked up, giving us the once over and sniffing slightly, as if she was trying to detect whether we were emitting an unpleasant odour.

"Yes?" she said, in a tone that implied that our visit was quite an inconvenience.

"Jenna Martin and Kris Redner," Jenna said in a no-nonsense tone. "We have a 1:30 with Ms. Chambers-Addington."

What Jenna would have preferred, I expected, was to pull out a badge and tell the bitchy little gatekeeper that she was police, but those days were behind her.

The woman, who hadn't introduced herself, turned to her computer to check whether such an appointment really existed, her long, red fingernails clacking on the keyboard.

Apparently seeing our names, she rose gracefully from her chair and indicated that we should follow her. We proceeded down a long corridor, then up a short staircase. Now I understood the 12-foot ceilings. The foundation had two floors in the office tower. The nameless assistant ushered us into a vast space that was flooded with sun, the west and south walls being all glass.

Miranda Chambers-Addington was already walking briskly across the room towards us, almost like she was glad to see us. She was an overly-thin woman, nearly six feet tall with full, curly grey hair and a tightly-fitted red dress. She reminded me of the red pencils they had handed out in school.

Jenna took the lead and said, "Jenna Martin. I'm the one who worked with your sister Pamela."

"Of course. She speaks highly of you. Nailed that slimeball of a CEO, I understand."

"I did," Jenna said.

"Long overdue. Pamela has been trying to get rid of him ever since she took over as chair of the board."

Then she turned toward me and extended a long, slim hand encrusted with rings. "You must be Kris Redner. Of course, I'm familiar with your work as a crime writer. Pamela says you're writing a book about Simon?"

"That's right, Ms Chambers-Addington, I am."

"Please just call me Miranda. The rest of it's quite a mouthful."

I nodded and said, "Sure, Miranda." I took it as a small but welcome sign that she might be human.

"We really appreciate you taking the time to see us on a Saturday," I said.

"That's not a problem, I've always worked Saturdays. It's actually the best time to see me. Fewer distractions, normally."

She motioned us towards a pair of couches that faced each other on either side of a gas fireplace. They were the same soft leather as those in the reception area. Maybe she had got a volume discount. We settled ourselves in and I pulled out my notebook, since we didn't need to use the writer and assistant ploy for this interview.

"So tell me about this book. Why are you writing it?" Miranda asked.

I hated it when the subject tried to control the interview, but it was a reasonable question.

"Change of pace for me. I want a break from writing about criminals and, from what I can gather so far, Simon is an intriguing subject. He's a major tech pioneer but he's also had an interesting and complex personal life."

"So a kind of tell-all, then?"

"I wouldn't put it that way. I think it's impossible to tell all about anyone. A biographer can never fully understand her subject, but what interests me is how he shaped technological development and the forces that drive him."

"I'm afraid I can't be of much help on his career in technology, really not my zone. You'd do better to ask Brendan Connor about that. The two of them have been connected at the hip for decades."

"He's certainly on our interview list."

"And what about Simon himself? Has he agreed to this book or is it an unauthorized biography?"

"The latter, in the sense that he won't get approval of the final text, but I'm confident he will be on board."

"Yes, Simon's favourite topic is Simon. I'm sure he will be flattered to be the subject of a book," Miranda said with a smile that reflected both affection and disdain.

"In my experience, that doesn't make him unique."

Miranda laughed and said, "Having spent my life studying the egotistical male, I can assure you that you're right."

"So you consider Simon egotistical?"

"Absolutely, but show me a real achiever who isn't. I consider it more of a characteristic than a flaw."

"OK. Let me confirm a few basics. You were married to Simon for two years, but divorced six years ago, correct?"

"Correct, and before we go any farther, I need to know if you intend to quote me in this book."

"I do, but feel free to go off the record any time if you have something that can add to my depth of understanding about Simon, but that you don't want attributed."

"All right. Proceed."

"How did the two of you meet?"

"In an odd way, I have to say. I represented his previous wife Paula in her divorce from Simon. It was hotly contested as poor Simon hadn't gotten a pre-nup. He's a romantic at heart, you know, always convinced that love will last. I'm afraid the statistics don't back it up."

I nodded. I couldn't argue with the numbers, but I found it interesting that he'd married his wife's divorce lawyer. Most divorced men I knew loathed the lawyer even more than the ex-wife. If I were really writing a book, I'd find it a useful plot twist.

"That has to be pretty unusual. How did it come about?"

"It was a matter of intellectual attraction. Simon said he fell in love with my mind, and I think it's true. I was certainly a contrast to Paula. Dreadful little woman. Their relationship was almost entirely physical. I'd prefer it if you didn't quote me on that, by the way."

"Of course. We're hoping to meet Paula soon. I'll form my own impressions."

"Best to try early afternoon. She will be hung over in the morning and back in the bag well before dinner."

I was sorry to hear that. Paula had been married to Brendan and then Simon. I hoped she would be able to tell me about the history between the two. My intuition said it had to have something to do with Simon's disappearance, or apparent disappearance.

Miranda picked up the thread of her story. "After the legal matters were resolved, Simon stopped by my office and brought me a dozen red roses. That was a first and it certainly caught my attention. Then he asked me to dinner. I should have said no. Here was a man who'd already had three strikes in the marriage game and I'd just taken him to the cleaners in the settlement. It seemed like an impossible relationship, but he's extremely charming, charismatic even, and rather handsome.

"I had never married. A side effect of being a divorce lawyer, I suppose, and I hadn't had a relationship for some time. I decided to treat myself. Something equivalent to a spa weekend, I thought at the time.

"I hadn't reckoned on Simon's ability to reinvent himself to appeal to the woman he's pursuing. Even before I ended up with this," she said, waving her hand at her opulent office, "I had begun to devote myself to philanthropy. I made a lot of money in my career, but all I had really accomplished was to help rich people tear each other apart. I wanted to do some good and Simon said he did, too.

"He said his sybaritic life was over and he seemed genuinely interested in diverting his attention to philanthropy. I wanted to believe him. Everyone wants to find a soul mate, wouldn't you agree?"

"I would," I said, and thought of Darcy. Was he a soul mate or just a lover?

"Let me clarify something. You said you cleaned Simon out in the divorce. Did he have the means to be a philanthropist?"

"Excellent question. When I first became involved with Simon, he was cash poor but he had a number of business ventures in development and a lifelong record of success. I figured he was just in a temporary downturn, one which I felt slightly guilty about causing by doing such a thorough job.

"Unfortunately, business opportunities that seemed promising didn't really pan out. That's the reality of the tech world, of course."

"I hear that he has something close to going to market, a green technology development that has huge financial potential."

"Does he? I hope so. When Simon is short of money, he becomes rather peevish and cheap. People in the media like to call him a tech billionaire, but he was barely a millionaire when I was with him. He was heavily leveraged, too. Mortgages and loans stacked up.

"It's what drove us apart, in the end. I was too old and too wealthy to be squabbling about money. I was quite content to pay for our life, but Simon wouldn't have it. He's intensely proud, you know."

Barely a millionaire. I reflected briefly on what it must be like to be so poor.

Miranda glanced at her watch. We hadn't set a fixed length for the interview, but I knew the signs well. She either had another appointment or was running out of enthusiasm for reliving her relationship with Simon. I had one key area left to cover and I got straight to it.

"As part of my research, I want to cast as wide a net as possible. I'm especially interested in lifelong friends or relatives. Pals, the kind of people Simon might reach out to if he was in trouble."

Miranda looked at me intently. I had her attention again.

"Is he in trouble?"

"Not that I know of. It's simply a figure of speech. What I meant was, people he feels he can rely on, especially those who knew him as a young man. I don't intend to spend a lot of the book dwelling on his early years, but they are a bit of a mystery at the moment."

"That's exactly the way Simon likes it. He really never talked about his life before Cambridge, although I know he grew up on a farm somewhere in the Ottawa Valley, rather a poor farm. I expect he wants people to see him for what he is now, not what he was."

"So no one at all, then?"

"The only name that comes to mind is his cousin Rob. I think he lives on the Ottawa River somewhere north of Arnprior. Simon would go up there occasionally and the two of them would go out on Rob's boat. Fishing, Simon said, although I think drinking was the main attraction. I never met the man myself."

There he was again, the Cousens cousin. I scribbled his name into my notebook and underlined it.

"Tell me," Miranda said, "have you met Simon yet?"

"I have," Jenna said. "I was at his wedding. The most recent one."

"Ah, the wife young enough to be his daughter. I have to say he's venturing into new territory there, although it's not difficult to see why he'd prefer her to a desiccated old thing like me."

Miranda gave a self-deprecating laugh, inviting us to contradict her. I passed.

She turned her attention to Jenna and said, "I suppose you must be a friend of the bride."

"She was a client, actually. That's how we met."

"Really?" I could see that Miranda was caught between the

desire to know why Simon's new wife had hired a private investigator and her unwillingness to admit that she was still interested
in Simon's situation.

She paused for a moment, then said, "Let me add one more thing.
I said that Simon reinvents himself to appeal to the next woman
he desires. I'm not sure that's entirely true. It's equally possible
that his periodic reinventions are all about him, and the women
he chooses just accessorize his new lifestyle. Whatever was behind
it, you need to understand that this reinvention is at the core of
who Simon is. He was fond of quoting George Bernard Shaw to the
effect that 'Life isn't about finding yourself. Life is about creating
yourself.'"

I couldn't argue with Shaw. What we needed to find out was
whether Simon was still creating his own story, or whether someone else had taken control of the plot.

 # Eleven

Jenna and I had stayed up late talking about what we had learned Saturday. In Jenna's view, it wasn't much. She was focused entirely on locating Simon, as she should be, and it seemed that neither Margaret nor Miranda had any recent communication with him. I wondered a bit about Miranda, though. She certainly had the means to help Simon and also some residual affection. If he was trying to raise money for Alicia's project, wouldn't she have been one of the people he would have turned to? I should have asked.

Jenna was disappointed, but for me everything was a story and I had found myself becoming more intrigued by Simon. In a world full of dull, predictable people, he was enigmatic and mercurial. Maybe I *should* be writing a book about him, or at least a long feature piece. Missing millionaires always attracted readers.

We knocked it off around midnight. I had encouraged Jenna to be optimistic about what we might find today. Margaret and Miranda were the two bookends of Simon's story before he met Alicia. They weren't the most empathetic pair I had ever met. The two wives in the middle seemed to be a different sort. Maybe we would have more luck today.

Jenna had spent the morning online finding out everything she could about Paula Connor and Marie-France Latour before we set off to meet Latour at her gallery.

It had taken us about 20 minutes to drive from downtown Ottawa to the gallery in the village of Old Chelsea. We slowed as we crossed the Macdonald-Cartier Bridge, taking in the power of the flooded Ottawa River as it raced and pounded under the bridge, water droplets misting up into the air like floating diamonds.

Once we had crossed into Quebec and headed north on Autoroute 5, the city disappeared in a hurry. It was one of the things I loved about Ottawa, the way the city receded so quickly and the forest took over, especially on the Quebec side. Old Chelsea was just at the entrance to Gatineau Park, a major tourist attraction. Latour had chosen wisely when she set up her gallery in the village.

By the time we had arrived in Old Chelsea, it was nearly noon and my thought had been to try a good restaurant and expense it to Alicia. Jenna, however, had brought sandwiches in a cooler, like we were on a stakeout. They were sliced chicken with brie and peach chutney on ciabatta buns, so I certainly wasn't complaining.

We sat on a bench across from the Gallerie Latour, ate our sandwiches and observed the place. It was a fantastic May day, crisp, blue-skied and still just a touch cool. The gallery had perhaps been a general store at one time, its display windows now full of jewelry and small framed pictures. The building itself was a ramshackle, two-storey structure painted bright red. Inside, we could see white walls and spotlights illuminating a substantial display of art. Tourists shuffled down the street looking at the shops, some going into the gallery. We hadn't seen anyone come out carrying art.

"I've never understood how an art gallery works," Jenna said, "especially in a little place like this. I know the owner gets a percentage but how much can she really sell?"

"Lots of Ottawa cottage money up here, tourists in both the summer and winter. People want something local. Maybe it's just a lifestyle thing or perhaps she got a bundle in the divorce from Simon."

"If someone gave me a bundle, I sure wouldn't be spending my time in some sleepy little Quebec village," Jenna said. "I mean, what could possibly happen here?"

"Not much. I expect that's what people like about it. Shall we go meet the second Mrs. Cousens?"

We crossed the quiet treed street and entered the gallery. A brass bell attached to the top of the door rang to announce our arrival. I was happy to see that, for the moment, there were no customers.

The gallery had a confusing jumble of smells. I identified oil paint, muffins, some kind of incense and the musty smell common to old buildings. On the right-hand wall there were large pieces with the swirls of colour that Margaret Radmore had belittled. On the left were dozens of smaller works, the usual scenes of Gatineau Park, the Wakefield covered bridge and the sweeping view from the park's Champlain Lookout.

Then a curtain was pulled aside in a doorway in the back wall and a middle-aged woman stepped into the gallery. She was short, perhaps five foot two, and full-figured. Like many women who had reached a certain age, her dress was more draped than fitted. Her hair was long on the right side, cut close on the left. Remarkably, it was pink. She sized us up with deep brown eyes that looked both wise and wary, not sure whether we were customers or trouble. She glanced at Jenna's business suit and briefcase, then said, "If you're lawyers, I really must insist that you take the matter up with my own avocat. I can give you the card."

I laughed. I was rarely mistaken for a lawyer. "A lawyer? I can't imagine it. No, I'm a writer, actually."

Marie-France relaxed, and showed a smile that was soft and teeth that were perfect.

"Sorry for the insult. I'm having a bit of a dispute with a customer over the provenance of an older piece I sold him. A deputy minister, thinks he's someone terribly important."

"I know more than a few people like that. Ottawa is full of them."

"Yes. So you're a writer. I hope you are here to talk about art."

"Not exactly. My name is Kris Redner, and this is my research assistant, Jenna Martin. I'm working on a book about Simon Cousens. I was hoping that you could spare us a few minutes."

"Ah, Simon. Yes, we have a history."

"I'm actually doing a series of books on the pioneers of Ottawa's technology industry, but I'm starting with Simon," I said, embroidering my cover story. "He seems such an interesting fellow."

"He certainly thinks he is."

"You disagree?"

Marie-France shrugged her shoulders and said, "Not really. It's only that Simon believes his life is a grand story, and he's the hero. He is an interesting man, though. I'll grant him that."

"I'd love to find out more. Can I steal a little bit of your time?"

Marie-France looked around the gallery. Although there wasn't a customer in sight, she said, "It's not a good time. Sunday is a busy day, people up for the weekend. Yes, there is a slight lull at the moment, but customers will drift in again soon."

"I understand. What if we just chatted until that happens?"

I figured that if I could get her talking about herself and Simon, she'd want to keep going. Most people were keen to tell interesting stories about themselves, and I was sure her time with Simon would be one of those. What was the attraction between the rising tech star and the pink-haired artist? Margaret Radmore had said it was just sex, but I doubted the story was that simple.

"Well, I suppose I could do that. Come upstairs to my studio. I can keep an eye on the gallery from there."

We followed her through the curtained doorway and up a steep flight of stairs, the steps worn in the middle from years of use. I imagined that the area had been storage space years ago, but Marie-France had removed most of a wall, leaving herself a view of the gallery below. The studio was all windows on the back wall, looking out over a treed garden that was a wild confusion of perennials and shrubs. Three large, incomplete works were on easels and brushes, knives and paints were scattered on a work table. Marie-France pointed us to two paint-flecked wooden chairs and then sat in an old, red upholstered chair that looked like it was from the 1940s.

"So, Simon Cousens. What do you want to know?"

"I'm trying to piece together the story of his early life. I should tell you that we spoke to Margaret Radmore yesterday."

"Ah, Margaret. I hope you didn't get frostbite."

"Well, she's certainly reserved, to put it politely. She was helpful, though."

"That's a surprise. Of course, I don't have a dispassionate view of Margaret. She detested me and my art and she made that very clear. I suppose it was understandable, under the circumstances."

"Which were?"

"Let's just say that there was a certain amount of overlap between Margaret and myself. In the latter part of Simon's marriage to her, I was his real woman."

Old jealousies died hard. Margaret and Marie-France were still carrying resentments over a man that neither of them had been married to for decades.

"Why don't we start with how you met," I said, offering an easy question to loosen her up.

"Simon attended one of my shows. When he stepped into the room, it was like there was a light shining on him. He was very tall and quite handsome, still just 30 years old. Five years older than me, but still a young man.

"We chatted and he was very friendly and admiring of my work. His wife was just the opposite. From the look on her face, she'd just eaten a pickle, then smelled something bad. Perhaps it is that sense women have, when they meet another who wants to take their man."

"And was that how you felt, then, that it was love at first sight?"

Marie-France's laugh was deep and genuine. "Love, no, not at all. Lust actually, but it's a reliable precursor to what we call love, as I'm sure you know."

I leaned toward her and nodded, trying to establish a connection and to draw her attention away from Jenna, taking notes. "I've had some experience with that myself," I said.

Marie-France sized me up, as if measuring my age and type, then said, "I'm sure you have."

"So how quickly did the overlap begin, if that's not too personal a question?"

"Well, this is all personal isn't it? You are going to put this into a book?"

That wasn't the track I wanted her on. Once people started thinking about their words in print, they became much more cautious.

"At this point, I'm just trying to get a better sense of Simon. There will be much more research and many interviews before the book is complete. I will check back with you to OK anything that involves you."

The expression on her face suggested she wasn't buying that, but she decided to answer my question. "Not immediately. I'm a passionate person and I place feelings over logic, but Simon was still somewhat cautious back then. I think Margaret had put his whole being in, what do you say, a chastity belt."

"But you were able to find the key."

"Oh yes. Simon was just beginning to acquire art. At first, we'd meet for coffee and I'd educate him about the market. I was young, so naturally I assumed I knew quite a lot. Then he began to buy some of my small pieces. When I delivered them, we'd have lunch. Eventually, lunch led to amorous afternoons. It wasn't difficult. I was a good looking woman then, and he was a handsome man with significant money. At first, our assignations took place in rooms at the Chateau Laurier, then it became suites. We began to see each other more frequently, and art was not the topic of interest.

"The fact that he was married really wasn't my concern. His wife seemed to spend most of the time in her lab. Simon was lonely and, I suppose, looking for an adventure."

It was a familiar story. I'd slept with a few married men myself. They were eager and had low expectations, but I hadn't yet found one who was worth the hand-holding it would take to get him through a divorce.

"But more than that, in the end. You married and had two children, right?"

Marie-France gave an expressive shrug, as if to say that of course she got her man, once she set her mind to it. "It wasn't difficult. Simon was starved for love, both physical and emotional. For my part, it was easy to fall in love with Simon. There's a certain sense of power in him. It attracts people, both men and women."

Marie-France paused and looked down into the gallery as if searching for customers, but her mind was far away, somewhere in the past. She seemed to gather herself, then said, "I loved him passionately, and he loved me. It lasted for nearly 10 years. I've never stopped loving him, really, but Simon's emotional attention span is relatively short. Finite, as he'd put it.

"Once we'd been married five years, I started to feel his interest diminish. At the time, I thought it was because of the way the children had changed our lives. Luc came along after we'd been together only two years, than Chantale quickly followed.

"Simon moved us to a house in Rockcliffe. It was ridiculously large but it had a wonderful conservatory that I used as a studio. I thought we would be happy there, but Simon missed the sexual adventure of our early days. There was quite a lively party scene in the city at the time, all young tech people on the rise. Simon wanted to be part of that, but I had the two small children to look after. He solved that problem by hiring a nanny."

Then Marie-France paused and said, "I don't mind telling you what happened next but I absolutely do not want it in your book."

I signalled to Jenna to close her notebook and prepared to hear a story about Simon and the nanny.

"Simon became addicted to the party scene and the cocaine and champagne that came with it. We were out four or five nights a week, until the clubs closed. Then sometimes we would go home with other couples to, let's say, share further adventures.

"Then it became complicated. Simon took a fancy to the wife of his business partner, Brendan Connor. Our little private parties quickly led to what we called wife swapping back then."

I felt like some major puzzle pieces had just clicked into place. Simon and Brendan Connor had a more complex relationship than I had thought. Did it play a role in Simon's disappearance?

"At first, all he wanted was to watch Paula and me together. This was new territory for me, but she was a very gentle lover. Then, we progressed to having sex in the same room with our own husbands. Brendan has one of those mansions on the rural edge of Kanata, and the master bedroom is like something from Versailles. It felt like we were making a movie. A pornographic movie, I have to admit.

"Then Brendan escalated things, demanding that the other two watch while I had rough sex with him. This was where I drew the line. I was devastated when Simon urged me to do it.

"I could tolerate sharing Simon with another woman. After all, I had already done it. This was different, though. Simon was basically demanding that I put on a show for his pleasure, and Paula's. And Brendan, he's a disgusting little man. Have you met him?"

"Not yet."

"Well, you're going to want a shower afterwards. Brendan's thing is dominating women. That's what turns him on. I'm talking about tying them up, spanking them, that kind of thing. Paula is submissive, so she was perfect for him until he grew bored with her. No challenge, I suppose.

"I remember him saying to me, 'You're a little hellcat, but we'll see how long that lasts when you start to feel my belt on your ass.' I think it probably made him hard just talking about it.

"That was it for me. I took Simon's keys, walked out and drove myself home. Simon showed up the next morning with a giant bouquet of flowers and an apology, carried away by the moment, that kind of thing. I decided to let it go. I was still in love with him and we had two young children."

Even though all of this had taken place years ago, the story had brought tears to Marie-France's eyes.

"God, I feel like a fool telling two strangers all of this, but my relationship with Simon is something that troubles me still. I could use a drink. Do you want one?"

Not wanting to seem anti-social, I quickly agreed. Jenna nodded her assent, too. Marie-France went to a fridge at the back of the studio and took out a bottle of white wine, then opened a cupboard and removed three glasses.

As she poured the sauvignon blanc, she said, "I don't normally drink while the gallery is open, but my assistant Anik will be in shortly."

"Wine and art seem like a natural pairing," I said.

"Very much so, but I'm getting fat."

It would have been polite to contradict her, but also insincere. Instead, I said, "So was that the turning point for you and Simon?"

"Looking back, yes. Our lives were out of control. I had stopped painting and all I could think about was holding on to him, but then I found out that he had kept partying with Brendan and Paula, while telling me that he was working late on a project. Somehow, out of all of that, he ended up marrying Paula. As I said, I think Brendan had grown tired of her, but still, I was surprised. I should tell you that Simon has a somewhat dominant side himself. I had never seen it as a sexual thing before that, but he's very confident, assured, convinced he's right. He expects others to follow his commands. Paula must have played on that. Me, I'm the sort that doesn't take orders from anyone. It was always a source of friction with Simon, but our infatuation with each other took the unpleasant edge off it.

"So that's the story of me and Simon. We separated, then finally divorced when he announced that he wanted to remarry. I'll admit that I had hoped he would grow bored with Paula, like Brendan had. She's actually not a very interesting person, once you get past the sex. I guess Simon finally figured that out, but it took him years. I think he was too proud to admit that he'd made a mistake.

"I went my own way, raised the children by myself. Simon was always generous with support, but I had to move out of the Rockcliffe house."

"Where are the children now?"

"They are grown, of course. Sadly, they have moved away. Luc is a petroleum engineer in Calgary and Chantale teaches French literature at UBC."

So not within easy range of a wayward father seeking refuge, I thought. I heard the bell on the gallery door ring, then footsteps coming up the staircase. A thin, boyish woman entered the studio. Anik, I assumed. She could have been anywhere between 18 and 25. Her hair was short and jet black, and she had dolphins tattooed on both forearms. A substantial ring hung from her nose and her tiny face had a "Who the hell are you?" expression.

"This is Anik," Marie-France said. "Anik, meet Kris and Jenna. They are working on a book about my former husband."

Anik greeted that news with a derisive snort, then leaned in to give Marie-France a lingering kiss full on the lips. So, the experience with the Connors had awakened something in Marie-France as well.

It was clearly time to wrap up the interview, but I had one more question. "When I write a biography, I like to get the fullest possible sense of my subject. Secondary sources can be important. Were there any good friends or close relatives he kept in touch with when you were together? I'm talking about the kind of person he might rely on if he was in trouble."

I wanted to ask the question the same way I had asked Miranda, to see how Marie-France's reaction compared.

As if on cue, she leaned forward, her face filled with concern. "Is he?"

"No, I don't think so. It's a way of putting things."

She leaned back in her chair, clearly not convinced. "The reason I ask, there was a man here two days ago inquiring about Simon and his friends, who he'd rely on."

That was a point she might have mentioned sooner, I thought. I shot Jenna a glance and said, "Who was he?"

"He said he was a detective."

"Police?"

"No, a private investigator of some sort. An older man with a cruel face and dark eyes. I remember that his hands were scarred, like he had been in a lot of fights."

"I assume he gave you his name."

"Better than that, he gave me his card. I have it here." Marie-France fished a stained canvas bag out of a box beside her chair. The bag looked big enough to hold all her worldly goods, but she found the card right away. Holding it at arm's length, she said "Paul Polanco, private investigator."

The she passed me the card and said, "You keep it. I won't be calling him."

"Did you tell him anything?"

"Only that I hadn't seen Simon in years and had no idea of what he was up to now. I'd be careful if I were you. I didn't trust him. There's something off about him, like he has a cruelty he's just barely keeping under control.

"Will you call me if you find out what this Polanco is up to?"

"Of course," I said, but my mind was already racing ahead. So someone else also wanted to find Simon and the $10 million. Who was it? I feared that what had looked like a harmless quest for information and an easy paycheque for Jenna had suddenly turned into something quite different.

 Twelve

We had nearly an hour's drive to get from Old Chelsea to Paula Connor's place in the wilds of West Carleton, on the far edge of Ottawa. That wasn't because the Quebec village was remote, but because Ottawa seemed to stretch on forever. It was one of the things I had found difficult to adjust to, after my years in the never-ending suburbia of Toronto. The part of Ottawa that people called the city was relatively compact. Then there were the suburbs, which were mostly found on the other side of a vast swath of government-owned greenbelt, which I was told had been preserved to prevent suburban sprawl. The plan had gone somewhat awry. Finally, one reached an area that was clearly the country, but still part of the city. Maybe it all made sense to someone.

We had passed most of the drive in silence, Jenna clearly deep in thought. Marie-France had given us a lot to think about. My gut told me told me that whatever had happened to Simon Cousens had something to do with the weird dynamic between him and Brendan Connor. The two men had shared a business for years, even shared each other's wives. Now Simon was gone and so was a big chunk of Brendan's money. Somehow, everything that had happened between them over the decades had led to this moment, but what was it, and where did Alicia fit into the whole mess?

And then there was this PI, Polanco, asking the same kind of questions we were and already out in front of us. What was his angle and who was his client? Brendan? I felt like Brendan and Simon had created a vortex and now Jenna and I were being sucked into it.

We had passed the last of the suburbs and were now heading north on Dunrobin Road. We were surrounded by farms and forest, and to our right we saw glimpses of the Gatineau Hills.

Finally tired of the silence, I said, "So what did you make of Marie-France?"

"I'm not a big fan of hippie-dippie people, but I liked her. You?"

"I liked her, too. She's certainly a contrast to Margaret and Miranda. It would be interesting to know why Simon left her, really, and with two kids."

"I don't know. How about men are beasts?"

"You really think that?"

"Maybe I've just known too many cops."

"Me too, but not all of them were beasts."

"I guess I've been unlucky then."

I knew very little about Jenna's romantic life before I met her. She never discussed it and I didn't want to pry. Maybe now was the moment. "You want to talk about it?"

"Not today."

I fought the urge to say something banal about the right guy coming along. Truthfully, I didn't even know whether Jenna was into guys or girls. When it came to that aspect of her life, she was about as open as a clam.

Perhaps to head me off, she said, "Things seem to be going well between you and Darcy."

"Yes, I think so. I'm still not sure where we're headed, but I'm enjoying the journey."

"Well, I hope it works out. I like the novelty of having parents."

"You will still have parents, whatever happens between Darcy and me."

"You know what I mean, parents who are a couple."

I nodded. It was good to know that she cared, that she was cheering for us. I decided to switch the topic before the whole conversation started to sound like one of those cheesy Hallmark movies.

"What do you want to do about this guy Polanco?" I asked.

"Right now, nothing. I'm going to talk to Alicia tomorrow to update her on our work. I'll mention Polanco. Maybe she'll ask me to look into him. I expect she will. We need to know what he's up to but it's not part of the job we have now."

It made perfect sense for Jenna to focus on exactly the work that she was being paid to do, but it wasn't the way I liked to proceed. More than 20 years in journalism had taught me to turn over every rock, follow every lead. I knew Jenna was trained to do the same, but I could see the consistency in her approach. When she was a cop, Jenna had stuck to the rules. Now, in her new job as a PI, she was following the rules for that job, as she interpreted them.

I was starting to see the downside of private investigation work. The investigator was really just a tool of her client. Either that or she didn't get paid.

"You don't want to know who he works for?" I asked.

"Sure I do, but it's got to be Brendan Connor, don't you think?"

"Seems a safe bet. It means that Brendan either knows or suspects that something is up with Simon. That's bad news for Alicia."

"Nothing she can't handle, I'm sure," Jenna said. "That woman is as tough as rawhide. The one I'm interested in meeting is Paula. Marie-France makes her sound like a sex doll and Miranda clearly wasn't a fan. I want to know what Simon saw in her."

"Me too, but I think the real goal of this interview has to be to find out more about the relationship between Brendan and Simon. I think everything comes back to that."

I slowed down as we passed through the village of Dunrobin, then turned left on Thomas A. Dolan Parkway. It was a grand name for a broken down stretch of rural road with little but woods and the occasional house on either side.

"It could," Jenna said. "It sounds like Brendan has been more of a constant in Simon's life than anyone else. Maybe the disappearance of Simon and the money has something to do with that relationship and nothing to do with Alicia.

"I'm not going to go blundering into Brendan Connor's business without a good reason, though. He sounds like a nasty piece of work."

"But aren't we already into his business? Brendan isn't going to be happy when he finds out you are working for Alicia, if he doesn't know already."

"Too bad. We're trying to find his money. He should be happy."

"Of course, we only have Alicia's version of what happened to Simon and the money. You trust her?"

Jenna's laugh was closer to a snort. "Not at all. She's already told us that she has an angle here. If Simon and the money don't show up, her big project and the chance to make a shitload of money are out the window. "

"You think that's her real angle?"

"I think it's one of them, but probably not the only one. I don't know Alicia well, but I do know her well enough to know that she's clever and calculating. She will do what's in her own best interests. Right now, that's probably finding Simon and the money."

The GPS on Jenna's phone interrupted our conversation, the computerized voice saying, "In 400 metres, turn right on Woodkilton Road."

I slowed the vehicle, made the turn, and then almost immediately, the voice said, "You have reached your destination."

Instead of a house, we saw a chain link fence that had to run a hundred yards. The thing was eight feet tall and looked like something from a prison, missing only the barbed wire at the top. On the other side, all we could see was dense bush, cedars mostly. I drove slowly along the fence. There had to be a gate. About halfway along, we saw it, two heavy stone pillars with a gate that looked heavy enough to stop a tank. Beyond it was a lane shaded by tall maples, no house in sight.

"Maybe we should have phoned ahead," Jenna said.

"Maybe, but from what we hear about Paula, I wouldn't necessarily expect a friendly reception. Better to catch her off guard."

The gate was set back about 10 feet from the road, and I saw a call button and intercom mounted on the left post. "OK, good news. We can ring back."

"What are we going to tell her?" Jenna said.

"Stick to our story."

I pressed the intercom button. No answer. Then I pressed it again two more times. My reward was a woman's voice squawking, "What the hell do you want?"

"Ms. Connor, my name's Kris Redner. I'm a writer working on a story about Simon Cousens. I'd really like to hear what you have to say about him."

"Is this an obituary?" the harsh, metallic voice asked.

"No."

"Then fuck off."

There was a click and she was gone.

"That went well," Jenna said.

"Maybe you should have told her you were the police."

"I could have, but there's only one problem. I'm not the police."

I turned off the car, then said, "Well, I'm not going to drive all the way out here without giving it our best shot. What do you think about climbing that fence?"

"I think I would call that trespassing."

"Technically, I suppose."

"Technically? She has an eight-foot fence around her property and she just told us to fuck off."

"You're the one who's always telling me you're not a cop anymore, so think like a PI. What do you suppose Paul Polanco would do?"

"I have no idea."

"He'd climb the fence, that's what he'd do. Let's go and ring her door bell. If she still tells us to fuck off, then we've got our answer."

"So this is what reporters do, just barge right in on someone who doesn't want to talk to you?"

"Absolutely. I couldn't tell you how many times I've walked into apartment buildings pretending to be a resident. Sometimes, I get to a door and say 'delivery'."

"All right. Let's do it then. Are you going to be able to get over the fence with that sore shoulder of yours?"

"Of course," I said, although I wasn't so sure. After talking her into it, I had to give it a try.

We got out of the car, locked it and then walked up to the fence. The chain link was small for a good toehold, but Jenna was up and over the barrier like she did it every day. I was a little more tentative. OK, a lot more tentative. My damn shoulder felt like someone was sticking a knife in it, but I tried not to grimace. I made it to the top, but then came the awkward part. While there was no barbed wire, the links did end in pointed, twisty tops that made it hard to hang on. I needed to swing my weight over the top and quickly grip the other side.

"You can do it," Jenna said. "I'll catch you if you fall."

What did she think I was, an old woman? I swung over the fence, ignoring the searing pain in my shoulder, latched on to the other side and let gravity work for me as I moved part-way down and then dropped to the ground.

"Hmm," Jenna said, sounding somewhat surprised.

We headed up the gravelled lane, our shoes crunching as we

went. The season's first serious cloud of mosquitoes soon identified our presence and swarmed in for a meal. After five minutes,
we saw a house at the end of the lane. I guess I had expected something grand, given the precautions taken to keep people out and the
fact that Paula Connor had been married to two rich men and had
gotten a big settlement from at least one of them.

Instead, we saw a dilapidated wooden house that looked more
like a cottage, one of those Viceroy prefab models. It sat on a small
rise and the front wall of the house was almost entirely glass, like
there was something special to see. It was surrounded by a wooden
deck supported by tall posts. On the left hand side, one had given
way, causing the whole thing to slump. The roof looked like it was
in need of an urgent re-shingling, and the finish on the wood was
peeling in strips, like a person with a bad sunburn.

"What a dump," Jenna said. "I didn't expect that."

"No. I wonder where all the money went?"

We walked up bowed stairs onto the deck. Rot had eroded its
surface, leaving a mottled pattern. "Watch your step," I said.

I approached a door that had once been red but was now a sad
shade of pink. There was no doorbell, so I pounded on the door.
That set off a chorus of barking. Small yappy dogs, at least three or
four from the volume of the barking.

We heard a harsh voice shout "Shut the fuck up!" The barking
turned into a chorus of whimpers. Then the door was wrenched
open by a woman who couldn't have been more than five feet tall.
Her long dark hair was streaked with grey and her face was puffy,
her features indistinct. It was mid-afternoon and I could already
smell wine on her breath. She was barefoot and wore black yoga
pants and a red sweater that emphasized her large breasts. I could
see how she might have once been beautiful but that was quite a
few cases of wine ago.

Paula looked us up and down, then said, "Didn't I just tell you
to fuck off?"

"Did you?" I said. "I'm sorry, we couldn't hear what you were
saying through that intercom. It sounded all garbled, so we decided
to come back and knock on the door. I hope we're not intruding.
I'm Kris, by the way."

I stuck out my hand and Paula took it, giving it a limp and

reluctant shake, then said, "Who's the young one?"

"That's my daughter Jenna. She's helping me on this book I'm writing."

Paula nodded. "I heard you mention a story about Simon. A book now, is it?"

"Yes, that's the plan. I have a lot of interviews ahead of me, but I decided to start by talking to his former wives. Who knows a man better?"

"Oh, I know Simon all too well."

"I'll bet you do. Here's what bothered me when I talked to the others. They were pretty mean in the way they described you. Nasty, even. Now, I don't believe everything I'm told. I thought I had better meet you, find out what you're really like."

The old "I want to hear your side of the story" line had been an interviewing staple for me for years. People usually responded to it. Besides, it was the right thing to do.

"Sounds like you've been talking to Marie-France."

"Yes, and Miranda, the fourth wife."

"The bitch lawyer."

"That's the one."

"They were just jealous of me. I took Marie-France's man and the other one was so old and shrivelled up that Simon quickly dumped her. She couldn't give him what he got from me."

I immediately thought infectious disease, but bit my tongue before I blurted it out. I could see why Miranda had called Paula a dreadful little woman.

"The bitch represents me in my divorce, takes a fat fee, then turns around and steals Simon. There has to be something unethical about that."

"Absolutely," I said, eager to find something that we could agree on. There was no point in questioning how a woman could steal a man that Paula had just divorced.

"Well," Paula said, "You're here. You might as well come in."

We stepped into a tiled entranceway full of cast-off boots and shoes. A dead palm tree sagged forlornly in the corner, spider webs pinning it to the wall. The dogs brushed against our legs and sniffed our shoes. There were three, all the same breed, something greyish that looked like a cross between a rat and a floor mop.

Paula clapped her hands and the dogs scuttled away toward the
back of the house. She waved us toward the living room, which
contained two blue and red plaid sofas whose cushions had been
torn up by the dogs, a floor lamp without a shade and a rag rug that
was closer to rag than rug. Jenna and I settled gingerly on one of the
couches, Paula on the other.

"Sorry about the place. It's a bit of a mess," she said. "No, who
am I kidding? It's a dump. I got it in my settlement from Brendan,
the cheap prick. He bought it years ago, intending to tear the house
down and build an estate subdivision on the 60 acres. Then he
decided that property development was beneath him, so he foisted
it off on me."

Paula looked at her hand, seemed surprised not to see a wine
glass there, and said, "Anyone want a drink?"

I was hardly going to say no. The more Paula drank the more I
hoped to be able to find out. Paula was already on her way to the
kitchen to get the wine bottle and she quickly returned with an
already-opened bottle of red and three glasses. There was only a
slim chance that the glasses were clean. Maybe the alcohol would
sterilize them.

Paula poured us each a modest glass, then upended the bottle
to drain what remained into her own glass. Settling back into the
couch, she said, "So, Simon. What do you want to know?"

Jenna pulled out her notebook, which drew a raised eyebrow
from Paula but no comment. I decided to start with an open-ended
question. "How would you characterize your relationship with
Simon?"

"Complicated. At first, he was just my husband's business partner. Then he and Marie-France became social friends of Brendan
and me. I'm sure she told you how that progressed. When things
started to go sour with Brendan, I thought Simon would be my
white knight. Wrong again. I've had a whole fucking troop of white
knights. They get dingy fast. I should have known better."

"But you were with him for quite a while, right?"

"More than 10 years. Simon took what was left of my youth,
if you can call your 30s youth. It looks young to me now. I didn't
always look the way I do, you know. When I walked into a room
back then, there wasn't a man who didn't want to fuck me."

It was a problem I had never encountered, but I nodded sympathetically.

"By the time Simon was done with me, no other man wanted me. I took him for a bundle, but my life is shit."

Definitely not someone Simon would turn to in a time of need, if what Paula was telling us was true, and I didn't think she had either the sobriety or the mental acuity to make it up.

"So, the bundle, what happened to that?"

"I was a frequent flyer at the casino over in Gatineau. At first, it was just something to do, a way to get out of the house. I thought maybe I'd get lucky. I was overdue, right? Plus, I had lots of Simon's money to gamble with. Then I started to lose and I did what losers always do, I doubled down to win it all back. I'm afraid I don't have very much left at all now. Just enough to get by."

"Help me to understand the relationship you had with Simon. It's somewhat unusual. What really drew you to him, at first?"

"Sex. I have a large appetite for it. It wasn't rewarding with Brendan. He's a small man, in every way. We got into swinging to try to add some excitement, but it wasn't enough. There were other problems, too. Brendan is a dominant person, cruel at times. He used to call me his sex slave and I was. I did what he asked, no questions. It's strangely erotic, being in the total control of another."

Her comment intrigued me. While I liked my men to be men, I had never played a submissive role in sex. Maybe I was missing out on a whole new twist, a way to freshen up a relationship. I reminded myself that most of my lovers didn't stick around long enough to get boring.

"And that was the nature of your relationship with Simon, as well?" I asked.

"Yes," she said, as if proud of it. "The relationship between the dom and the sub can be subtle and complex. It's something I brought out in Simon. Once he discovered his true nature, he couldn't get enough of it."

"So what went wrong?"

"I got older. Simon got bored. He always does. Look at the pattern of his marriages. I hear he's on number five now. Good luck to her. I predict she doesn't even last as long as the bitch lawyer, although she's a lot younger. Simon has always been trying to discover who he is, and thinks he can do that through a relationship with a woman. It's like he's trying on different personalities but he can't find one that fits."

It was an astute summary of what we had learned about Simon so far. Paula might be a broken-down drunk, but she wasn't stupid.

"It seems like the only relationship that Simon has been able to sustain is the one with Brendan. They go back a long way."

"Yes, I sometimes thought that Simon loved Brendan more than he did any of his wives. They started out as two kids in their 20s, both with the dream of making it big. For Simon, it was about ideas, the problems he could solve, the things he could accomplish. For Brendan, it was about the money. That's how he keeps score. He's not an ideas man, he's a salesman, even though he likes to be called a tech pioneer. They were opposites in most ways, but somehow it made them a good team."

"Any idea how they get along now?"

"Why would I?" she asked. "I haven't seen Brendan in years."

Paula said that quickly, almost defiantly, answering a question I had not yet asked. It made me want to probe for more.

"That's too bad. You don't talk to Brendan at all?"

"God no. I avoid him completely. I put up that ridiculous fence to keep him out. He's a dangerous, nasty man."

"Dangerous? In what way?"

"You don't cross Brendan Connor without paying a price. I found that out when I told him I was going to leave him. Ten minutes later, he pushed me out the door with a single suitcase and I had to fight for everything I got. The prick had already made up his mind to dump me, too. I'm sure of it. It had to be his idea, though. He didn't like Simon getting his wife, either, even if he was tired of me.

"Brendan has been keeping some kind of mental tally of his success versus Simon's for decades. Anything good for Simon is automatically something bad for Brendan."

"That's odd, because we've heard the two of them are on the verge of going into a big business deal together."

Nothing in Paula's expression betrayed any knowledge of the deal, or the missing $10 million.

"Well, if that's true, it would have to be a deal where Brendan made out big time and Simon got screwed," she said. "Brendan has always set things up to benefit himself over Simon, taking advantage of the fact that Simon isn't as focused on money as Brendan is."

"And Simon, I assume you don't talk to him any either."

"Right. Did you hear me when I asked if he was dead?"

"That must have been part of what was blocked out by the static. Why would you think he was dead?"

"I didn't think it. I just hoped it. The sooner Brendan and Simon are dead, the better. Between the two of them, they ruined my life."

It seemed like Paula had done most of that herself, but I had to be somewhat sympathetic to another person who drank too much and made bad choices when it came to men. I could see her mood was starting to sour, so I decided to wrap it up.

"Look, we really appreciate your time today. You've been a big help. Last thing I wanted to ask you, did Simon have any long-time friends or relatives, people he still stayed in touch with?"

"Just that cousin of his, Rob. He has a nice place on the river up past Arnprior. We went there a few times. I have no idea whether they still talk."

Paula drained her glass of wine, then placed it somewhat unsteadily on the floor. "This book you're working on, you get that I'm a victim of these two men, right? I don't want you portraying me as some kind of whore."

"No, of course not. The situation is way more complex than that, just like you said."

Jenna closed her notebook and we both got up to leave.

"I'm sure you can find your way out," Paula said. "I'll open the gate for you. You must have climbed over the fence, right?"

"We did."

"I'm glad you came by. It has been a while since I talked to someone other than the dogs. It's lonely here."

"You could move."

"Yeah. Maybe I will, but first, I'm going to have another drink."

We let ourselves out. As we walked down the driveway, Jenna said, "What a sad mess she is. Brendan and Simon really screwed her up."

"Up, down and sideways, apparently. I don't see her as a victim. The woman married two millionaires."

"It didn't buy her much happiness, in the end, just a weird, spooky house and a big, gloomy country property."

"A perfect place to hide out."

"Or to bury a body."

I looked at Jenna in surprise. "You think she's capable of that?"

"Probably not, but her former master Brendan sounds like he would be."

"You think we should be taking all of this to the police?"

"Not yet. All we have is a bunch of conjecture. Something wrong has happened, though. I can feel it."

"If we're smart, we'll keep our noses out of it," I said. I had absolutely no intention of taking my own advice.

 # Thirteen

I took a long sip of Smoking Loon cabernet sauvignon and sank back into the bath tub. It was a huge claw-foot relic that had been around so long it had become trendy again. The water was as hot as I could stand it, just the way I liked it, and I had added some bubble bath solution. It felt luxurious, but more important, I did some of my best thinking in the tub and it had been a day that required careful thought.

I had found myself intrigued by Simon and his constant ability to recreate himself. I realized that, in at least one respect, he reminded me a bit of Colin, my former boss and lover. Colin was also one of those distinguished and authoritative men, and he loved to get married. He had fallen just short of Simon's score, with four wives. I could have been the fifth, if I had wanted it. Colin and I had been comfortable together, but for me, the passion just didn't last. Perhaps that was the way of all relationships.

Of the wives, I had preferred Marie-France and her candour and embrace of life. The frosty Margaret Radmore wasn't exactly my type and Miranda Chambers-Addington had been friendly enough, on the surface, but she wasn't someone I would want to cross.

Paula Connor intrigued me in a way I hadn't anticipated. She was a ruin of her former self, clearly an alcoholic, and yet she understood the dark and complex world of dominance and submission that underlay so many relationships between men and women, even if not in the stark, sexual ways she had experienced it. Paula was a risk taker, and while most of her risks hadn't paid off, she had the courage to take them. Her apparent willingness to place herself entirely under the control of one man, and then another, was something foreign to me. I really couldn't imagine that, but the idea had excited some dark corner of my psyche. I had never tried it, or even seriously contemplated it. Maybe I was missing out on something. It could get complicated, I was sure. The story of Paula,

Brendan and Simon was proof of that.

The thing that concerned me most was Polanco, the private investigator. Jenna and I had discussed that at length on the drive back from Paula's house. I had half-heartedly suggested that we pull back from the Simon investigation until we found out more about Polanco and what he was up to, but Jenna disagreed. She still had a cop's confidence, the belief that she could handle any situation. I envied it. I used to have that kind of confidence myself, but I had come close to death one time too many. Maybe I was losing my edge.

We had done a quick Google search on Polanco and at least he looked legitimate. He was a former police sergeant and had been a PI for nearly 25 years. He was a tough-looking bastard, though, the kind of man who exuded menace, even in a photograph.

I drained my glass of wine and reached down to pour myself another, then turned the hot water on to keep the temperature up. I thought I would get slightly drunk, then shave my legs and go to bed early. Jenna had gone out for the evening. She didn't say where and it wasn't my place to ask. She was 26, after all, and had been living her life quite competently without me looking over her shoulder.

Then I heard footsteps coming up the stairs. It must be Jenna, home sooner than I expected. Fuck. The bathroom door was open. I thought about jumping out of the tub to grab the white terry robe that hung on the bathroom door, but decided to sink beneath the bubbles instead.

"In here," I shouted.

I was surprised when Darcy appeared in the doorway, not Jenna. He was carrying a bouquet of red roses and wore a look of anticipation.

"Hey, I didn't expect you tonight."

"I thought, it's Sunday night. What am I doing up in Round Lake when you are here in Ottawa?"

"Glad to see you, too. As it turns out, I don't have anything on."

"I can see that, but I'd like to see it better."

What the hell, I thought. I stood up in the tub, then slowly turned around, water and bubbles sliding down my naked body. Darcy didn't wait for an invitation. He set the roses on the floor, then quickly stripped off his blue T-shirt, jeans and boxer shorts. Although he was 46, Darcy looked 20 years younger.

"Before you get in, I was about to shave my legs. Can you get the razor and cream from the medicine cabinet?"

"Sure and I'll do better than that. I'll shave them for you."

"You're an expert at that, are you?"

"I wouldn't say that, but I've had some practice."

I fought off the urge to ask him who he'd practised on. Darcy had had a busy sex life before I came along, but the less I knew about that the better. What mattered was now, not what either of us had done in the past. Besides, I was now the beneficiary of his various forms of sexual expertise.

I lowered myself back into the water and he stepped in.

"Jesus, Kris. This water is hot. What are you trying to do, boil lobsters?"

"If you don't like it, you could always get out."

"Not a chance. This is exactly where I want to be."

He reached out of the tub, picked up the wine bottle and refilled my glass, leaving about one-third of the bottle. He took a long gulp straight from the bottle and set it back down on the floor.

"Let's get to those legs," he said.

I raised my right leg and he ran his hands over it appreciatively. I didn't have a lot of good features, but I did have good legs. I settled back, closed my eyes and then heard the whoosh of the shaving cream leaving the container, immediately followed by its lemon-lime smell. Darcy lathered my leg, spending considerable time working the cream around. Then I felt the smooth glide of the razor as he took the first stroke from my ankle to my knee.

"How was your day?" he asked.

"Weirdly sexy."

"Oh yeah, tell me about it."

"Yesterday we interviewed one of Simon's former wives. She had an unusual story to tell, a kinky wife-swapping tale. Then today, we met the other woman in the foursome, another former wife of Simon's."

"Really?"

"Turns out Simon and Marie-France, the second wife, were into swinging back in the '90s. Ultimately, they hooked up with Simon's business partner, Brendan Connor and his wife Paula."

"That must have led to some uncomfortable days at the office."

"Apparently not. The way Marie-France tells it, Connor was growing tired of his wife and was happy to see Simon take an interest in her. Simon's wife Marie-France was the one with the issue. At first, she went along with it. Brendan was the director of their little drama. He wanted to see Paula and Marie-France make love to each other, so they complied."

Darcy kept looking at me, then at the leg he was nearly finished shaving, paying close attention to my story. He gave my leg one last swipe with the razor then I lowered it back into the water and rested my foot in his lap. It was clear that he was enjoying what he was hearing.

"You ever try anything like that?" he asked.

"Lesbianism or swapping?"

"Either."

"Hard no to both. I'm a serial monogamist," I said, although that wasn't strictly true, "and I know which team I play on."

"Maybe you need to be more open-minded."

I took a long gulp of my wine and tried to decide whether to be pissed off by that comment, or intrigued. "And you have tried this kind of stuff, I assume?"

"Back in my early days in the NHL, the single guys had some pretty wild parties. I guess I'd call it more a case of sharing than swapping. There was no emotional involvement, although I'd think that would be part of the turn-on, watching your woman with another man."

"So I'm 'your woman,' now, am I?"

Darcy gestured to indicate our situation in the tub and said, "I sure hope so."

It was something we hadn't explicitly discussed. I thought we were too old to be talking about being boyfriend and girlfriend and the term partner had always seemed a bit lame. I decided to push him a bit. "Is that something you'd like to see, then, me with another man?"

"I can't say it's a preoccupation."

"Good. I didn't want to get your hopes up."

"So what spoiled it all for the happy foursome?"

"Brendan Connor pushed Simon's wife too far. His own wife was submissive and apparently they enjoyed a little BDSM. When Connor told Marie-France he was going to spank her ass with his belt, that was it for her. She walked out, but the relationship between the other three kept going."

"Everyone has their limits."

I lay back into the bubbles, my tiny tits rising like islets above the foam, my nipples standing to attention. To my surprise, the story had aroused me, no doubt because I was telling it to my lover while we shared a bubble bath and a bottle of wine.

I wasn't sure what I wanted from Darcy ultimately, but I knew what I wanted right now. I felt like taking a chance and pushing our lovemaking beyond its safe and predictable pattern. I wondered what my own limits were.

"Would you ever spank me?" I asked.

Darcy looked at me like he sensed it was a trick question, then said, "Only if you wanted me to."

"What if I had been bad?"

"Have you been?"

"I'm about to be," I said, then I turned around in the tub, got on my hands and knees and raised my ass in the air, presenting myself to him.

"Do it," I said.

Fourteen

I turned around and stared at the reflection of my ass in the bathroom mirror. It was still pinkish, but not red like it had been last night. After I had requested a spanking, Darcy had given me two hard slaps, one on each buttock. Then he asked me if I wanted more. My answer was more of a growl than a yes, but he got the picture. He gave me two more, than repeated his question. We kept going until I had taken a dozen whacks on my rear.

After that, things got rapidly out of control. Our flailing sent water flooding over the top of the bath tub. I can't say that I was too concerned about it at the time.

When we finished in the tub, I thought that was it, but Darcy picked me up like I was a feather, carried me to the bed and started over again, this time slower and face to face. It was as if my switch from willing to wanton had triggered a vast, pent-up lust in him. I wasn't complaining. I hadn't had such enthusiastic sex in years.

I hadn't thought, just acted. Now, in my usual over-thinking way, I was wondering what I had set off in him, and more important, in me. I had crossed a bridge that I didn't know existed and gone into unknown territory. I would have thought that being dominated by a man was the last thing I would have wanted, but the lack of control had somehow been arousing, even exhilarating. I didn't know why I wanted it, just that I did, even now that I was more or less sober.

Our love making, if you could call it that, had been a weird echo of my first time with Darcy, when I was 16. He had pinned me up against a tree at a bush party, pulled my pants down and taken my virginity. It had changed the course of my life. I had become pregnant with Jenna and had given her up when she was three days' old. For years, I had considered what had happened between Darcy and me to be rape, or the next thing to it. I did have to admit that I wanted him back then, but not like that. He had been my hero, the boy I lusted after in high school. I hated what he had done to me and it ended any connection we had, back then.

Now, suddenly I wanted him to be rough with me. Had our first encounter created some kind of mental switch that none of my other lovers had been able to find? Then I realized the difference between what happened last night and my first time with Darcy all those years ago. This time, I had demanded, and gotten, what I wanted. Was I submitting to Darcy, or was he submitting to me?

I stepped into the shower and turned the water on as hot as I could stand it. I was sore and tender all over, and I couldn't remember the last time I had felt so good. I let the water hammer on my tight hamstrings. Darcy had stretched my legs into positions where they wouldn't normally go. If we kept up like this, I was going to have to take up yoga.

I had left the bathroom door open and I could see Darcy, still asleep in my bed. He was sprawled on his back, the covers pulled down. His image was misty through the shower doors, but there was no mistaking his strength and his fitness. All his years of training as a professional athlete had built up his physique and the work he did now putting up log houses kept him in top form.

I looked down at myself and thought I couldn't claim a similar level of fitness, but optimistically my skinniness probably made me look somewhat younger than 42. At least I wasn't showing signs of middle-age, yet. Whatever I had, it certainly seemed to work for Darcy.

I gingerly soaped my buttocks and wondered if spanking was something I wanted again. Maybe I would let Darcy decide. Why did I have to be the one to initiate things?

It was certainly a pleasant surprise to know that Darcy had a sexual imagination. My last lover, Colin, was a gentle man but entirely predictable in his lovemaking. Young J.T, the cop I had met down in the Adirondacks, had enormous enthusiasm but little experience. Darcy had found my sweet spot.

I stepped out of the shower and began to dry myself with a fluffy white towel, a small indulgence that I had allowed myself when I moved into the house. I wondered how Jenna was making out with Alicia. I had assumed that I would accompany her on the morning update trip, but she'd soon straightened me out on that, and good for her. I had never wanted to play second fiddle to anyone and neither did she.

I did worry about what she was getting herself into, though. I didn't trust Alicia or believe a word she said and the appearance of Polanco added a whole new level to the situation. What did he want and what was he prepared to do to get it?

I was just about dry when Darcy walked into the bathroom, naked and looking a little worse for wear. We'd killed two bottles of wine last night. I glanced down and saw that he was semi-hard. Again, already?

He smiled and said, "Don't worry. I just have to take a piss."

He then proceeded to do just that. Clearly, we had crossed more intimacy boundaries than I realized.

"What do you want to do today?' he asked.

"Don't you have to work?"

"Eventually."

"Maybe something less strenuous, then."

"Works for me. I'm not as young as I used to be."

"Good thing. I don't think I could have taken any more."

He smiled, then took me in his arms and gave me a kiss, not the good morning type, either.

"Hey, I just had a shower, and I think you need one."

"Scrub my back?"

It was tempting, but if we kept going at the pace of last night, I would end up needing physio. "Not right now," I said. "You go ahead and I'll put together some breakfast."

He smiled at that. "You, make a meal?"

"You think I didn't eat before you came along?"

"All right. I'm sure it will be delicious, whatever it is."

Delicious? I had some boxed cereal and a few grocery store muffins in the freezer. I was going to have to be creative.

I dressed quickly in jeans and a T-shirt and headed for the kitchen. Opening the fridge, I saw that I was in luck. Darcy had brought a bag of oranges and there were a dozen eggs on a shelf. I knew how to fry an egg. If I put orange slices on the plate and microwaved the muffins, it would look like a real breakfast.

I slipped a Starbucks pod into the Keurig and was instantly rewarded with the gratification of coffee. I set the eggs out on the counter to let them warm up a bit. I vaguely remembered that it was the right thing to do. I took out the muffins and decided the freezer burn was really minor.

We could go out, but I didn't feel like facing the world this morning. Right now, Darcy was my world and that was all I needed.

I was slicing oranges when Darcy came into the kitchen wearing only a pair of khaki cargo shorts. He ran his fingers through his still-wet hair and said, "Oranges? This is fancy."

"Only by my standards."

"Will Jenna be joining us?"

"No. She's gone to meet with that Alicia woman, the one with the missing husband."

"Right. I'd like to meet her, form an opinion. From what you tell me, she sounds like a problem."

"Probably, but a well-paying problem for Jenna."

Darcy nodded. "The customer is always right, or at least, you have to pretend that he is. You wouldn't believe some of the assholes I've met in the home construction business. People who want to tell me how to do my job, but they can't tell one end of a hammer from the other."

I nodded, but I didn't want to talk about Darcy's business. Instead, I found my mind drifting to our future. Did we have one? I reminded myself that Darcy was a guy who had never had a single sustained relationship in his entire life.

People could change, though. I had. I had spent more than 20 years as a deadline-driven newshound. I thought I couldn't live without the adrenaline of chasing a story. I was wrong. Instead of pounding out columns, I was working on a book, the biggest and most laborious thing I had ever attempted. I was being a mother to Jenna, to the extent that my limited maternal instincts allowed. But who would have thought that I had any such abilities?

I was opening myself up to Darcy literally and figuratively, in ways that I wouldn't have imagined possible. Listening to Marie-France and Paula made me realize that my own view of sex was too narrow, and worse, I had usually let my limits be set by someone else.

"Kris, have you wandered off somewhere?" Darcy said.

"The future."

"How does it look?"

I wasn't sure what to say so I went with my heart. "Pretty damn good."

Fifteen

Jenna Martin's RAV4 accelerated up the Catherine Street onramp and merged smoothly with westbound Queensway traffic. The small SUV didn't have the punch of the big police vehicles she was used to, but it was measurably better than Kris's old Honda Accord. Jenna didn't get why Kris drove around town in such a beater. It had been embarrassing pulling up in front of that snooty Margaret Radmore's house in a car that looked like a homeless person lived in it.

There were a lot of things about Kris that Jenna didn't fully understand yet, but she was working on it. There wasn't really a playbook for how to handle meeting your mother for the first time when you were 25. One thing Jenna did know was that Kris was pushy and she was going to have to call her on it. Yesterday had been ridiculous, her sitting there taking notes like some kind of junior secretary, not a private investigator. Her idea of putting Kris front and centre as a non-fiction writer had been a reasonable cover for their efforts, but she'd barely had a speaking role in the little drama.

Then last night, Kris had announced that she'd be accompanying Jenna for the update meeting at Alicia's house. That was where she had to draw the line. She was the investigator, the former cop, and this was her business and her client. It was hard enough being a young woman in a line of work dominated by retired male cops without giving the impression that you had to take your mother with you to a client meeting.

Kris had been miffed. As she explained, she was used to working alone, calling her own shots. Jenna had reminded Kris that for this case, she was on a team and she wasn't the captain. Kris hadn't liked that very much, but she didn't put up a vigorous argument, either.

Clearly, the idea of a morning at home was attractive to her and Jenna thought she knew why. From the looks Kris and Darcy were giving each other, something special was happening between them. They always focused on each other when they were together, but they'd had that can't-stop-smiling look people got when they were in love. Jenna wondered if they really were. Her parents' relationship had been an odd one. A high school crush, a one-night stand, 25 years of no contact and now they were back together again. Maybe they were meant for each other, although Jenna didn't really believe in all that romantic bullshit.

Still, it would be nice if it were true. Growing up thinking she was an orphan, all Jenna had wanted was parents. Now she had them, and not just adoptive parents, but her real parents. It was a turn of events she couldn't have imagined. In their own way, the three of them were forming a kind of family, but it all depended on Kris and Darcy. She knew they'd both had a lot of partners. If they drifted apart, it would become one of those awkward divorced parent scenarios, not that her parents had ever been married.

Jenna had been trying to give them space, going out most evenings just for a walk, getting to know the city, sometimes stopping for a beer. Last night, she'd had a couple with Carol Stillwell, her former staff sergeant when she was with the Ontario Provincial Police. Like Jenna, Stillwell had been disgusted by the way the brass had handled the Madawaska Mills case, keeping the truth about a killer buried to make themselves look better. While Jenna had quit in reaction, Stillwell went another direction, transferring to the Ottawa Police. She'd landed a good gig, staff sergeant in Major Crimes, but the way Stillwell told it, her new shop was just as big a rat's nest of sexism and politics as the OPP.

Jenna shook her head, as if to clear those thoughts from her mind. She needed to focus on how she was going to handle Alicia and she had only 20 minutes to do it. She was already approaching the western suburb of Kanata and Alicia's house was somewhere in the woods to the north of it. The GPS would show her the way.

Truthfully, they'd come up pretty dry in their interviews with Simon's wives. The background they offered was interesting, but their marriages to him had been years ago. If Simon was looking for a place to hide, he wouldn't turn to Margaret Radmore, surely. Marie-France was a better bet, but she hadn't shown any indication of recent contact with Simon. Paula Connor certainly wasn't a fan and Miranda was too smart to get tangled up in Simon's troubles.

The cousin up past Arnprior might be a possible source of refuge for Simon, but with his resources, he could be anywhere in the world.

The important thing to focus on was Paul Polanco. Someone else had a reason to find Simon or they wouldn't be spending money on a PI. Her bet was that it was Brendan Connor, the guy who was out the $10 million. Jenna wondered how Alicia would handle that news.

It was really none of her business, but Jenna still wanted to understand the real dynamic behind the Simon-Alicia relationship. The guy's first wife seemed prim and proper and the second was some kind of flower child. The third had brought out a dominant side in Simon. It was hard to see how that would work with Alicia. Jenna could see her wielding a whip, or whatever they used, but not submitting to one. Maybe she was overthinking it. The simple exchange of youth and beauty for money was the simplest explanation and that made it the one most likely to be true.

Jenna exited the Queensway at Terry Fox Drive, passed a big box mall and a cluster of suburban condos, then turned left onto Richardson Side Road, then right on Huntmar. Suddenly, she was in the country, farmland on either side. The corn crop was just starting to poke up through the dark soil. A small river ran beside the road, its banks still overflowing from the wet spring. Jenna powered the driver's window down part way and took in the smell of trees and plowed earth. Low grey clouds were advancing toward her and it looked like rain was not far off.

The RAV easily handled the steep grade as Huntmar climbed what Jenna knew was the Carp Ridge. She'd been to a house party out in this area once, back when she was stationed in Pembroke. She didn't remember much about it, except waking up in the morning and finding herself on the living room floor. The drinking was legendary at cop parties.

She glanced at the view to her left. Ottawa was mostly a flat city and any kind of elevation was a novelty. There was nothing to see but farms and trees, but their green expanse beat downtown high rises.

The GPS told her that her destination involved a right turn in one kilometre. She slowed and watched for the sign for Oak Ridge Drive. As soon as she turned on to the road, she could see that it was big money. Estate homes, they called them, vast outsized places each nestled on a wooded acreage. She saw the number 477 mounted on the right hand pillar of an impressive set of stone gate posts and turned down the winding paved lane. The house came into view and it was immediately clear that it was built to impress. Jenna didn't know much about architectural styles but the term stately manor house came to mind. The four-car garage was bigger than most houses and the attached main structure loomed three full storeys, the roofline full of crazy angles and the front domi-nated by a stone-clad entrance area that rose to the full height of the house. It certainly made a statement, and that was "I'm richer than you."

Jenna pulled the RAV up in front of the garage and paused to gather her thoughts. She had decided to lead with the other PI, then talk about the wives. She flipped down the visor and looked at herself in the little mirror. She'd thought about makeup but decided to go without. She wasn't sure it was professional and she didn't want to compete in any way with Alicia, although Jenna *had* chosen her navy power suit with a white blouse. It lacked the authority of a police uniform with a gun on the utility belt, but it would have to do.

She got out of the vehicle and walked across the driveway to the front door, noting the immaculate state of the lawn and shrubber-ies. Not Alicia's doing she was sure. Jenna stepped into the stone entranceway, which was so tall and looming that it made her feel like a child in a fairy tale. Jenna looked for a doorbell, but there was none visible, just a door knocker that looked like it weighed about ten pounds. She would bet money that there was a door cam alert-ing Alicia to her arrival, but lifted the knocker and gave it a couple of heavy smacks on the door anyway.

The sound was greeted with the low, throaty growl of a dog, then Jenna heard paws scratching at the door. Rex, she presumed.

Alicia opened the door and grabbed Rex by the collar. "Don't worry, he's just a big baby. He can't wait to meet you."

Jenna stepped in and the dog nuzzled her legs, slobbering on her navy pants. She'd have to remember to expense the dry-cleaning bill.

"Rex, crate," Alicia said and the dog trundled off to another room. Jenna wondered how he managed to master the place without a map. The house's entrance hall alone was large enough to hold a couple of dozen people. It was dominated by a broad wooden staircase that rose to a second-floor landing, then continued to the third-floor rooms above.

Alicia looked as polished as the chandelier that lit the entrance-way. She wore black designer jeans, heels and a tight white sweater. Was she expecting more company or was this always the way she dressed at home?

"So, what have you got for me?" Alicia said, like Jenna was there to drop off a parcel.

She put on her professional smile and said, "Let's sit down, then I'll run over the progress so far."

"All right. Follow me."

Alicia led the way past the kitchen and formal dining room to a wood-ceilinged sunroom that looked out on the pool and the woods beyond.

"Nice house," Jenna said, implying that she'd see plenty nicer.

"Oh well, that's all Simon's doing. If it were up to me, we'd be living some place far more modest."

Still a mansion, Jenna was sure, but a smaller one. Alicia pointed to a wicker chair and took the identical one on the other side of a glass-topped table.

"So, you've met the wives then? Any leads?"

"I met with Radmore and Latour. I think it's safe to say that neither of them has seen him in years and isn't particularly worried about it."

"Surely you've got more to tell me than that."

"Of course, and this is the thing I wanted you to know about. When we talked to Latour, she said that another investigator had been there before us, asking about Simon's whereabouts."

"Shit," Alicia said, displaying a quick flash of anger.

"He's a guy called Paul Polanco. Runs his own agency. He's a former cop, been around forever. You know him?"

"No, no, of course not," Alicia said quickly. The look on her face told Jenna that it wasn't the first time she had heard the name.

"Who's he working for? That's the important question. Do you have an answer?"

"Not yet. I wanted to consult with you before pursuing that

angle. I can try to find out, but it could alert Polanco that we're on to him."

"It's Brendan, it has to be. Who else really cares if Simon is gone?"

It was a bleak question, but not one for which Jenna had a ready answer.

"Did the second wife tell Polanco anything?"

"She says not. I think she's telling the truth. She doesn't seem like the kind of person who'd co-operate with anyone in authority."

"All right. Good. What about the other two wives?"

"Miranda Chambers-Addington was very slick. No surprise there. She's been a lawyer forever. I think she looks on her marriage with Simon as a mildly regrettable mistake, quickly corrected. She claims not to have heard from him, either. I believe it.

"The more interesting one was Paula Connor. You know the story of her, Brendan and Simon, I'm sure."

Alicia nodded curtly, as if the semi-question was so stupid it wasn't worth an oral response.

"She's a bit of a ruin. Too much drinking. There seems to be no love lost for either Brendan or Simon. It's always hard to tell if an alcoholic is lying, though. It's a lifestyle for them. She has a big rural property. Someone could hide out there if they wanted to. We couldn't exactly search the premises.

"One other thing. Some of them mentioned a cousin Rob who lives up past Arnprior. It was the only name of a friend or relative I was able to get."

"Yes, Rob. I've met him. Valley boy. So was Simon, of course, but he moved past it. I want you to talk to Rob, see what you can find out. I think he would lie for Simon, though. If anyone was going to help Simon in a pinch, besides me, it would be Rob."

"I can definitely track him down, get a read on him."

"Good. What's your next play?"

"Let's discuss that. I assume you haven't heard anything from Simon, nothing happening on the credit cards or bank accounts."

"Not a thing. It's like he's disappeared into thin air."

Jenna nodded. She was almost certain that Alicia wasn't telling her everything, but would calling her on it make a difference? She made eye contact with Alicia, but didn't say a word.

The uncomfortable silence was a proven interrogation technique. Maybe it would work here.

Alicia looked away, then feigned interest in her backyard. Finally, she said, "I haven't been entirely honest with you."

Jenna imagined there were quite a few layers to that particular onion. How many would Alicia peel back?

"There's more happening with Simon. He's under a lot of money pressure. The house is heavily mortgaged and the incubator he runs is draining cash every month without producing marketable ideas. My emissions project is really the only thing he has on the go. I know he's been to all the banks and his network of private lenders, trying to raise the $10 million he needs to cover his stake in the new company. He assured me it was going well, but he was secretive about the details.

"For Simon, this plan is more than another business venture. For one thing, he promised me that he could do it, no problem. He's a proud man and he'd see failure as a virility issue. Have you ever had a relationship with an older man?"

"No, but I understand the dynamic."

"Right, then you realize that they see everything as a test of their manhood, an opportunity to prove that they're still potent, powerful.

"Then there's Brendan. Simon would never want to admit to him that he was short of money. If he did, it would be the final chapter in their long rivalry. Game over. Simon loses."

"So to avoid all of that, he grabs the $10 million and what, heads for a Caribbean island?"

"Or Central America. Easy to disappear there."

"Look, if you really think he's left the country, then this is all well beyond my scope. You would need an agency with international connections. Better still, my advice would be to report this to the police and let them use their resources."

Alicia switched from confiding to commanding in a split second. "I need to take this in logical steps. That means starting with the simplest explanations, checking those out and eliminating them one by one. That's the job I've asked you to do. Simon's passport is still in the house. I don't think he'd blow up his whole life, take the money and run. I can't rule it out, but I just don't buy it. I'm searching for answers here. Don't take everything I say literally."

Jenna felt like she'd just had her knuckles rapped. She took a deep breath before saying, "Whatever you like. That leaves the issue of Polanco. What do you want me to do about him?"

"Nothing. I'll make some discreet inquiries of my own, but I think we're safe to assume that Brendan has been trying to reach Simon, can't, and is now digging around. He's always been a suspicious type, Simon says. Most dishonest people are, of course."

Jenna recognized the voice of personal experience. Alicia had many qualities, she was discovering, but honesty was unlikely to be one of them.

"All right, we're up to date then," Jenna said, getting up to leave. "You want me to look into the cousin, or not?"

"Fine. Do that. You can show yourself out. Keep me informed if you find anything substantial."

Jenna headed down the long hall, in a rush to get as far away from Alicia as she could, as quickly as she could. She couldn't really afford to drop a well-paying client, but Alicia really was a bitch. She hadn't offered the most obvious reason for Simon packing his bags and hitting the road. He had a habit of leaving wives and perhaps his patience with Alicia had worn out quicker than average.

That still didn't explain what happened to the $10 million, though. Her guess was that Jenna knew more about that than she was letting on. Maybe she was the one who was planning a one-way trip to Central America. On the other hand, she had only Alicia's word that the $10 million had ever existed.

Sixteen

Alicia Jameson took Rex's lead from the hook in the mudroom and clipped it on his collar. She had to get out of this great, freaking cage of a house and think. Walking the dog was her favourite way of doing that. She certainly wasn't going to let him go bounding around in the bush behind the house, like Simon allowed him to. With the skunks and porcupines they had on the property, that was irresponsible, but then Simon was irresponsible. She was starting to think that it was his dominant characteristic. He had been gone almost a week and not a word. Had he double-crossed her or had something terrible happened to him?

She pulled on an old red Eddie Bauer rain jacket. Heavy grey clouds hung over the woods surrounding the house, but there wasn't a breath of wind, like the storm hadn't decided what to do yet. Rex surged ahead, but she hauled back on the leash and said, "Heel!" The dog turned to stare at her with a sheepish look. He knew what to do, but he always liked to test her. Accepting her dominance, he walked meekly beside her, matching her pace.

Alicia was beginning to think that she had made a mistake in choosing Jenna Martin to help track down Simon. She needed someone who worked quickly and didn't ask too many awkward questions, but she worried that Jenna wanted to understand the whole picture, even though she said she was doing exactly what Alicia asked. It was the ex-cop in her. That should have been Alicia's warning. If you're sailing close to the wind, don't bring in someone trained to look for laws being broken.

Alicia still thought she had been right to hire a private investigator. She could hardly let Simon disappear and take no action at all, and going to the police was out of the question. Jenna simply wasn't the right person for the job. Her task had been so simple. Interview the wives and report back. Instead, she had taken an interest in Paul Polanco, Brendan's favourite thug. Despite strict instructions to the contrary, Alicia was certain that Jenna would dig into Polanco on her own, but calling her off completely now would look suspicious and there was nothing to stop the investigator from independently pursuing the truth behind the disappearance of Simon and the money.

Worse still, she might take the whole thing to some buddy of hers in the police. At least there was a bit of jurisdictional insulation. Simon's situation wouldn't be a matter for Jenna's former colleagues in the OPP, but a city police responsibility.

Was Jenna loyal? That was the question. Alicia's experience with loyalty had been mixed at best. Rex was loyal, beyond that everything was uncertain. She had trusted Simon when she turned her project over to him and when she had married him. Was that another miscalculation?

Alicia realized she had what her therapist called "trust issues." Who wouldn't, when their parents were murdered and the crime was never solved? What else could she conclude but that the people you were supposed to trust to fix things weren't reliable? Ever since that day when the man walked into her room, she had vowed not to trust a soul. It still seemed like a smart first line of self-defence, but she had broken her own rule with Simon.

As Alicia walked down Oak Ridge Drive, she glanced at the pompous homes of her neighbours, all larger than any family could possibly require, all meant to one-up the people next door. She didn't know even one person on the street, and she didn't care to. The only virtue of a street like Oak Ridge was that people minded their own business.

She had vague, hazy memories of spending the early part of her childhood on a street much like it, before the murder of her parents, but those happy times were so far away now they seemed like a fairy tale, one that ended with a monster and a little girl hiding under a bed.

Rex bounced along contentedly beside her, but Alicia felt tired. She hadn't slept well since Simon had taken off. She knew she must look haggard. She certainly felt it. Her mind couldn't stop working the problem of Simon, Brendan and the missing money. Her forte was solving problems, but she was lacking key data. What was Simon doing? Whatever it was, it wasn't something she had planned or anticipated. And why had he taken the money? It didn't make sense. The missing $10 million was certain to spark a dramatic response from Brendan. She hoped that he didn't know about it, but surely he must. Why else send his goon looking for Simon?

As the days went by without Simon reappearing, Alicia had become more certain that her original plan wasn't going to work. She thought of the gun she kept in a case in her underwear drawer. It was a Smith and Wesson .38 calibre revolver that had belonged to her father: if only it had been close by when he needed it. Using it would be a drastic, blunt plan that would effectively end her own life, as she had imagined it. She hoped it wouldn't come to that, but if it did, she was prepared to act.

Alicia still had had a card to play. She took out her cell phone, went to contacts and tapped on the number of the one person who might be able to help.

Seventeen

On the drive back from West Carleton, the rain had started in earnest, first big drops splashing on the windshield, then a heavy, steady downpour. The wipers were on high, but visibility was still poor. The real world seemed as murky as the one she had gotten into with Alicia. The question was what to do.

Jenna missed some things about her old job and one of them was its clarity. As a cop, she had investigated crimes and helped to build a case that would put criminals away. It was a black and white kind of world, the way she had seen it. Now, as a private investigator, her world was turning a murky sort of grey. What was she trying to accomplish? Was the job just about making a buck or was she supposed to do some kind of good?

She knew which way she'd prefer it to be, but the situation with Alicia reminded her that her new life wasn't as simple as her old one. Alicia was paying her $1,600 a day, double her usual fee. The smart move would be to bill another day for talking to the cousin and if she didn't find him and Simon sitting on the porch having a beer, then send Alicia an invoice and hope she'd pay it. Despite the fancy house, it didn't sound like there was a lot of money floating around.

Part of her brain, maybe the smart part, said get the hell away from Simon, Alicia and Brendan and whatever they were up to. The other part of her brain, maybe the bigger part, said this wasn't something she could just walk away from. There was every possibility that Simon had been murdered and that she was being used by Alicia as a way to buy time or maybe even hide Alicia's own culpability. The first possibility didn't sit well with her and she knew she couldn't live with the second. Not only was it wrong, but if Alicia had killed Simon, Jenna was getting perilously close to being in a position where she could be charged with being an accessory to homicide.

She needed to consult with Kris, that's what she needed to do. If she was putting herself in danger, her bright idea of getting Kris involved was endangering her, too.

Jenna was almost home now. The rain hadn't arrived yet, but the sky was dark and ominous. Rather that drive down Frank and park in front of the house, she decided to swing down Gladstone, the street that ran on the other side of St. Luke's Park, one block south. It was time to start taking smart precautions and one of them was remembering her police training. Never drive down a street without keeping a sharp eye for anything that looked out of place.

She parked the RAV under a big maple tree and took a pair of binoculars from her glove compartment and started to scan Frank, looking for anything unusual. Maybe she was just being paranoid, but she remembered one of her instructors at the police college saying that paranoia kept cops alive. Unfortunately, she didn't have a good view of Frank. A group of adults was playing pickup basketball in the park and closer to Kris's house a playground was crawling with little kids using the structures. She decided to take a slow roll down Frank itself.

Three houses before she got to Kris's, Jenna spotted a man sitting in a newer bronze-coloured Lexus sedan. He had the windows up and was reading a newspaper, or pretending to. Who did that on a May morning?

She shot a quick glance at the man as she slowly drove past, and saw that he was checking her out, too. He was older, short grey hair, face that looked like it was chiselled from granite. Jenna had worked with enough cops to spot someone who was one, or used to be. Polanco? He looked like guy in the picture on Polanco's website, but she had only caught a glimpse of him.

She kept moving, turned on to Elgin, then back to Gladstone and around the block to Frank. She parked on the side of the road opposite the Lexus, maybe six car lengths back. Pulling out her cell phone, she went to Polanco's site and looked at the picture of him there. Then she picked up her binoculars and zoomed in for a closer look. Same guy, she was 90-per-cent certain. Whoever the fucker was, he was surveilling the house, no doubt about it, doing a lazy, arrogant job too, sitting so close like they were too stupid to make him.

Jenna fired up the RAV and moved quickly down the street, parking tight to the Lexus and blocking it in between other cars parked front and back. She reached under the passenger seat and took out a tire iron she kept handy, just in case. She opened her door and walked briskly around the RAV to the Lexus, approaching on the passenger side. She could see the driver swivel around, trying to figure out what was going on.

Jenna tapped on the passenger side window with the tire iron and the driver powered it down. Before he could speak, she said, "Paul Polanco, I presume."

He gave her a look of cold, controlled fury, then said, "Jenna Martin. So nice to meet you, at last. I have to ask, what the hell do you think you're doing?"

"Trying to find out why you're watching my house. What did you think?"

"Who says I am? I'm just sitting here enjoying the day."

"Really? Maybe I've got it wrong. Maybe you're here to watch the kiddies across the street." She pointed to an expensive-looking camera with a long lens that was sitting on the front seat. "Doing a little photography are you? Maybe I should phone it in, report a strange man taking pictures at the children's playground."

Polanco laughed, a kind of harsh bark. "Nice try. I was a cop for 20 years. I've got lots of friends on the force. They know what I do and how I do it.

"The better question is what are *you* doing? You're in over your head, kid. My advice, get out while you've got the chance."

Jenna saw red. It was just the kind of smug, patronizing shit she had put up for five years from her so-called superiors on the OPP. Polanco wasn't a superior, though, and she didn't have to take it.

"So let me see if I've got this straight. If I don't drop my client, you're going to do what?"

Polanco looked Jenna slowly up and down, spending a little extra time on her breasts, then said, "You really don't want to find out." He flexed his hands, which were as big as hams and heavily scarred, just like Marie-France had said. The guy had been in a few fights. Didn't mean he'd won them.

Then Polanco switched gears, giving her a smile that clearly required seldom-used facial muscles. "You're new and keen. I get it. I used to be like that myself. Once you've been around for a while, you learn to read people. Your girl Alicia? She's nothing but a gold-digger who backed the wrong horse. Simon Cousens is a con man who has taken off with a large quantity of my client's cash. When I find him, and I will, we're going to have a frank conversation that will lead to an informal resolution of the problem. Trust me, that is not something you want to get involved with.

"Let it drop and go back to the cheating husbands and insurance cases. Do it today."

"Says the guy who's so fucking stupid that he gets made on surveillance and pinned in his car by some dumb rookie woman like me."

"Don't make me come out that passenger door and deal with this."

"Of course not. I wouldn't want to see you throw your back out, at your age. You have a nice day, Paul."

Jenna turned and walked around the back of the Lexus. She took the tire iron and smashed the passenger side tail light. It felt so good she did the same on the driver's side.

This prick Polanco thought he knew Jenna, but he didn't know the half of it. A competitive spirit burned inside of her. She didn't lose a game without giving it everything she had, especially to an opponent who liked to talk trash.

Polanco had accomplished one thing. Jenna hadn't been sure whether she wanted to keep working for Alicia. Now she was, 100 per cent.

 Eighteen

Darcy and I sat side by side on the beaten-up paisley couch I had picked up for $100 at the Habitat for Humanity store out in Stittsville. The couch was somewhat comfortable, provided you were careful about exactly where you sat. We were re-experiencing the quiet pleasure we had come to love when I had been recuperating at his lake house, spending time together engrossed in good books, no talking required. I had been devouring true crime books to help me focus on the one I was supposed to be writing. I was halfway through *In Cold Blood* by Truman Capote, a book that was older than I was but one that most agreed had defined the genre. Darcy's reading choices had surprised me, but I quickly learned that he read non-fiction compulsively. As he put it, "You don't need to go to university to be educated." Right now, he was reading *A Short History of Nearly Everything* by a guy called Bill Bryson, a former journalist. It explained everything one needed to know about science in 600 pages, a feat I couldn't even imagine attempting.

Darcy put his book down on the pine coffee table and said, "What do you want to do about lunch? Should we walk down to the Market?"

I looked out the window at the park across the street and saw that it was just starting to rain. A group of basketball players made a dash for their cars and wind whipped the street trees like second-rate umbrellas. This wasn't going to be a shower.

I pointed out the window and said, "I don't fancy a walk in this. Maybe we should order in."

"Sure. Will Jenna be joining us?"

In answer to his question, we heard the front door slam. Either the wind had caught it or Jenna was exceptionally pissed off. I heard her feet banging on the steps as she came up to my apartment. I thought I had my answer.

Jenna stepped into the living room, her short, dark hair wet from the sudden storm. She looked tense, pumped up, like she had just been in a fight or was about to be. If something had gone wrong at Alicia's, it must have been big. She'd have had a half-hour drive during which to cool off.

I closed my book and said, "It didn't go well at Alicia's, I assume."

"No, it didn't but that's not why I'm so pissed."

"Why don't you start with that," Darcy said.

"I rolled down the street checking things out, just standard paranoia, when I see a guy in a parked car looking at our house through binoculars. He looked familiar so I went around the block, parked and checked the website photo of the private investigator, Paul Polanco, the one who has been sticking to our shoes like dog shit. Bingo."

"That's disturbing," I said.

"What did you do?" Darcy asked.

"I double parked tight to his driver's door, blocking him in. Then I went around to the passenger side and we had an exchange of views. He told me that Alicia is a gold-digger and Simon Cousens is a con man. Polanco admitted that he's working for Brendan Connor and said that he was going to track Simon down for what he called 'an informal resolution' of the problem.

"He had some advice, too. He told me I was in over my head and that I should get out while I still could."

"What an asshole," I said. "What did you say?"

"I told him where he could park his advice. I happened to have a tire iron with me, so as I returned to my vehicle, I took the opportunity to demolish both of the tail lights on his Lexus.

"He actually called me kid! If he could have reached, he'd probably have patted me on the head. Fuck, I hate men like that."

"I've met a few myself. Most of them are bullies who back down when you call their bluff."

"I'm not sure Polanco is that type of bully. He's a tough-looking bastard."

"You should have called me," Darcy said. "I'd have been happy to come down there and straighten him out."

"I don't need you to fight my fights, but thanks."

"Good job," I said. "I'm sure he's just as pissed off as you are. Pinning him in his car couldn't have made him too happy."

"No. He looked like his head was going to explode." Then Jenna laughed, the anger dissipating. She collapsed into an overstuffed red armchair across from the couch.

"So what did you learn at Alicia's? Are we working for a gold-digger who's looking for a con man?"

"Maybe. I wouldn't rule it out. She did tell me that she hadn't been completely honest with me. Shocking, eh?"

"Totally. Specifically what was she dishonest about?"

"Simon. Apparently, he's short of money. I'm sure that's true because we heard the same thing from Miranda. He hasn't been successful in raising the money to match Brendan's investment and Alicia says it's like a big virility issue with him. He and Brendan have been competing for decades and Simon doesn't want to fail."

"What do you think, motive enough for Simon to declare victory in their game, grab the money and run?"

"Maybe. When she said it, I was wondering if there ever had been $10 million, but with Polanco chasing it, I think we have an answer to that question. I asked her if she knew who Polanco was by the way, and she denied it. That's almost certainly bullshit."

"Does Alicia want you to stick with the case?"

"For now. We're supposed to interview that cousin, Rob, the guy who lives up past Arnprior. See if maybe Simon is hiding out up there."

"Then what?"

"I say we don't sit back and wait for Alicia to tell us what to do. Polanco's appearance on our doorstep escalates things. He ordered me to drop Alicia's case. I'm not going to get pushed around that way."

"Damn straight," Darcy said. "One thing I learned in hockey, when you're up against a bigger, more aggressive opponent go right after him, pin him to the boards, get in his grill. Don't wait for him to line you up."

I wasn't as convinced as Darcy that hockey was a guidebook for real life, but I couldn't disagree with his advice. "Makes sense," I said. "We need to find out everything we can about Brendan Connor and about Alicia. What's her real angle and how does he operate?"

"Exactly," Darcy said. "Scouting."

"Right. I'll find someone I can talk to about Connor. Jenna, can you dig deeper on Alicia?"

"Just what I planned to do. I'm going to talk to some people I know about Polanco, too."

Then Jenna's cell phone rang. She pulled it from her pocket and reacted to the number with surprise. She answered the call and put it on speaker.

"This is Alicia. I've just heard from Brendan. He's moved the meeting up to Wednesday morning. He's bringing things to a head. I'm going to need you to come with me. Do you carry a gun?"

"I'm happy to come," Jenna said, "but I can't bring a gun. PIs can't legally carry one in Canada."

"Fine. I'll bring my own. I'll text you the details."

Then she was gone.

 # Nineteen

A quick examination of the *Ottawa Citizen* database told me that Brendan Connor had been mentioned in 173 stories, the vast majority of them by Vic Dwyer. I vaguely remembered Dwyer. He had been the paper's tech industry reporter since the 1980s, but was one of the people who took a buyout shortly after Colin and I arrived at the paper. The corporate thinkers at head office had reasoned that news about businesses in the community where the paper was actually published could be easily replaced by business stories that were generic enough to run in all of the chain's papers.

Personally, I didn't much care about business news, but I remembered vividly Colin's anger that one of his first tasks as the new editor was to reduce the staff, which made the paper worse. My main memory of Dwyer was that he always wore dark suits to the office and that he gave a rather long speech at the farewell lunch at The Newshole, the pub next door to the paper.

I remembered hearing that he had quickly joined the vast consulting industry downtown. A Google search revealed his work email at Hill+Knowlton and he got back to me quickly. I had offered to buy him a late lunch in exchange for whatever he could tell me about Brendan Connor, and Dwyer had quickly agreed. One thing I had learned in more than 20 years in the business is that most journalists found free food and drink to be irresistible.

Now I was waiting for him at the Red Dart, the cheesy faux English pub that was on the ground floor of my old apartment building on Elgin. The food was OK, beer was beer, it was right around the corner from my house, and it was still raining. He was working from home and said he'd walk because he needed the exercise. I nursed a pint of Lugtread and hoped Dwyer would be reasonably punctual. He was already 10 minutes late.

Then I saw a bald, heavy-set man come through the door, shake out his umbrella and start looking around the half-filled pub. I recognized Dwyer from his photo on the corporate web site, but it must have been taken on his first day of work. He looked worn out in that way that people in late middle age often did. The flesh on his face drooped, what was left of his hair was colourless and his squint told me that he needed glasses but was too vain to wear them. I was surprised to see that he had jeans on, but his button-down white shirt and blazer were within the acceptable bounds of corporate casual.

I waved to get his attention and Dwyer noticed me, then lumbered towards my table with a bear-like gait. He had been right about needing the exercise.

He held out his hand and said, "Vic Dwyer, but I guess you must know that."

"Of course. How could I forget?"

"Easily, I would think. If I remember correctly, I was going out the door at about the same time that you and Colin were coming in."

"Yes. Glad to know that you landed on your feet."

Dwyer sat down, motioned for the server, and pointed at my beer, ordering one of the same. Then he said, "Landed on my fat ass, more like. My new employer formed the notion that all my years covering the industry made me an expert on tech business communications. Who was I to contradict them? Terribly boring work, but well paid. Still, I miss the newsroom."

"There's not that much left of it now. My advice is to remember it the way it was."

Dwyer nodded in agreement. "I'm sure you don't want to reminisce about the good old days."

He had that right, at least in regard to what life was like at the *Citizen* before I worked there. "I do in a way," I said. "I'm trying to get a handle on Brendan Connor and I understand you know him pretty well."

"Ah yes. The tiny tech titan, as the Sun once called him. I wish someone had put that headline on one of my stories. I've been covering Brendan since he was a brash upstart. Mind if I ask why a crime columnist is interested? I smell something juicy."

This was the part that would be somewhat challenging to finesse. "Trying to help a friend with some research," I said.

Dwyer looked at me skeptically, then nodded, perhaps realizing that it didn't really matter why I wanted to know about Connor, so long as I was picking up the lunch tab. "What's your overall take on the guy?" I asked.

"Brendan is a puffed up, egotistical little prick, but I had to be kind to him in print. He gave me a lot of good insight into what was happening in the tech world back then."

Dwyer clearly belonged to what I called the suck-up school of journalism. The theory was that flattering a source and avoiding controversial stuff would get you some great scoops. I was more the put the fear of God into them type.

"Of course. Remind me how he got started."

"He was an engineer at Nortel. You remember Nortel?"

"Big company, went broke, burned a lot of local people."

"That's the one. Brendan was either lucky or smart enough to get out before all of that happened. He and his pal Simon Cousens had come up with an innovation in telephone switching gear. I won't bore you with the details, but it was a big deal back in the 1980s. A lot of money was made digitizing phone switching and Brendan and Simon were in on the ground floor. Their little Kanata company became a big player almost overnight. They were both multi-millionaires in short order."

"Then what?"

"Years of flailing about, frankly. They sold their company before the tech became outdated and did rather well. Then they were up against the challenge of every person who has one good idea. What next? They stayed in telephony, forming a series of corporations over the years. Gradually, they moved from being inventors with a solid product to sellers of hope who were skilled at persuading investors that their new company would be the next big thing. None of them were, but the two of them were adept at selling out before that became apparent. Have you heard the joke about what Brendan calls his company?"

"Can't say that I have."

"Conn-Tech, one part tech, one part con. Are we eating, by the way?"

"Sure. Get whatever you like."

The server appeared again and Brendan ordered a cheeseburger with fries. I chose a Cobb salad.

"So as I was saying, their timing was better than their products."

"Beats the reverse, I'm sure. Tell me a bit about this Simon Cousens. How did their partnership work?"

"Brendan and Simon have a symbiotic relationship, like algae and fungus. Together they make lichens, or in this case, money. I'm not sure one would be much good without the other. Simon is the real engineer, the ideas man. He's not interested in sales at all. Brendan, on the other hand, might have played a role in the first idea, but he hasn't had one since. He's the salesman, the one who gets the investors on board. Smooth as silk, Brendan is, when he wants to be. An aggressive boor when he doesn't."

"Tell me more about that."

"Brendan is famous for lording it over his staff. Demands total obedience, which he prefers to call loyalty. Quite a terror at staff and board meetings, cutting people off in mid-sentence, mocking them, belittling their appearance."

"An asshole, then. Why do the rest of them put up with it?"

"Money, plus Brendan rarely hires anyone who is uncomfortable with being dominated by him."

I thought of Paula and her sexual relationship with her former husband. Talk about taking your work home. It was the kind of detail that I knew Dwyer would enjoy, but I decided to keep it to myself.

"And Simon Cousens? What's your take on why he stuck with Brendan all this time?"

"Brendan looked after all the stuff Simon had no interest in doing and made them both a lot of money while he was at it. Simon thinks worrying about money is beneath him, although he doesn't have any problem spending it. Quite the lifestyle back in the day."

"Do tell."

"Simon was a fixture at all the city nightclubs in the first heyday of the tech industry. Quite a ladies' man, too."

"And what about Brendan, a partier, as well?"

"Not so much, and I believe he has had only one wife. Divorced now."

We paused while the server put the food on the table. Then I said, "What are the two of them up to now?"

"Brendan has become kind of a godfather of the local tech business. Serves on a lot of boards, invests in startups, that kind of thing. He still owns a number of companies but none of them are really in the forefront. Simon has some kind of incubator but nothing is coming out the other end. I'm out of the news business, of course, but I stay on top of tech developments because of clients. Simon seems to have gone off the radar in recent years. Enjoying his millions, I suppose."

"Not an option either one of us will ever have, I'm sure. I've heard some things about the way Brendan does business and what you're telling me substantiates them. Would you consider him dangerous in any way?"

Dwyer nodded, starting to understand why a crime columnist might be writing about Brendan Connor.

"What's he done?"

"Probably nothing. I'm trying to get a sense of his limits."

Dwyer waited for me to tell him more, but when I didn't, he said, "Brendan Connor is certainly not physically dangerous. He's a diminutive fellow. He has a thug who's always lurking in the background, though. Ex-cop. On one of the rare occasions when I wrote a story Brendan didn't like, this fellow showed me from the premises when I arrived for my next interview, and not in a gentle way."

"Paul Polanco."

"That's the one. You're working on something aren't you?"

"No, just helping someone out. I'm actually on leave writing a book about something else entirely." As I said it, the obvious hit me. Instead of pretending to write a book about Simon Cousens, I needed to dig into the whole Alicia-Simon-Brendan situation and get it into the newspaper. There was a story there, maybe a huge one. I knew I could sell it to my editor, Soupy Campbell, just by telling him the headline could be Mystery Man Vanishes With $10 Million.

"You asked about Brendan being dangerous. There is one thing you might want to look at. Sometime in the early or mid-90s, two senior employees of the company that Brendan and Simon ran were killed. Shot to death in their house somewhere out in rural Kanata. The crime was never solved, but I always felt that it might have something to do with Brendan. Strictly a hunch, you know? Like I said, Brendan can't stand so-called disloyalty and he has a volcanic temper. I've seen that in person."

This was a new and intriguing piece of information. "What were their names, do you remember?"

"I'm sorry, I don't. I didn't cover the story and it was a long time ago now. I'm sure you can find out easily enough."

"I will, of course."

In fact, I wanted to find out right now, but first I had to watch Vic Dwyer finish his lunch. Fortunately, he was attacking it with great vigour.

* * *

Jenna had thought finding out more about Alicia Jameson would be relatively straightforward. Women her age were almost invariably active on social media, especially upwardly-mobile business strivers like Alicia. Facebook turned up 20 Alicia Jamesons. There were artists, realtors and cocktail waitresses, mostly living in the U.S. None of them were striking, red-headed tech entrepreneurs. Instagram was a bust, too, even though the site catered to good-looking women with handsome dogs. The only place the relevant Alicia Jameson appeared was on LinkedIn, the business networking site. Even there, the profile was barebones. Alicia had stated her education simply as Masters Degree in Computer Science, University of Waterloo. She listed six previous employers, all companies that Jenna had never heard of and described her work with job titles like product development specialist or research officer. She listed her current employment as BrightFuture, which Jenna knew was Simon's idea development factory. Her official title there was senior vice-president, knowledge development. Jenna wondered whether the big job title came before or after she had married Simon.

Maybe Alicia was just a really private person. Nothing wrong with that. Still it was odd, and frustrating, not to find even a single reference anywhere to any friend, any family or even where she was from. Jenna hadn't expected Alicia to post photos of what she looked like in goofy animal ears or shit like that, but most people felt compelled to show others at least some pictures of how wonderful their lives were, especially people with as much ego as Alicia.

When it came right down to it, Alicia's only visible human connection was to Simon Cousens and he wasn't exactly available for an interview. She could maybe find out something from the other people who worked at BrightFuture, but it was a high-risk strategy because word of her inquiries could get back to Alicia pretty quickly. Right now, Alicia still offered their best window into whatever was really going on, even if it was one that was maddeningly opaque.

Then Jenna had a better idea. It meant taking someone else into their confidence, but it might just be worth it. Kris wouldn't like it, but she wasn't going to sit around and wait for approval.

Her call to the Addington Foundation was answered by a frosty receptionist, but Jenna adopted her stern police voice and reminded the woman of her recent meeting with Miranda and said she was calling with an important follow-up question. Miranda had invited her to do so at any time, Jenna said. It wasn't true, but the receptionist was unlikely to know that.

The line clicked and hummed briefly, then Miranda came on, her tone crisp, but not unfriendly. "Jenna Martin. Here you are again. Something more about Simon?"

"In a way. There's a bit more to the story, beyond what we told you about."

"There always is when it comes to Simon."

"There's a situation that involves Simon and I could use your help. It would have to be in strictest confidence, though."

Then was a brief hesitation, then Miranda said, "All right, but if you are asking me to do something that would be against Simon's interests, the deal is off."

"Fair enough. I think what I want to tell you is actually very much in his interest. First, you should know that Kris is not working on a book."

"That does not overly surprise me, although I think Simon is worthy of one."

"And getting more so by the minute. As you know, I'm a private investigator. In this case, my client is Alicia Jameson."

"Really? What's her angle?"

"Simon is missing, and has been for a week."

"Good Lord. You say missing. Can you be a little more specific?"

"Alicia says she hasn't seen him since last Monday morning. She went off to work but when she got home, Simon wasn't there and neither was their dog. She assumed he'd gone off somewhere for a ride in one of his sports cars, taken the dog with him. Then he didn't show up for dinner or return at all that night. By then, she was angry more than anything. Then the dog came back on its own the next day. On Friday, she came to me asking for help."

"Why you?"

"She had hired me to vet Simon before the wedding," Jenna said, omitting the fact that Alicia had gotten cold feet on the vetting.

"Really? I wouldn't have thought she was the one who should have been suspicious."

"Just worried about his long track record of marrying and divorcing, she said."

"I suppose that's legitimate."

"There's more, though."

"Is he in trouble?' Miranda asked, concern apparent in her voice.

"I think so. And there's another thing. Ten million dollars are missing."

There was a brief pause, then Miranda said, "All right, what do you need?"

"I need you to find out who the hell Alicia Jameson really is."

 Twenty

After the lunch with Vic Dwyer mercifully ended, I decided not to waste my time searching for online coverage of a murder from more than 25 years ago. I didn't need to, because I had access to the best human encyclopedia of homicide in Ottawa. Mike Reilly had headed the Ottawa Police major crimes unit for decades. There was little he did not know about homicides in the city, solved and unsolved.

Reilly had been a frequent contact for years, but we had worked especially closely on a story involving a missing Chinese spy and a senior cabinet minister. Reilly had gone well outside the normal bounds of policing to solve it, but his triumph was so great that his enemies in the police brass had no choice but to promote him to inspector, something that was long overdue.

I brought up the contacts on my phone and hit his number. Reilly answered on the first ring. "Reilly," he barked. I was used to his customary impatience. We hadn't spoken in months, but his gruff, hurried manner hadn't changed despite his recent retirement.

"Mike, it's Kris."

"Ah, Redner. I thought you had forgotten about me, now that I'm just another old washed-up cop."

"Not a chance. I need some information. It's about a case from the 1990s, unsolved."

"Jesus Kris. You aren't going back to dig up some old case to rake me over the coals are you?"

"You know me better than that. Can I swing by?"

"Sure. You remember where I live?"

"Of course. I can be there in 10 minutes. That OK?"

"I'm not going anywhere."

It was a short walk to Reilly's apartment. It was an older brick building painted a dingy white. Probably dated back to the 1960s, I thought, and it had the air of a structure being left to rot while the

landlord waited for demolition. It wasn't the kind of building most
people would expect to see a police inspector living in, but Reilly
had some tough times financially after his divorce and he'd once
told me that he'd reached the point in life where he just didn't care
about where he lived, as long as the shower worked and there was
beer in the fridge. It had to be a big adjustment, going from having
a hand in every big crime investigation in the city to being a retiree
cooped up in a small apartment. I wondered how he was handling
it.

Reilly was on the fifth floor and I decided to take the elevator
up. It had a worrying mechanical groan and a grimy air about it.
I stepped out into a hallway with well-worn red carpet. Someone
had cooked fish for lunch, judging by the smell in the hall.

I rang Reilly's bell and he opened up immediately, then gestured
for me to enter. Reilly's faded Celtic good looks hadn't changed. His
hair was a bit greyer, though, and he was wearing a pair of khaki
shorts and a navy T-shirt. I thought it was the first time I had seen
him without one of his trademark dark suits.

The biggest surprise, though, were the stacks of large cardboard
boxes that filled the small apartment.

"Finally moving to a better place?"

"Damn straight. I'm moving to a Caribbean island."

That stopped me. Reilly had spent his whole life in Ottawa and
his family went back generations in the city. The idea of him leaving Ottawa was unbelievable. He laughed at what must have been
a look of obvious shock on my face. Then I said, "You're kidding,
right?"

"Not a bit. I've got nothing to keep me here now and I've got an
inspector's pension and all the freedom in the world. Why would I
want to sit around and gripe about what a shitty job the next gen-
eration of cops is doing, just like every other guy who packed it in?"

"But a Caribbean island? To do what? How much sun and sand
can you take?"

"I guess I'm going to find out. I want to go someplace where I
can be whoever I want to be. I'm tired of other people holding me
back."

It sounded pretty good when it he put it that way.

"So when's the big move?"

"Two weeks."

"Wow. That's sudden. Where are you headed exactly?"

"I'm not sure yet. I'll see where the wind blows me."

My knowledge of Caribbean islands was limited. I wasn't exactly the type who took week-long package trips.

"Wow. Congratulations. It takes some nerve to pull up stakes like that."

"I'm not leaving much behind, just memories. That's not what you came to talk about, though. So an old case, which one?"

"Double murder of a high tech couple in Kanata in the 1990s. They worked for one of Brendan Connor's companies."

"John and Eve Tarrant. I remember it well. It was in 1995, the year when all the local police services merged. It was one of the first cases I handled in Kanata. It had been OPP territory before.

"They lived in one of those big estate homes in the country. Beautiful place except for the two corpses we found in the hallway. They had both been shot, single tap in the head. It was a pro job. Out-of-town hitter, we figured at the time."

"Why was that?"

"There wasn't so much as a sniff about the shootings on the local criminal grapevine and his style suggested it wasn't his first time. The guy didn't leave us any useful forensic evidence. We had the slugs that were in their brains, but that was it. He picked up his brass and must have worn gloves. There wasn't a print anywhere, other than those belonging to the family and a few close relatives. We don't get operators like that in Ottawa."

"Motive?"

"Unclear. They were a successful couple with a fair amount of money but nothing was taken. No obvious enemies. Kept mostly to themselves. We interviewed Connor, of course, and their colleagues but if there was a workplace motive, we didn't find it."

"What was your take on Connor?"

"Nasty little prick. Didn't seem upset about two of his employees being murdered. He was more concerned about who would pick up their work. Some telephone switching thing.

"We worked it hard for a year and didn't get to first base. Then it started to slide down the priority scale. You know how it is. The worst part was the little girl."

"What, they had a kid?"

"Yes, and she was in the house when the shootings took place. She didn't see them, but she told us that the killer came up the stairs, then found her hiding under her bed. He dragged her out, then told her to run. Good advice. She took it."

"She must have gotten a look at him, then."

"She did, but all she could tell us was that he was older, hadn't shaved and had bloodshot eyes. It wasn't of much value, but she was only eight."

"Do you remember the child's name?"

"I can't forget it. We let her down. Ashley Tarrant."

"What happened to her, do you know?"

"She went to live with a relative and after that, I don't know."

"Relative's name?"

"Jesus, Redner. You're asking me for secondary details on an unsolved that's more than 25 years old. I think the relative was her mother's brother. I can't remember his name off the top of my head. If I think of it, I'll let you know."

"All right. Thanks Mike. You've been a big help."

"Good, now send one back my way. Why are you digging into this case after so many years have gone by?"

"Something is going on that involves Brendan Connor and his partner Simon Cousens. A former colleague filled me in on Connor's background and he mentioned the unsolved killing. I've got absolutely nothing to suggest that it's related to what's going on now, but I'm looking at Connor from every angle."

"Well, that's unfortunate for Connor," Reilly said. "You got time for a beer?"

I knew I should, for old times' sake, but I needed to keep moving. "Not today, but let's catch one before you leave. I'm going to miss you."

"You are a member of a very small group, then. I think the brass had a party after I retired."

"You *were* a pain in the ass."

"I take that as a high compliment, coming from you. You're the biggest pain in the ass I ever met."

"Well, thank you. It's a gift I have."

Reilly nodded in agreement, then said, "Watch out for this guy

Connor. He didn't feel right to me. Rich asshole who thinks he rules the world."

"That's what I hear. Oh, one other thing. Paul Polanco, a PI who is Connor's hired muscle. You know him, I'm sure."

"I do. We were on the job together. Polanco spent most of his time in vice. Seemed like a natural fit to me. The guy's bent in some way. He always played close to the edge, which tells me he went over it but didn't get caught. Somehow he came up with enough money to start his own business. That's difficult to do on a sergeant's salary. My theory is that he roughed up drug dealers, relieved them of their cash. Tough to do now that everyone has got a cell phone, but some guys got away with a lot back then. Polanco's a big guy, and he used it to advantage. His own advantage, I think. Avoid him if you can."

"Too late for that, unfortunately. He was casing my house yesterday."

"Jesus. That's not good. You want some help? I can make a few calls."

"I think I've got it handled. If I find out different, I'll let you know."

"Don't leave it too late, Kris. You like to get too close to the fire. You're not going to get lucky every time."

I thanked Reilly for his help and as I rode down in the elevator I thought about what he said about my luck running out. I used to think I could take on the world singlehandedly. Now I knew I couldn't, but I had Darcy and Jenna behind me. Together, we had already taken out a vicious killer. Surely we were up to whatever Brendan Connor could throw at us.

Twenty-one

I sat at the kitchen table with a yellow legal pad and a glass of merlot, not my first of the evening. I often found that a diagram helped me to see the real shape of a story, especially one with so many confusing links. On the legal pad, I had drawn a circle in the centre and written Simon's name on it with a red Sharpie. I had then drawn somewhat smaller circles with the names Brendan and Alicia. I used a black Sharpie to draw a dark, heavy line between Simon's circle and Brendan's. Then I put a second heavy line connecting Alicia and Simon, followed by a lighter line connecting her and Brendan, with a question mark on top. I depicted Simon's former wives like a cluster of small planets circling his star and connected them to him with yet another line. All except for Paula. She warranted her own circle, with lines of equal weight to Brendan and Simon. Finally, I added Polanco, orbiting Brendan like the moon.

Those were the characters in the story I was trying to understand, but grasping what connected them was far, far more complicated than drawing lines on a piece of paper. I was surest of the connection between Simon and Brendan. It was long, complex and multi-faceted. They had shared careers, fame, wealth and wives. Their relationship was perhaps the most important in this whole affair, but everything I knew about Brendan was second hand. I wanted to assess him directly, but Alicia would have to approve it if I was going to be part of the meeting Wednesday.

What Alicia meant to the two of them was more of a mystery. She was Simon's latest wife and his new business partner, of course, but there was something more there, something larger and darker. I could sense it. According to what Jenna had been able to find out so far, Alicia seemed to have suddenly sprung into existence, a woman without a visible history. That set off alarm bells, but what were they trying to tell me? Alicia seemed like the key to everything, but in what way?

I had dug further into the 1995 Kanata killing that Reilly and I had talked about. The Tarrant homicide had been page-one news in both the *Citizen* and the *Ottawa Sun*. The tabloid headline read Tech Stars Shot, Killed. I would have expected something snappier from the Sun, then in its heyday. The *Citizen* had been ever more prosaic with a head of Double Slaying In Kanata.

I had spent the rest of the afternoon and the early part of the evening reading everything that Google and the *Citizen* database had. I discovered that the Tarrants were as dull as the headlines describing their rather spectacular demise. John Tarrant was 36. The newspaper pictures showed a slight-looking man with wire-framed glasses and a prematurely receding hairline. If you typed in computer nerd, Tarrant's picture would have come up. He certainly didn't look dynamic enough to have done anything to justify homicide. Eve Tarrant was a different type altogether. She was a 30-year-old blond who looked more like an actress than a tech worker. Big smile, big lips, big eyes, big hair. While her husband seemed lifeless, even in life, Eve burst off the newspaper page.

I drew another circle at the bottom of the page, as far as possible from the rest and wrote Eve and John, then added "Affair?" Eve Tarrant was clearly the kind of woman that a lot of men would desire. She was beautiful and apparently brainy, judging by her job. Maybe this was a familiar story, a lover, then a jealous wife. I knew the killing wasn't the direct work of a woman, but it could be someone acting on her behalf. Reilly's speculation about the hit being a professional job supported that idea.

Was there some link to the Tarrants' work at Brendan Connor's company, or was it just a coincidence? It was always easy to see connections that were apparent but not real. Still, I drew a faint black line from the Tarrants to Brendan.

It was a surmise not based on much. The police had released few details of the killings and according to what Reilly told me, it wasn't a case of holding back, they just didn't know what happened. With a lack of new angles, the double homicide dropped from the news coverage quickly. There had been a story on the first anniversary of the killings, then another on the fifth. Then the news trail ended. None of the stories mentioned the child, Ashley. Police wanted to protect her, I assumed.

I decided not to waste too much time on the Tarrants. If the story behind their killings couldn't be broken by the police at the time, what hope did I have now?

What I needed to find was the catalyst that had set all these recent events in motion. How could it be the killing of the Tarrants, after so much time had passed? No, it was something big, something that connected Brendan, Simon and Alicia. Money was part of it, but it wasn't as simple as that. It was just possible that the story that Alicia had told us was largely true, but I wasn't going to bet on it.

Suddenly, I had the feeling that I was being watched. I looked up and saw that Darcy was standing in the kitchen, looking at me. "You gave me a start," I said.

"Sorry. You looked like you were deep in thought. I didn't want to interrupt."

"Just trying to work out the relationship between Simon, Alicia and Brendan Connor."

Darcy pointed at my pad and said, "So, have you solved it?"

"Hardly," I said, although I felt that the diagram had at least given a shape to my uncertainty.

"I think I'm going to head to bed," Darcy said.

"What time is it?"

"10:30."

He came over to the table, laid a hand on my shoulder, then bent to kiss the top of my head. "Are you sleepy?" he whispered.

"Not yet. My head is full of this story. Having Polanco almost on our doorstep changes things. I've got to help Jenna get to the bottom of it."

"But not tonight."

"No. You go ahead. I'll be right along."

I watched him leave the kitchen, admiring his ass, as I always did. It was pretty clear what was on Darcy's mind, but I wasn't so sure it was on mine, even though I felt like we'd taken our sexual relationship into new territory last night. I was tired and I wasn't sure what to do next. I didn't want our next time together to be a let-down.

By the time I got to the bedroom, Darcy was already in bed lying on his back shirtless with his hands behind his head, sheet pulled up to his waist. It was a position that flexed his chest and arm muscles in a way that I liked, as I was sure he was aware. He was nude, no doubt. In the time that I had known him, Darcy had never worn a pair of pyjamas. I was a nightgown girl. I felt less vulnerable that way.

I crossed the bedroom, which was dully lit by his bedside lamp. I turned my back to him then pulled my T-shirt over my head.

"You aren't suddenly shy are you?"

"What did you expect, a striptease?"

"Well ..."

I thought about what to do next, but not for too long. I had drunk three glasses of wine and there was a naked man in my bed. Fuck it. I was only going to be youngish once. I turned to Darcy and said, "Turn on some music."

Twenty-two

The view of the Ottawa River from Rob Cousens's patio was spectacular. The river widened north of Arnprior, looking more like a lake dotted with several small islands. A brisk, late morning breeze gave the water a chop but the sky was pure blue and the forest beyond stretched as far as I could see. Although Jenna and I were just an hour from downtown Ottawa, it felt more like we were on the edge of a wilderness. Our view was enhanced by the fact that Rob's 19th century stone house was on the side of a hill that swept down to the river.

Rob had gone into the house to get coffee and muffins, leaving Jenna and I a moment to talk. "What do you think?" I asked.

"Seems like a friendly guy and we didn't have to climb a fence to get in, so that's an improvement. At the very least, it was a beautiful drive up here. I can think of tougher ways to make $1,600."

"Yes. We'll soon find out if Cousin Rob really knows anything. He doesn't seem as devious as the wives."

When we called ahead, Rob had seemed eager to talk. We had agreed that it was time to drop the pretence of my working on a book about Simon. Brendan Connor was already well aware of who we were and what we were up to. Instead, Jenna explained that she was a private investigator trying to help Simon. If he formed the impression that we were working for Simon, who were we to contradict him? Rob had invited us to 'come on up straightaway' and we had done just that. I was glad of the quick invitation, because the meeting with Brendan Connor was set for tomorrow and Rob was our last hope of finding useful new information. He had welcomed us like old friends and insisted that we have refreshments before we got down to business.

So now, we waited. Although it was a perfect May morning, the breeze still made it a little cool on the hill. I was glad that I had brought my yellow cotton sweater and I pulled it on. Jenna was wearing a short-sleeved T-shirt and jeans.

"Are you cold?" I asked.

"No, Mom. I'll be fine," she said, giving me a look that said drop the mothering mode.

"Sorry. Just a question."

We both turned at the sound of a screen door slapping shut and saw Rob Cousens heading our way. He was a stocky man, but powerful, not fat. I figured he was in his late 50s, with greying ginger hair and a whitish goatee and moustache. His green T-shirt was a little tight, but his muscular arms were already tanned, as if he spent a lot of time outdoors. In all, he seemed like a capable, masculine sort of guy, a familiar type in the Ottawa Valley.

Rob laid a tray with a coffee pot, three cups, cream, sugar and a plate of muffins on the round, glass-topped patio table. Noticing my sweater, he said, "I should have asked if you ladies were comfortable enough outdoors. It is a bit fresh yet."

"We're fine," Jenna said, offering her very best smile. Rob smiled back with equal enthusiasm. There was no sign of a Mrs. Rob and I expected he didn't have a lot of attractive younger women dropping around for coffee. Jenna certainly seemed to draw his attention a lot more than I did. I was getting used to it.

Rob poured the coffee, then settled into his own chair and said, "So, what's Simon gotten himself into now, more woman trouble?"

"Not exactly," Jenna said. "Actually, he's missing. His wife Alicia hasn't seen him in more than a week."

Rob nodded and smiled again, apparently relieved that the problem was something so minor.

"He will be on one of his road trips, then. I guess the new bride isn't aware, but Simon likes nothing better than to jump in one of those old cars of his and let the road take him where it will. It's when he does his best thinking, he says. No distractions from the home or work front."

"That's what Alicia thought, at first, but she hasn't been able to contact him. His cell phone is still at the house. She hasn't heard a word, so of course, she's worried," Jenna said.

"He'll turn up. He always does."

'There's something else, as well. Some money is missing from one of the business accounts. Quite a lot, actually."

"You're not telling me that Simon is stealing his own money?"

"No, someone else's. Not to say that anything has been stolen. It is just presently unaccounted for."

Rob shook his head and raised his hands, as if he were shooing away this information. "I don't pretend to know anything about high finance or Simon's deal-making. I just know him as my brilliant cousin who made a shitload of money doing stuff I don't understand."

I could see that Rob was taking the information about the missing money as an attack on Simon, and that we were on the verge of losing him.

"The money is an interesting detail," I said "but it's not like we understand all of that stuff either. The real point is that Simon's wife wants to find him and we agreed to do what we could. We came to you because we hear that you're the person who has known him longest and you're his best friend. Alicia is really hoping you can help her."

Rob nodded sympathetically. Over the years, I had found that a simple request for help brought out the best in most people.

"Simon and I grew up together, right around here. He's a couple of years older but we were tight as ticks, back in the day. We stay in touch but I don't see him more than three or four times a year. He likes to drive up in the good weather, have a couple of beers. Sometimes we take out my boat, do a little fishing."

"Sounds like you'd like to see him more," I said.

"Sure, but I know he's busy. Always up to his ears in big ideas and big projects. My life has been a lot simpler. I ran an electrical contracting business in Arnprior, sold it a year ago and did pretty well. Not Simon Cousens kind of money, but good for me."

"Well, you picked a great spot to retire."

"Oh, I didn't pick it. The house picked me. This old house has been in the Cousens family for more than 150 years. I grew up here. Summers, Simon would come down and stay with my family for weeks at a time. His father was a farmer, but he made his money as a carpenter and it was his busiest season. Simon's mother died when he was only five, so it was just him and Uncle Fred.

"We were a regular pair when we were kids. Simon always shone brighter, even back then. He was tall, good looking and smart. Everything I'm not," Rob said, chuckling. "People used to refer to me as Simon Cousens's cousin Rob Cousens, like that was my claim to fame. I suppose it was. People still call me that to this day."

"When was the last time you heard from Simon?" Jenna asked.

Rob rubbed his goatee and made a show of thinking. Maybe too much of a show, I thought. Then he looked out at the river, like he might find the answer there.

"I think it was mid-April. Yes, it must have been. The river was terrible high. That's why Simon came up. We've both been river rats forever. He loves the power of the river in the spring, but this year, the flood was the highest it has been in our lifetimes. It's still high, what with the snowy winter and the wet spring. We took a walk down to the river, then followed the bank as far as we could. My property goes right to the river."

"Good thing the original builders didn't go for waterfront," Jenna said.

"No, they were too smart for that, and being close to the road was more important. No cars back then, of course."

Rob seemed a little more relaxed, but I felt that he was drifting away from the topic of where Simon was now. "It must be great to have such a strong family connection," I said. "If Simon was in trouble, you sound like the first person he'd turn to."

"Well there you have it. He hasn't turned to me, so I guess he isn't in trouble," Rob said. "Simon Cousens knows how to take care of himself, that I can assure you."

"I'll bet he does. Still, you can imagine why his wife is worried. She's young and they haven't been married long. Oh, and I forgot to mention the dog."

"What, Rex is missing too?" he said, showing more alarm than he had over the idea of his cousin having disappeared. "That's not right. Simon doesn't go anywhere without that dog."

"Rex has turned up," I said, "but he was gone for a day, came back full of burrs, like he'd gotten lost in the woods."

"Ah, so maybe a coincidence then."

"Maybe, but it all happened on the same day that Simon disappeared. Rob, can you help us or not? Alicia is really worried and getting more so with every day that she doesn't hear from him.

Maybe he's done this kind of thing in the past, but he has never dropped out of contact with her for so long."

"I can see why she's concerned," he said. "Thinking back, I'd say that most of Simon's road trips took place once the marriage of the day was starting to burn out. It's a little early for that."

"Yes, it is. With the two of you being so close, you can see why we would think that maybe he turned up here."

"Hasn't though. Look, if I could help, of course I would. Leave me your card. If I hear anything, I'll let you know."

I sincerely doubted that. If Rob Cousens did learn where Simon was, his loyalty would clearly be to Simon, not to his new wife or two investigators he had just met.

Jenna stood, then handed him a card and said, "We've taken up a lot of your time, Rob. It was really great to meet you." She stretched her hand to shake his and he responded reflexively. Jenna held his hand just a little longer than normal and gave Rob a particularly intense look. I appreciated the technique. Despite his denials, I thought that Rob knew something and if we couldn't get his conscience to motivate him, maybe the thought of spending more time with Jenna would.

It wasn't much of a hope, but at least it was something.

Twenty-three

By 8:45 Wednesday morning, Jenna and I were at a table at the Brwd 4 U coffee shop in Kanata. As a writer, I found the spelling offensive, but it was the nearest place to the tech towers of Kanata and only five minutes' drive from Brendan Connor's office in the Conn-Tech Building. Alicia was to join us at nine to set strategy for the meeting with Brendan. Jenna had made it pretty clear that Alicia would exclude me, but I came along anyway. I was in this now just as deep as Jenna and my protective instincts had kicked in, too. I wished I knew more about what I thought I was protecting her from. Brendan Connor, surely, but was it just him? The Connor meeting was the most important of all that we had done in the last week and I wanted to meet him, to see how the stories married up with the reality.

The coffee shop was busy with laptop-carrying tech workers coming and going. It wasn't a private setting, but the bustle created a kind of white noise. Outside, the sky was an ominous grey, as if rain were not far off.

"Let me take the lead with Alicia, Kris," Jenna said, not asking. "She's my client, as I am always reminding you and she didn't ask you to come along. I hope that you will be able to, but if she doesn't want it, that's it."

"Sure, I understand," I said, vowing to show Alicia that she needed me in the session.

"I guess the only real news we have for her is our take on the chat with Cousin Rob. We on the same page there?" Jenna asked.

"Nice guy. Allegiance would be 100 per cent to Simon. He seemed surprised when we mentioned the dog not being with Simon. Shut us down pretty quick after that. I just don't know whether he has seen Simon or not. He certainly wouldn't tell us if he had."

"I'm in agreement with all of that. If someone is helping Simon, my money would be on Rob. I don't see any of the wives doing it."

"Especially not Paula."

"No. Even if you thought her hostility toward Simon was fake, she's a mess. Doesn't seem like the kind of person you could trust if you were in trouble."

"I wouldn't, that's for sure," I said. "She had some kind of hold over Simon, though."

"Right, until she didn't."

"I wish we knew more about Alicia. I'm still not sure of her angle. Is she a distraught wife or a black widow?"

"You really think she killed Simon?"

"There is no direct evidence of it, but no one has seen him alive lately. What if she's the one who drained the business account and then eliminated Simon to cover her tracks? The longer she delays going to the police, the more credible all that seems to me."

Jenna shook her head, unconvinced. "No, it's something else. I just don't know what yet. If she had killed Simon and taken the money, the smart move would have been to head to the airport and disappear. No, whatever Alicia is doing, it's not over yet. I think it's just getting started."

I could see her point. Brendan was wound tightly into all this intrigue, too, I was sure of that. Before I could say it, the door of the coffee shop swung open and Alicia stepped inside, scanning the room. She wore a black pant suit, white silk blouse and a single strand of pearls. It looked like the outfit she had on the first day I met her, although she might have had a closet full of them. Her long red hair was pulled back tight and twisted into a bun. It made her look sleek and ready for battle.

Spotting us, she favoured us with a brief nod and headed toward our table. "Jenna," she said, then looked at me disapprovingly. "It's just going to be the two of us," she said, taking the chair beside Jenna, as far away from me as possible.

"I think another set of eyes might be helpful," Jenna said. "Strength in numbers, too."

"I don't need numbers for strength. Your mother has played her role. She can wait here."

I wondered, not for the first time, what in the world Simon Cousens saw in this woman. Maybe I was looking at it the wrong way. He had quite a track record of bad judgment when it came to women. Alicia fit that pattern.

"The cousin," Alicia said, speaking directly to Jenna. "What did you find out?"

"He and Simon are certainly tight. He acknowledges seeing Simon up at his house in mid-April. Rob professes not to be surprised at Simon taking off for a period of time, although I saw a flicker of concern when we told him that Rex had come back on his own."

"Bottom line?"

"I don't think he knows where Simon is, but I can't be certain. If this comes down to sides, he will be on Simon's."

"Fine. Let's move on. When we sit down with Brendan, I will take the lead, of course. I don't think there is any point in trying to bullshit him. With his boy Polanco snooping around, I'm sure that Brendan is aware that both Simon and the money are gone. I'm going to present that as a problem that we have a mutual interest in solving. Brendan will help me if he sees a financial benefit in doing so."

"You sure?" Jenna asked. "He and Simon go back so far that it's hard to see Brendan working against him."

"Don't presume to know more about Simon than I do. Now, let's go. I want to be early, although I'm sure he will keep us waiting regardless."

Alicia stood up, gestured for Jenna to follow and said, "You stay here. Jenna will pick you up when we're done."

I forced my mouth into a smile that I suspected was closer to a grimace and said, "Good luck." Now I knew how a dog felt when someone tied its leash to a parking meter outside a store.

* * *

Jenna got into the Lexus and closed the door. It had that heavy, solid sound that was the hallmark of ridiculously expensive vehicles. The SUV smelled of fresh leather and Alicia's perfume, something faint and unrecognizable.

"Before we go," Jenna said, "I have to make sure that you didn't follow through on that personal protection plan you mentioned."

"You mean the gun?"

"Yes, the gun. Bringing it would be illegal and dangerous. Tell me you don't see this as a shootout."

Alicia shook her head, as if she had never heard such nonsense.

"Of course not. And I should assume you are unarmed as well, right?"

"I'm not carrying a gun, no. It's illegal for PIs to do so."

"Do you miss it? The gun, I mean."

She did. With her utility belt on, Jenna felt strapped up and ready to rock. Her use-of-force training would still enable her to handle most situations, but seeing a gun on your hip helped keep people in line. "I never used it as an officer, but it was always good to know it was close to hand."

Alicia put the car in gear and then pulled out into the March Road traffic. "Think of this as a battle of wits," she said. "We need to be able to outsmart Brendan, probe at his weak spots."

"And what are those?"

"Like a lot of successful men, he's insecure. He can't believe he has gotten as far as he has based on his actual abilities and he's worried that everyone will find out that he's a fraud. That's why money and power are so important to him. They keep self-doubt at bay."

"I didn't realize that you knew him that well."

"I don't, but Simon does. That's his take on Brendan. No one knows him better."

Jenna saw an opening and decided to take it. "You came to me five days ago, worried about what had happened to him. We still don't know. Isn't the worry eating you up?"

Alicia glanced across at Jenna and said, "I am not allowing that to happen. Worry is an unproductive emotion. We need to focus on the problem at hand. If we get Brendan on our side, he will help us find Simon."

She was a cool customer. Jenna had to hand her that. Maybe that's the way engineers thought, all rationality, no emotion. Alicia was the first Jenna had ever known.

The Conn-Tech Building loomed ahead of them, 15 storeys of silvery glass surrounded by a cluster of similar but smaller buildings, most with names that sounded vaguely familiar.

Alicia pulled the Lexus into a visitor parking spot and said, "When we get up there, let me do all the talking. I just want them to know that I'm not totally on my own, that I have personal security."

"Is that what I am now?"

"For today, at least. I assume Polanco will be there. If he glares at me, you glare back at him."

Jenna knew she could handle that. The hard-eyed stare was one of the first things she had mastered in her time with the OPP. She hoped Polanco was in the meeting. The prick hadn't done too well in their last interaction, and her presence would remind him of that.

A chrome elevator emblazoned with Brendan Connor's corporate logo whisked them to the 15th floor. They stepped into a small waiting area, no more than 10 feet by 15, with a thick maroon carpet and a row of black leather chairs along one wall. Jenna expected some kind of receptionist, but there was no human watchdog, just an empty desk. The inner office had a heavy black door with a chrome plaque saying Brendan Connor CEO. It was closed, but quickly swung open, Paul Polanco filling the doorway with all the grace and presence of a gorilla. Polanco looked at his watch and shook his head at their premature arrival. Jenna was surprised that he could tell time. Polanco eyed them like a couple of mutts that had walked in off the street, then stepped back into the office and waved them forward.

The room they walked into was more like the living room of a mansion than an office. It had the same maroon carpet and three couches were grouped in a semi-circle around a fireplace that was big enough to roast a hog in. Above the black mantelpiece was a portrait of a middle-aged man with combed-forward grey hair, a strong chin and a smile of self-satisfaction. The portrait was a head only, and yet it was six feet tall. A miniature version of the same man was seated on one of the couches, staring intently at some thick corporate document. He held up one finger signalling them to wait. It reminded Jenna of the charity boss, Vic Walker. Was there some kind of executive training program that taught men to control women with hand signals?

Alicia glanced at Jenna and smiled. Perhaps they shared the same thought. They were early, so Brendan had to make it seem like he was too busy to see them. The little charade went on for about two minutes then Brendan closed the report and put it on the coffee table in front of him with a thud.

Now in salesman mode, he jumped to his feet and walked briskly toward them and reached to shake Alicia's hand. He couldn't have been more than five foot four, but his confidence worked like elevator shoes. "Alicia, so good to see you again. We have a lot to discuss."

Then Brendan glanced at Jenna and said, "And who is this?"

"My associate, Jenna Martin. Perhaps Mr. Polanco mentioned her."

Brendan finished his inspection of Jenna, sniffled slightly, then said, "He might have done, yes. Now please, everyone take a seat."

When they had done so, he said, "Let's cut right to it shall we Alicia? I don't know what story you came here intending to tell me, but I know that Simon has been missing for quite some time. More than a week, if I am not mistaken. I also know that the $10 million I put up as seed money has been withdrawn from the corporate account."

Brendan paused, to see if Alicia would contradict any of this. When she didn't, he leaned forward, pointed a finger at her and said, "Perhaps you'd like to tell me what the fuck happened to my best friend and my money."

Alicia's expression hadn't changed, as if Brendan had told her nothing more concerning than that rain was forecast. "I think we both have a problem," she said calmly.

"We? I didn't make Simon disappear and I certainly didn't steal my own money."

"Of course not, and neither did I."

"I'm afraid I'm not seeing any other suspects, Alicia. When Simon first told me about you, I was afraid that you were a gold digger, but I never imagined that you would be a grave digger. On the face of it, it seems that you have killed Simon and taken my money."

Alicia shook her head and said, "Brendan, Brendan, think it through." Her tone was one that might have been appropriate when addressing a dull student in elementary school. The tightening of Brendan's lips and the look he gave her made it clear that he didn't like it.

"I'll indulge you, just for a moment then," he said. "Please, do tell me what I'm missing."

"Simon is just as valuable to me as he is to you. He's my husband and I love him. On top of that, he's the key to my career and to getting my idea into production. Without his connections, I'd just be another young engineer with a good idea and nowhere to take it. Remember, the plan that you put that $10 million into is going to make us all rich and Simon's technological credibility is the key to its success."

Brendan sat back into the grey couch and gave Alicia a dismissive little smile. "Really, is that the best you can do? Simon and I are already rich. You're the one trying to turn our credibility into a fortune."

"Yes I am. Wouldn't you do the same in my position?"

"I suppose I might, but that doesn't tell me where Simon and my money have gone."

"I don't know. I wish I did. I'm just as worried as you are."

"Hah, I doubt that. By my calculation, you aren't out a penny and all you've lost is a husband you scarcely know. Simon is like my brother, we've been best friends, more than best friends, for decades. Now, I ask again. What have you done with him?"

Now Polanco, who was sitting on the far end of the same couch as Brendan, decided it was his turn to enter the discussion. "I know what you did," he said, his voice deep and gravelly. "You killed him." Then he pointed at Jenna and said, "Now you've brought this amateur in to help you cover it up. It's not going to fly."

Alicia stared at Polanco and said, "I'm not sure, weren't you a police officer at one time? Maybe they didn't rely on evidence or motive back then."

"Don't get smart with me," Polanco growled.

"Someone has to get smart here. Why would I kill the man who is my own meal ticket? Even if I had grown to hate Simon, and I haven't, I know that his disappearance will kill my project. This new corporation he started has the rights to it. If he doesn't reappear, my plan will remain in limbo for seven years, until the courts rule him dead. By that time, the tech will be hopelessly outdated. Believe me, I need Simon alive as much as you do."

"All right, let's say I accept that, just for the sake of argument," Brendan said. "That doesn't explain where the $10 million went. As you know, I've got a shitload of money. I'm not the kind of guy who would miss $10 million, but I'm also not the kind of guy who'd let anyone con me out of ten bucks, much less $10 million. There's no way that Simon would take my money. That only leaves you."

"Why are you so sure Simon wouldn't steal your money? The way I hear it, you've been stealing the credit for his ideas for years."

"What? That's bullshit! Simon has always gotten full credit for everything he did. Maybe you don't know the nature of our partnership, but Simon is the ideas man. Everyone knows that. I'm the guy with the magic to turn those ideas into reality."

'Yes, I'm aware of how the two of you work. Are *you* aware that Simon is just about out of money?"

Brendan's head jerked back against the top cushion of the couch, as if he had been slapped. "What are you talking about? Simon has made hundreds of millions of dollars over the course of his career."

"Yes, but sadly he has also made bad investments. His incubator has produced a lot of bad eggs, costly bad eggs, and living like Simon Cousens isn't cheap. Did you not wonder why he didn't put in the $10 million that was supposed to be his share of the seed money? He doesn't have it and he couldn't raise it."

"I don't believe it."

"I'm happy to show you all his personal accounts. Now, can we get down to the real purpose of this meeting? We need a plan to get Simon back, locate the $10 million and get this new company back on track."

"What, and act like this is all some kind of misunderstanding? You put the cookies back in the jar and I pretend you never stole them? And then there is the issue of Simon. Mr. Polanco has been engaged in a vigorous search for him without any results. I understand that your little bloodhound has been doing the same, although I expect it's all for show.

"No Alicia, I'm not buying it. Only one person knows where Simon Cousens is, and that's you."

"You're partly right. Only one person knows where Simon is, and that's Simon. If I knew where he was, we wouldn't be sitting here now."

Brendan shook his head, not bothering to hide his frustration. "I'm sure you are familiar with Occam's razor, Alicia. The simplest explanation is usually correct. I can see it clearly. I'm looking at a con woman who has killed Simon, stolen my money and is now trying to brazen it out. You've got some nerve, I'll give you that."

"I'm sorry you feel that way. I was hoping you could use your power to fix this problem. As you say, Simon is your best friend. Surely you are the one best placed to find him, with the unlimited resources at your disposal."

Brendan gave a little nod, acknowledging her admission of his omnipotence, then said, "I'm a reasonable man and, as you say, not without resources. Let's give it until Friday, shall we? If neither one of us has discovered Simon and the money by then, I'm going to take all this to the police. I'm afraid that won't go very well for you."

"So you accept my deal then?" Alicia said. "We will both work towards solving this problem."

"Oh, I wouldn't put it that way," Brendan said with a lizard-like smile. "I'm merely giving you some additional rope so that you can complete the process of hanging yourself. Don't leave town Alicia. We'll be watching."

Polanco lumbered to his feet, ready to escort them out. "Pro tip," he said, "for a problem of this size you might want to find an investigator who is a little more experienced."

Alicia didn't respond, but rose and headed for the door, Jenna following and Polanco trailing behind. Once they were back in the reception area, Polanco leaned down to Jenna and whispered in her ear, his stale breath stinking of yesterday's garlic and beer. "Watch yourself little girl," he said. "I owe you one, and you're going to get it."

Jenna didn't say a word, just turned to Polanco, darted out her right hand, grabbed his balls and squeezed with all of her considerable strength. The big private investigator doubled over in pain and shouted "Fuck!"

Twenty-four

When Alicia and Jenna got to the lobby of the Conn-Tech Building, they saw that it was raining heavily, the kind of downpour that would soak them in seconds.

"Let's make a run for it," Alicia said. She took out her key fob, unlocked the Lexus and they dashed out the door. Jenna got there first. Smarter shoes and better conditioning. She pulled open the big door and jumped in. Alicia was only a few seconds slower.

As they both brushed water from their clothes and hair, Jenna said, "So what did you make of all of that?"

"We bought an extra two days. I'd call that a win. There was no way Brendan was going to agree to work with me and I didn't want him to. I only put that out there so he could take charge and make me settle for less. You did OK, too. That was quite a move on Polanco. I really enjoyed that."

"So did I. The guy told me he owed me one and I was going to get it. I don't put up with shit like that."

"I guess he owes you two now, then."

"Good luck to him."

"I like your style, Jenna. You know how to handle yourself. I'm going to need security 24/7 for the rest of the week, maybe longer. I'll pay $3,000 a day. You up for it?"

It was too much money to turn down. "Of course," she said. "I'll just need to go back to my house, get a few things."

"Excellent. Were you being straight with me when you said that you didn't have a gun?"

"Yes. Like I said, as a PI I can't legally carry one and I'm not going to risk my licence by breaking that rule."

"No problem. I have a small handgun, the one I mentioned before. I'll bring it. I'm sure we won't need it, but I like to plan for any eventuality. Now, what's your take on Brendan's plan to watch me? You think that's real?"

"It takes a lot of resources to really keep tabs on someone especially if they are moving around. This is an unusual case, though. They aren't trying to do it surreptitiously. They want you to know they are there. That makes it easier for them. Polanco's agency is big. They could probably handle it."

"All right. Let's not make it easy for them. After I drop you off, I'm going to ditch this car and set up in another location. I'm tired of wandering around in that big empty house anyway. I'll just have to make an arrangement for Rex. I'll text you the details."

"Sounds good, but what are we going to do to find Simon? I've already tried all the obvious investigative angles. He doesn't have a phone with him and we don't have the resources to locate his car. Maybe we should beat Brendan to it, take all of this to the police ourselves."

"No!" Alicia said. Then, in a more normal tone, "That's not what I want. You know what the police are like. They'll spend days filling out forms and trying to figure out where first base is. That's not going to cut it."

Jenna couldn't contradict her. Instead, she said, "All right then, but what's the plan?"

"I don't have one yet, but I will. I have to."

It wasn't a persuasive answer, but there was still the three grand a day, assuming Alicia actually paid her. If things went south, that was far from certain. It still beat an insurance job, not that she even had one of those in hand.

"All right. I'll trust you to do that," Jenna said, hoping she could persuade both of them.

"That raises a point. Can I trust you Jenna, I mean absolutely trust you?"

"Yes," she said. There was no other viable answer.

Alicia paused, watching the windshield wipers slapping away the rain. Maybe yes wasn't a good enough answer.

Then Alicia said, "Trusting people isn't in my nature, Jenna. I won't get into why right now, but let's just say that I have had some bad experiences. On the other hand, I need to trust someone and you're the best bet.

"Let me start by saying that I haven't told you my whole story. I've kept it need to know, but maybe we've reached the point where you need to know more. Let me think about that and we can talk about it when we meet later today."

"All right, but what about Kris? Is she in on this? We've worked together on everything so far and she's a really good digger."

"No, just you. The fewer people who know the whole story, the better and I have to insist that you not tell her anything that I tell you in confidence."

Jenna quickly agreed, not at all sure that she would keep that promise.

Alicia put the car in gear and headed back to the coffee shop, so that Jenna could pick up Kris and her car. She knew she was going to have to make a quick decision about what to tell her mother.

* * *

Paul Polanco went back into Brendan Connor's office, wincing a bit as he walked toward the couch where Connor sat waiting.

"I heard you shout," Connor said. "What happened?"

"Stubbed my toe," Polanco said. "What a pair of shifty young bitches those two are."

"No doubt, but they aren't going to outsmart me."

Polanco noted that he had not been included in the group that was too clever to outsmart. Maybe that was fair. He wondered if he was losing his edge. That was twice now that Jenna Martin had made him look like a clumsy old man. He needed to prepare for their next encounter, make sure it was one she would never forget.

"How do you want to play this boss?" Polanco asked, settling on the couch across from Connor, trying not to make the pain in his balls too obvious. "Safe to assume that you were kidding when you threatened to take all this to the police."

Polanco knew Connor liked it when he was called boss. Strictly speaking, the little guy was a client, not his boss, but Brendan Connor had owned his ass for decades. It was something Polanco tried not to dwell on.

"Yes, obviously," Connor said. "The last thing I want is cops rooting through my personal business. We tail her, like I said. I want to know where she's going, what she's doing and I want to know it in real time. You have the people for that?"

"Of course." It was true if the question related only to numbers, but the tricky part was that only one of Polanco's people was not an ex-cop. Most of them liked to stay on the right side of the law. He'd have to give them a well-laundered version of why they were following Alicia Jameson.

"Good. Get on it ASAP. That's phase one. I know she's stalling. She's not going to walk in here Friday with Simon Cousens and $10 million. She doesn't have the one and she won't give up the other unless she thinks her life depends on it."

"Does it?"

"I'll have to think about that. Would I rather have the money back or put an end to the Alicia problem?"

"When you say put an end to the problem, what did you have in mind?" Polanco thought he knew the answer, but he wanted it spelled out explicitly.

"We eliminate her. Do I need to make myself clearer?"

"No, but what about Martin and her mother, that snoopy journalist?"

"We need to assume they know too much. Alicia certainly does. She doesn't seem like the confiding type, but I'm not going to take a chance with that kind of knowledge."

"Three killings. That's a lot. We might want to bring in an outside guy, someone who can do the job and disappear."

"No, you'd have to do it yourself. We need to keep this tight."

"It's going to bring incredible heat. Martin is an ex-cop and Redner is a well-known journalist. The media and the police will dig in on those killings and not let up. Let me try to find out just what Martin and Redner know."

"Sure, but don't waste too much time on it. I'd rather be safe than sorry. I'm not worried about the heat. What's all this got to do with me? I had a potential business deal with Alicia Jameson. It wasn't advancing as hoped so naturally I met with her to discuss it. I liked the deal so I would be sorry about her untimely death and concerned about the disappearance of my friend Simon."

"OK, but the $10 million will look like a pretty obvious motive, even to the dimmest detective."

"What $10 million? The money was transferred to Simon from an untraceable offshore account and it's not there now. I don't know a thing about it."

Polanco nodded, then said, "But your main concern must be Simon."

"Of course it is. She killed him. I can feel it in my bones. I won't believe otherwise unless she can prove that she didn't. The fact that you can't find Simon tells me that he's not alive. He's an egghead, not an undercover operator."

Polanco leaned back into the couch and nodded. It was a tricky situation, but Connor was a smart little prick and he had a lot at stake. He'd figure a way out of the hole he was in. Polanco was going to have to trust the guy. If that didn't work, he had an option, but it was one that would take him down, too. He liked his life and he wanted to keep things as they were. Maybe there was one other way to play it.

Twenty-five

I was just starting my third cup of coffee when I saw Alicia Jameson's black Lexus pull up in front of the Brwd 4U. My legs were jumpy and it wasn't just the caffeine. It was a cliché, but it was still fair to say that I was worried sick over Jenna and what she had gotten herself into with Brendan Connor and Alicia Jameson. I was reacting like a mother stranded on the beach while she watched her daughter swim in shark-infested waters. Even though I had been swimming in similar waters for years, it was different when it was Jenna. Was I having a brain-changing flood of hormones 26 years after giving birth?

I was relieved to see Jenna get out of the SUV and make a dash for the coffee shop through the still-pounding rain. She smiled when she saw me and walked across the coffee shop as calm and confident as ever. For the hundredth time, I reminded myself that I was lucky to have a daughter who knew how to take care of herself, one who had skills that I did not possess.

Jenna got another coffee for herself, then sat down and said, "Well, that was interesting."

'Tell me more."

"Brendan Connor knows all about the missing money and the disappearance of Simon Cousens. He wants Simon and the money back and he's given Alicia until Friday to produce them both."

"And if she doesn't?"

"He says he will take the whole thing to the police. His opinion is that Alicia is a con woman who has killed Simon and stolen the $10 million."

"What if he's right? Maybe we're on the wrong side here."

"Maybe, but I'm not convinced. Besides, it's too late to pull out now."

"Why?"

"I just told Alicia that I would give her 24/7 protection for the rest of the week, maybe longer. She admitted that there was more to her story, stuff she hasn't told us, and I think I'm getting close to finding out what's really going on."

I knew just how powerful the desire to scratch that particular itch could be. A good journalist didn't walk away from a story without getting to the bottom of it and neither did a good cop, even an ex-cop.

"The other thing," she said, "Brendan Connor can't possibly be the good guy. He's a domineering little man who thinks his money gives him the right to treat everyone else like shit. The kind who'd stab his mother in the eye for ten bucks, you know what I mean?"

"I do, but that doesn't make him guilty of any crime here. On the face of it, he's lost his best friend and a big sack of money. It would be easier to make the case that Alicia *is* a con woman than that Brendan is behind all of this."

"I don't know what Brendan Connor did, but he did something. It was big and he's covering it up. He's not some regular business guy. He had his goon Polanco with him. We're leaving and the guy leans into me, his stinking breath blowing right in my ear. He says, 'Watch yourself little girl. I owe you one, and you're going to get it.'"

"What an asshole. What did you say back/"

"Not a word. I just reached out, grabbed his balls and squeezed as hard as I could. Like one of those stress reliever balls for me, but it didn't work so well for him. Doubled him right over."

"Jesus, when you go into the woods do you look for bears to poke?"

"Only if they poke me first. Besides, it's a can't-miss technique. I don't know why the Trojans were so focused on Achilles's heel. All they had to do was go for his nuts."

"You read Greek mythology?"

"No. It came up in a sports injury course. I wanted to find out who the hell Achilles really was."

"More important, what's Brendan Connor's critical weakness?"

"Ego," Jenna said without hesitation. "Guys who believe they're smarter than everyone else always make mistakes because they think no one can keep up with their giant brains."

"I've met a few of those. So, how's this personal protection thing going to work?"

"Alicia is changing cars and moving to another location. She'll text me the address. Brendan and Polanco say they will be watching her every step of the way. Of course, she doesn't want that."

"No, she wouldn't, but what about you? Are you supposed to be some kind of bodyguard? You aren't trained for that are you?"

"Not specifically, but it won't be that hard. I will need to keep an eye out for their surveillance. It won't be difficult, if they locate Alicia. They want to be seen. Besides, most of Polanco's people are middle-aged ex-cops. I can spot those guys a100 metres off."

"What if there is a confrontation?"

"There won't be. They will give her until Friday to find Simon or cough up the money. It's pretty clear that Brendan and his thug can't accomplish that on their own."

"She have a plan?"

"Not yet. I'm sure she's working on it."

"That's not entirely reassuring. What happens if Friday comes and no Simon, no money?"

"Then Brendan will either go to the police or get dirty."

"Maybe we should be taking this to the police ourselves."

"No. For one thing, Alicia is a client. I have no clear evidence that she committed any crime. There is even less to support the idea that Brendan has done anything wrong."

She was right and I nodded my agreement, but that didn't mean I had to like it. I would have preferred to take all of this to Mike Reilly, but he was out the door and thinking of the Caribbean.

"There's one other thing," Jenna said. "Alicia doesn't want you involved in her situation from this point on. She made that very clear. It's just me and I will be with her all the time, so we aren't going to be able to work together."

I felt like I had been kicked. "That's no good," I said.

"It's not up to me. She's the client. Of course, I'd rather have your assistance, but maybe we've dug out as much as we can together."

"Not at all. You're forgetting one big thing. We don't know who Alicia really is or what her angle is. I'm not comfortable with you tying yourself to someone that slippery and mysterious."

Jenna sipped her coffee, clearly taking time to formulate a diplomatic response. Then she said, "I don't disagree with a word of that, but it's what it is. I can take care of myself, but if it would make you feel better, why don't you keep looking into Alicia? Text me with anything you find out."

"Count on it. Whatever happened with your request to Miranda Chambers-Addington? Wasn't she supposed to help dig into Alicia's murky past?"

"She was. I'll text you her number. Why don't you follow up on that? Just to be clear, I don't trust Alicia any more than you do, but I think we're stuck in this now. We know too much to walk away and not enough to take it to the police. We need to get to the bottom of things if we can."

"All right then," I said, knowing I had no other option. I wasn't happy about being pushed to the side and leaving Jenna on her own. Not happy at all.

"So what next?"

"We head back to the house, I get a few things to carry me through the week and then I report to wherever Alicia tells me to go."

"Am I going to know where that is, at least?"

Jenna hesitated for just a second, then said, "Sure."

I knew having her mother looking out for her was the last thing Jenna wanted. We had never talked about it, but her kidnapping and confinement by a killer last winter had dented her self-confidence and sense of invulnerability. The last thing she needed now was me feeding her self-doubt.

"All right," I said. "Good plan. Let's roll."

 Twenty-six

I watched from the kitchen window as Jenna left the back door of the house. The rain had stopped but puddles lay like mirrors on the paved backyard of the property. Jenna looked appropriately non-descript, wearing jeans, a blue T-shirt, an unzipped black jacket and a navy ball cap with no logo. She wore a small backpack, just like any young woman out for a walk. She scaled the six-foot wooden fence at the back of the yard, swung herself over the top and disappeared from sight. I caught just a glimpse of her as she headed down the neighbour's driveway, then she was gone. I wondered when I would see her again.

The plan was for her to walk up a couple of blocks to Minto Park and catch an Uber she had already called. It all seemed a bit cloak and dagger to me, but Jenna said that's the way Alicia wanted it. Apparently she had gone to some trouble to disguise her new location and she didn't want anyone tailing Jenna straight to it. Jenna hadn't even told me where she was heading, except that it was a suites hotel downtown. She promised to send me the details.

I hoped Alicia knew what she was doing. I had the impression that her whole life was a series of calculated moves. Now, she had to improvise. Or did she? For all I knew, Alicia had a fake passport, airplane tickets and a suitcase full of cash in some storage locker, just in case.

My job now was to wait. It happened to be the thing that I was worst at. I had already called Miranda, following up on her promise to dig into Alicia's past. Her snooty receptionist or secretary, whatever she was, had put me off saying, "Ms. Chambers-Addington is in conference," as pompous people say when they mean in a meeting. She did assure me that my call would be returned promptly.

It was just about noon and I figured I had better eat while I had the chance. I wasn't hungry, but who knew what the day would bring?

I slapped some deli turkey between two pieces of rye that could have been fresher and tried to overcome the deficiency with too much mayonnaise. Darcy was fond of saying that I'd starve to death without his cooking and maybe he was right. He'd left for Round Lake Tuesday night, saying he would need two or three days to supervise the crew that was working on a log house outside Killaloe. Before he got tangled up with me, I knew Darcy had worked ridiculous hours trying to get his business up and running. He was stretching himself now, trying to spend time with me in Ottawa while still keeping things under control up in the valley.

I had no intention of asking him to stop. I felt that I was at the point where I wanted to wake up beside him every morning, but that wasn't what our lives allowed, not yet. Still, I ached for him. It was partly physical. I had to admit that I wanted him inside me, regularly, repeatedly. It wasn't just that, though. When I was with Darcy, I felt protected, calm, centred in a way that I had never felt in my life. If someone had told me a year ago that I would feel that way with anyone, I would have been deeply skeptical. I would have bet a million bucks that if I did, it wouldn't have been with Darcy Lamb, not given our brief and unpleasant history.

Life was full of surprises, but the biggest one for me was that some of those surprises were good.

I bit into my mediocre sandwich and tried to get myself refocused on the problem at hand. I wasn't going to do Jenna any good by worrying about what she and Alicia were up to. The best thing I could do was to get the goods on Alicia, so that Jenna would know for sure who she was working for. I understood all the stuff about the client being the boss, but I thought Alicia had layers of secrecy and motive stacked higher than a snowdrift in January. I was ready to start shovelling.

I was just finishing my sandwich when my cell phone rang. I could see that it was Miranda's number. I answered and before I could speak, Miranda jumped in. "Kris, I have news for you."

I could tell by the tone of her voice that it was good news. She sounded quite pleased with herself. That was all right with me.

"So I have sunk my teeth into this Alicia Jameson matter. I do love a good mystery. I put a number of calls out and had my former investigator do some legwork only to discover that Alicia seems to have dropped from the sky fully formed as an 18-year-old University of Waterloo computer science student in the early 2000s. Outstanding marks, dean's list, scholarships but nothing about her personal life, either before that moment or since. No friends, no family, no selfies on social media. We were able to track her education and employment but it's more like a CV than a picture of a real person. I understand that some people like to keep themselves to themselves, but it was almost like Alicia Jameson didn't exist before she was 18. That's the part that really puzzled me.

"Then I thought, what if that were really the case? What if Alicia was someone else altogether? It's complicated to create a truly false identity, but there's a simpler path. I've seen clients use it on the back side of a bad divorce."

"I'll bite. What do they do?"

"A legal name change. It's surprisingly easy. All you have to do is fill out a provincial government form and pay $137. Here's the good part. The name change is included in the Ontario Gazette, the government's publication of record. I had a friend at the courthouse look into it and wouldn't you know, there is the first mention of Alicia Jameson, age 16, on a Change of Name Act Form 5. That's the earliest one can change a name without parental consent."

"What else does this form tell us?"

"Quite a lot, including the name of the parents. In this case, I assume the adoptive parents. Alex and Kat Jameson. They live on one of those crescents in Kanata. Or they did. I don't know if the address is still current. Can I leave it with you now?"

"Sure. Do you have the form?"

"Yes, I can send you a copy. That's everything I know. I hope it helps."

"I'm sure it will. Just out of interest, what was Alicia's original name?"

"Tarrant. Ashley Alicia Tarrant."

Holy fuck, I thought. That was the little girl whose parents were murdered, the ones who worked for Brendan Connor's company.

"Thanks Miranda. Send that right away please. I've got to go."

"Kris? Does the name mean something to you?"

"I'll let you know."

Twenty-seven

Jenna and Alicia looked at the Smith &Wesson Model 10 .38-calibre revolver that lay on the hotel bed between them like an unspoken threat. It was in pristine condition, its bluing neither scratched nor worn and its chequered walnut grip as shiny as the day it was made. Jenna could see that the revolver was loaded. It was the kind of gun police officers carried for decades but it was laughably quaint compared to the weapons even the average street punk carried these days. It wasn't what you wanted in your hand in a shootout.

"Where did you get this thing?" Jenna asked.

"It belonged to my father."

"Did he ever shoot it?"

"I don't know. I inherited it when he died."

"How long ago was that?"

"June 10, 1995."

When Alicia was a child, then. Maybe losing her father explained her mistrustfulness and need to control everything. "This the original ammunition?" Jenna asked.

"Yes, it's what came with the gun. Will it still be any good?"

"Maybe." Ammunition would definitely last 10 years but 25 years could be a stretch. Would it work? It wasn't a question Jenna wanted to be thinking about if she had to point this gun at someone with serious intent, but then, she didn't see that happening. If the gun made Alicia feel safer, then it would have done its job. Jenna's main goal was to make sure it didn't go off accidentally.

"I guess I should have thought of that," Alicia said. "Can we get more?"

"Not easily. Don't worry about it. We're not going to need the gun. At the very most, I might have to point it at someone. He won't know how old the ammunition is."

The other parts of Alicia's plan seemed more sound. She had

driven the Lexus to the airport and left it in long-term parking, then taken an Uber to the Prince George Suites Hotel on Slater near Bay, on the western edge of downtown. It was a good choice. Slater was a busy one-way street with parking restrictions. Not an easy place to set up surveillance, if Polanco did locate them. The hotel was older and catered to long-term guests in the city on government contracts. Strangers coming and going would stand out and there was front-door security. The guy was the usual rent-a-cop, but at least he'd had the sense to quiz Jenna about who was expecting her rather than let her go right up to Alicia's suite on the fifth floor. There was a back entrance, too, leading into an attached parking garage with multiple exits. Jenna had checked all that out soon after she had arrived and found it all satisfactory.

Now, she watched as Alicia went to the window and peered out, like she expected to see Polanco standing on the street with binoculars. She wore a light summer dress in a blue flowery pattern and sandals. A large straw hat and sunglasses sat on the bureau. It was a reasonable disguise, if they had to go out, but Jenna's thought was to rely on room service. She would do whatever fetching and carrying was needed. She was sure Alicia would expect nothing less, not at three grand a day.

"So, what now?" Jenna asked.

'We wait."

Surely not two days of waiting, Jenna thought. She had been hoping for something a little more active. The suite was spacious and had two bedrooms but she'd be climbing the walls no later than tomorrow.

"Wait for what?" she said.

"For Brendan to make a move. Once he and Polanco figure out I'm not at the house, they will assume I have made a run for it. Polanco might not be the smartest guy in the world, but he'll check the airport to see if I've dumped my car. If we're lucky, he will have had someone put a GPS tracer on it while we were meeting with Brendan."

"OK, but how will we know if they've found it?"

"Dash cam. I have one that records what's happening in front of the car and inside, too. It connects straight to my laptop through an app. I'm monitoring it now."

"All right, good. So they find the car. Then what do you hope will happen?"

"At that point, Brendan will conclude that I've moved his $10 million offshore and skipped the country. Then we'll see what he does."

"OK, but if he thinks you've left the country, what's he going to do? Do you see him mounting an international search to get his money back?"

"No. First we enrage him, then I reappear. That will bring matters to a head."

"How does that solve your problem?"

"That depends what you think my problem is."

Jenna wondered what she was missing. A powerful and ruthless businessman and his no-boundaries thug were hunting Alicia down. Her husband was missing and $10 million was unaccounted for. Was there another problem?"

"It seems obvious, but I guess you'd better tell me."

Alicia looked at Jenna with a flash of impatience, as if surprised that she couldn't keep up. "Simon, of course," she said. "I've got to get him back."

Not wanting to appear stupid, Jenna nodded like it all made total sense. Unfortunately, it didn't. How was compelling a dangerous man to act going to make Alicia's husband return, especially if it was a return from the dead, as Jenna was starting to strongly believe. Alicia had always seemed logical, almost machine-like. What if she was actually crazy? Jenna picked up the .38 and tucked it into her waistband, first making sure there wasn't one in the chamber.

"You don't get it, do you?"

"To be honest, no."

"If Simon thinks I'm missing and in danger, he'll come out of hiding. I'm sure of it. Protecting me is one of his strongest instincts."

"Sounds good, but don't you think he should have popped up by now? Things haven't exactly been going to plan."

"How do you know that?"

Jenna gestured at the room, as if the situation they were in required no additional explanation.

Alicia nodded, conceding the point. "It's true, I've been forced to improvise, but this will work. I'm sure of it."

Just like she'd been sure the rest of her plan would work, whatever it was.

"You must be convinced that Simon is still alive."

Alicia looked like she had been slapped. "Of course he's still alive. Why wouldn't he be?"

"Well, he has been missing for 10 days."

"It must be part of his plan."

Ah, a second plan. "I don't suppose you happen to know what that plan is?"

"Not yet, but we will soon. Simon will have a plan, he always does."

Jenna felt like it was time to come back to that not telling her the whole story comment Alicia had made that morning in the car.

"You said there was more to your story, things you hadn't told me. Are those things what make you so certain that Simon will reappear?"

"Not entirely. I'm not going to get into the exact nature of my relationship with Simon except to say that he started as my mentor, then became my lover and finally my husband. In each of those roles, he has seen himself as the wise and powerful older man whose duty it is to guide and protect me."

"And is that how you see him?"

"It's a comfortable arrangement for both of us."

Jenna's phone buzzed and when she glanced at it, she saw it was a text from Kris. She clicked on it. The text read "Alicia not who she says she is. Stay alert. More to come."

 # Twenty-eight

Alex Jameson's address had been easy to confirm in Canada411, the online phone directory. He was still in the same house that he had been in 20 years ago, when Ashley Alicia Tarrant became Alicia Jameson, no middle name.

I wasn't sure whether I would find him or his wife Katherine at home on a Wednesday afternoon, but Ottawa was a city dominated by the public sector. Most of those people retired by their mid-50s and Alex would certainly be in the age range, if not older. I had his phone number but decided not to call ahead. I had no legitimate-sounding reason to ask about his adopted daughter and he was likely to tell me to mind my own business. That was always harder to do when looking a person right in the eye.

I decided to drive straight 73 Palmer Street and see what I could find out about the mysterious Alicia Jameson. There had to be a reason why her adoptive parents never appeared in anything online and she had never mentioned them, even though they lived no more than 10 minutes' drive from Simon's house. Maybe it was just ordinary family estrangement, but I needed to know. It was the first real crack I had found in Alicia's shiny fake image and I intended to open it as wide as I could.

It didn't take me long to get to Kanata, but I made a couple of wrong turns trying to find Palmer. It didn't help that every other street was a meandering crescent and that they were all named after vaguely familiar golfers. I finally had to resort to the GPS on my phone.

Palmer was a street like all the rest, big brick houses with garages protruding from the front, mature trees and that broken-in look that subdivisions got after 40 years or so. I pulled into the driveway of number 73, walked quickly up the front steps and rapped on the door.

My knock was met with the barking of what I took to be a small but highly agitated dog and then I heard a man's voice say, "Buster, shut up." Then, "I've got it Kat."

The door swung open and I saw a stocky, middle-aged man in a blue short-sleeve dress shirt and a pair of khaki shorts, the type that were covered with special pockets and zippers. It was as if he hadn't decided whether he was going to work or for a walk in the woods. He had thick red hair and his face looked friendly, what little I could see of it behind his dense, greying beard.

He looked at me quizzically and said, "Can I help you?"

"Alex Jameson?"

"Yes, but if you're selling something, I'm not interested."

"It's about Alicia."

His expression turned from genial to alarmed in an instant. "Who are you, and what do you know about Alicia?" he asked.

"My name is Kris Redner. Alicia and my daughter Jenna have gotten themselves into a tricky situation. I could really use your help. You are Alicia's father, are you not?"

"Adoptive father. What kind of trouble has she gotten herself into?"

"Large trouble, I think, and now my Jenna is in it, too. Can I come in? I'd be happy to explain."

"All right," he said. "My wife and I were just going to have a drink on the back patio. Follow the path around the side of the house and I'll meet you there."

"Sure," I said, although I'd have bet even money that he had just found a clever way to get rid of me. I noted that Alex Jameson didn't seem particularly surprised that his adoptive daughter might be in big trouble. Was that because she had been in it plenty of times before, or because he didn't particularly care?

I followed a path of large concrete paving stones around to a wire mesh fence. I unlatched the gate and stepped into a shady backyard that looked out onto a golf course. I never understood why people paid a premium to have other people hit golf balls into their backyard, but it wasn't the right time to ask.

The patio was made of the same old concrete slabs, heaved up and down like a country road after the frost got to it. On it was a round, glass topped table surrounded by four beige mesh sling-back chairs. In one of the chairs was a bleach-blond who I figured was late 50s, but wanted you to think a decade younger. Kat, I assumed. Her hair was long and curly and she had rings on every

finger and her thumbs, plus an ankle bracelet. I had read somewhere once that an ankle bracelet on the left leg was supposed to
mean a woman was sexually available, but maybe that was a myth.
Even if not, the overly large breasts that squeezed out of her white
tube top sent the message. Not original equipment, I thought. A
part bottle of white wine and a full glass sat on the table in front
of her.

Kat looked me up and down as if I were a stray dog that had
wandered into her yard, then said, "Who in the world are you?"

"Hi. I'm Kris Redner. I just spoke to your husband at the door
and he said to come around. My daughter is a friend of Alicia's."

"Alicia? Well, that's unfortunate for your daughter then."

Before I could ask her to expand on that, there was the sound
of a sliding patio door and Alex came out onto the small deck that
overlooked the yard, carrying two wine glasses and another bottle.
"Kat, this is Kris. She's here about Alicia."

"Good to know she's still alive," Kat said.

"Let's not get into all of that," Alex said. "Kris says Alicia is in
trouble."

"What a surprise. You aren't going to get sucked into this again,
are you?"

I decided to jump in before the family feud got out of control.
"Let me explain why I'm here," I said, sitting down without wait-
ing to be invited. "First, just remind me, Alex, when did you adopt
Alicia?"

"Well, it would have been 20 years ago now, but we took her in
when she was eight. She didn't have anyone else to turn to after the
killings, so I felt it was our duty to look after her, being her aunt
and uncle. She changed her name to Jameson when we made the
adoption formal."

"Of course," I said, like I'd known that all along, Alicia and Jenna
being such pals, after all. Maybe Alicia's name change held no
mystery at all, simply something one would do to formally become
part of an adoptive family. And yet, Kat's tone and comments told
a different story.

"That's when it all started to go wrong," Kat said, "right after
the adoption. Alicia, as she then chose to call herself, announced
that she had a life plan, a rather bizarre one. She was going to get
a computer science degree at a good university, develop original

products and marry a millionaire."

"I don't suppose she'd be the first teenage girl to want to get a good education, a good job and a rich husband," I said.

"No, but Alicia's plan wasn't that simple. She wanted to marry a particular millionaire, a high-living low life called Simon Cousens, a man already in his 40s and married more than once. He was a playboy, pictured in all the papers dancing in clubs and living it up.

"Why would a 16-year-old girl set her sights on a man like that? I thought she was mentally ill and suggested she get therapy but of course, Alex said no. He has always been a sucker for her. Men usually are.

"I'm afraid I'd had it with Alicia at that point. She was clearly the sort of person who was going to do exactly what she wanted, no matter what we said. And she did, of course. She's married to him now, as you know."

"Why Simon Cousens, out of curiosity?"

"She's obsessed with the murder of her parents," Kat said. "Simon Cousens was a partner in the company her parents worked for. Maybe she thinks he knows something about it, maybe she's looking for a replacement father. Who knows what goes on in her twisted mind?

"We certainly don't hear from her unless she needs something. Not even a card at Christmas. We had a wonderful life until Alicia came along and ruined it. All Alex does is worry about her and she's not even ours."

"Don't blame Alicia for what happened to her," Alex said, his voice tense. "It's not her fault that her parents were killed and let's not forget that Eve was my sister. Her murder was horrible for our family. That's the real problem, not Alicia."

Having repeated a statement I was sure he had been making for years, Alex said, "I don't think Kris wants to hear about all of that. Let's get to the point. What kind of trouble is Alicia in and what can I do to help?"

I knew all about what the murder of a parent can do to a family. The killing of my own father had set my family on a ruinous path that only I had survived. This wasn't the place for a therapy session, though.

"It's about Simon, actually," I said.

"Dumped her has he?" Kat asked.

"No, but he's missing and so is $10 million."

"Good God," Alex said. "I assume the police have been called in."

"No, Alicia doesn't want that."

Kat gave Alex a knowing look and said, "She probably did him in. She has the capability, you know."

"Don't be ridiculous Kat. Alicia adores Simon. Marrying him was her life's goal."

"Well, now she's achieved it. Maybe it's time to move on with Simon's money. Besides, what do we know about their relationship? It's not like we were invited to the wedding."

"You wouldn't have gone if you were," Alex said. "Please excuse us, Kris. As you can see, Alicia is a matter of some contention between us, but you came here because of your daughter Jenna, right? What's her connection to Alicia?"

"It's a bit unusual. Jenna sometimes hires herself out as a bridesmaid. She's just getting started in her main business and the cash helps. Jenna responded to an ad Alicia placed online and Alicia hired her. As the maid of honour, actually."

"A complete stranger?" Kat said. "What did I tell you, Alex? She hasn't a friend in the world."

"Shut up Kat," he said.

Smiling like everything was normal, I said "I know it sounds weird, but apparently it's something that young people do these days. It's actually Jenna's main business that brought them back together. She's a private investigator. She took that up after a few years with the OPP."

"And Alicia has hired her to find Simon?" Alex asked.

"Yes, but they haven't been able to locate him yet. Here's the worrying twist. That missing $10 million is not Simon's. It belongs to Brendan Connor. He and Simon were forming a corporation to invest in one of Alicia's ideas. The money is gone from the corporate account. It's not exactly clear how, but Brendan is rather keen on getting it back."

"Brendan Connor is bad news," Alex said. "I always thought he had something to do with the murders of John and Eve. They both worked for a company owned by Connor and Simon Cousens, you know. They had for a few years. Eve was in corporate communications but John was an engineer. He worked closely with Connor and Simon on some kind of telephone switching technology. What exactly, is way over my head. I was in the public service, 35 years in human resources. Not a techie at all. In any case, just weeks before the murders, Eve told me that John and Connor had gotten into a big fight over credit for this invention. She said that John made the key discoveries but that Connor now wanted to take personal credit for the whole thing. The dispute turned around something that John had patented before he even started to work for Connor.

"The way Eve told it, the truth would be extremely embarrassing for Connor, and Simon Cousens too, I suppose. John and Eve were considering a lawsuit. Then they were both dead, shot in their own home not 15 minutes from here. I'll never forget that day. Alicia, Ashley as she was then, was in the house when her parents were killed.

"She ran and hid in some bushes but she didn't know what to do, so she went back in the house and called me. At first, I didn't understand what she was trying to say. It was too outlandish. I got in the car and raced over to Eve's house. It was a June day, sunny, one of those days when life seemed perfect, and then, the nightmare.

"When I got to the house, the door was open and I could see John's body. He was clearly dead. I rushed inside, calling out for Eve. She was in the kitchen, lying on her back, a hole in the centre of her forehead. The floor was covered with her blood, a big pool of it. There was a muffin tin on the counter and a mixing bowl. She was just about to bake. I don't know why I remember that detail.

"Alicia was curled up on the kitchen floor in the fetal position, near the phone. I dialled 911 and the police came quickly. It was too late for John and Eve, of course. The investigation dragged on for months. I told them about the dispute between John and Brendan Connor and the possible lawsuit, but they told me they had interviewed Connor, who denied all of it.

"The killer hadn't left a trace, they said. Alicia actually saw him but she was never able to describe him properly. He pulled her out from under her bed. Can you imagine how frightening that must have been for a young child?

"Then he told her to run. The police told me that the killer was a professional, but why would he do that? Wouldn't he have wanted to eliminate all witnesses?"

"Most people would draw the line at killing a child," I said.

"But he had just slaughtered John and Eve," Alex said.

Kat reached over and laid a comforting hand on his arm. Tears had begun to run down his face. The pain of losing a family member that way never really ends.

"I think it's time for you to go," Kat said. "We've told you all we can about Alicia and why she's the way she is. She is obsessed with finding her parents' killer. I think it's what drives her every decision.

"Here's my advice to your daughter. Get out while she can, before Alicia drags her down, too."

I thanked them, went back to the car, then drove down the street for some privacy. I sent Jenna a text. "Alicia thinks Connor killed her parents. Out for revenge. Call me soonest."

 Twenty-nine

Jenna's phone buzzed. She pulled it out of her jeans pocket and saw a text from Kris. The message was short but alarming. Alicia's parents? Where did they fit into this? Jenna knew nothing about them and now Kris had dropped this bombshell. What had she learned?

Jenna put the phone back into her pocket without responding to the text and did her best to keep a neutral expression.

"Who was that?" Alicia asked.

"Kris. Wondering how we were doing. Mothering me."

"Aren't you getting a little old for that?"

""You'd think, but Kris and I were separated for a long time. It's a complicated story."

"We all have issues."

Jenna thought Alicia might take her statement as an invitation to find out more, but she reminded herself that it would be out of character for Alicia. Jenna was a means to an end for her, not someone she wanted to get to know.

"Aren't you going to respond?" Alicia asked.

"No, it would just encourage her to keep pestering me. I think I'll take a walk, check out the parking garage, see what's happening at street level. If Polanco and his team do find us, we will have to adjust our strategy."

"Fine. I'm going to take a bath. I have to do some serious thinking. Leave the gun here, would you?"

"You won't need it. They aren't going to batter down the door and I will only be gone a few minutes. They want to track you, not abduct you."

That could come later, Jenna thought, but better not to say it.

"All right then. Don't disturb me when you come back unless you have some urgent news."

"Of course."

Jenna let herself out of the room, glad to be free of Alicia and desperately curious to know more about what Kris had found. She headed out the back door and then to the third floor of the parking building, an aging concrete structure that squatted behind the hotel itself. There were few cars parked at that level, leaving her with a clear field of view and no chance of being overheard.

She pulled out her phone and hit Kris's number.

"That was quick," Kris said.

"Your text sounded urgent. Tell me about the parents. What did you find out and when?"

"Miranda called after you left. She's cracked part of the mystery of Alicia. She's actually Ashley Alicia Tarrant. She legally changed her name when she was 16."

"OK, but that doesn't tell us much."

"It gets better. I just talked to her adoptive parents, who are actually her aunt and uncle. Let me backtrack for a minute first. On Monday, I talked to Mike Reilly about a double homicide in Kanata back in 1995. You remember Mike. Major crime guy in Ottawa forever. The victims were a couple who worked in tech, John and Eve Tarrant. They were gunned down in their home and the crime was never solved."

"And these are Alicia's parents?"

"Yes, and get this. They both worked for Brendan Connor's company. Actually, Brendan and Simon's company at the time. Mike says Connor was questioned but nothing came of it. There were no solid leads and the case eventually petered out."

"Wait a minute, you say you found this out on Monday. When were you going to tell me?"

"When it came to something. I had no reason then to think there was any link between Alicia and the killings."

"Still, it would have been good to know. I'm an investigator, remember?"

"Sorry, old habit. I never take anything to an editor until I'm sure it's solid."

Jenna hesitated long enough to make her point, then said, "Fine. Tell me the rest. Why did you go to Reilly in the first place?"

"I was trying to find out more about Brendan Connor, so I had lunch with a guy who used to work at the *Citizen*. Covered tech for ages. He told the story about the killings. Reilly is the expert on killing in Ottawa."

"So really, you've been conducting an entire investigation on your own."

"Yes, but I haven't gotten to the best part yet. When I tell you that, you will know everything I know."

"Revenge, right? Alicia thinks Brendan Connor, and maybe even Simon, is responsible for the death of her parents and she wants to get even."

"Yes, and it's not just supposition. Alicia's step-mother, the aunt, told me so in as many words. Alicia has been obsessed with avenging her parents since she was a teenager and get this, even back then she had plans to marry Simon."

"Whoa. So it wasn't some chance meeting at Simon's company."

"Not according to the aunt. No love lost there, but even though the uncle is clearly still a big Alicia supporter, he didn't contradict her. It fits with what we know of Alicia. She's the kind of person who makes meticulous plans and sticks to them. Up until now, at least. Now she seems to be winging it."

"I wouldn't be too sure of that. I just finished talking with her and she told me the plan now is to place herself in danger so that Simon will be compelled to come out of hiding and save her. It didn't sound like she just came up with that today."

"So it's all about getting Simon back?"

"So she says."

'You believe that?" Kris asked.

"It's possible, but only if it doesn't negate getting revenge on Brendan and laying her hands on $10 million. Those are pretty powerful motives."

"Surely she's going for all three. Alicia isn't a bronze medal kind of gal."

"Agreed," Jenna said. "The other thing that concerns me is that Alicia has brought a gun, an old .38 that belonged to her father. Don't worry, I have the gun."

"Jesus, that's not good. I think it's time to call your friend Stillwell at Ottawa Police. We're getting in over our heads here."

"Maybe, but there's still no hard evidence that a crime has occurred."

"I get that, but I'm worried. What if the aunt is right and this whole thing is about taking revenge on Brendan Connor? Alicia has been planning all this for years. We don't know what evidence she has on Connor, but if there's any, she would be the one to find it.

"She's going to want someone to do her dirty work for her, or at least help her out. What if that's the real reason why she's keeping you close, to set up some situation where you have to kill Connor and take the fall for it."

"That's not going to happen."

"I hope not, but we're not controlling the play here. Alicia has been moving us like chess pieces since the first day she met you."

"I guess that would make me pretty stupid, then."

"You know that's not what I'm trying to say."

"Let me think about it. If your theory is correct, I think we need to give Alicia a little more time, at least until we get something solid enough to take to Carol.

"Keep your own head up and let me know right away if you find out anything more about Alicia," Jenna said.

"All right. You do the same."

Jenna hung up. She could hear the reluctance in Kris's voice. Of course she was worried; she was a mother. On the other hand, Kris had been in a lot of tight spots. Her concerns couldn't be dismissed out of hand.

Alicia wasn't the only one who had to do some serious thinking.

 Thirty

Alicia sank deeper into the tub, letting the warm water caress her and feeling her muscles start to relax for the first time in days. For just a moment, she considered how easy it might be to just slide under the water, breathe in and end all of her troubles. Then she looked at the photo of her parents, the one she had brought in her bag and propped up on the bathroom vanity. It was their wedding picture. Her father stared into the future, the way newlyweds do, handsome in a white tuxedo with a blue bow tie, his brown hair thick and dark, his moustache trim. Her mother looked excited, clearly not anticipating what the future would bring. Who would? Her wedding dress was traditional, white and lacy, with a high neck. It was eerie how much Alicia and her mother looked alike, although Eve Tarrant had been a dozen years younger than Alicia when the photo was taken.

Alicia shook her head, rejecting the idea of the easy way out. Although her parents were just vague memories to her, she had to get them the justice life had so cruelly denied them. She had come too far, worked too hard, to lose her nerve at the last minute, and the last minute was fast approaching. She knew that. Brendan Connor was ruthless and she was an existential threat to him. He'd take action. He had to.

If she had read Brendan right, he would fall into the trap she had set. She had baited it with Simon and a large amount of money, his two favourite things. It wasn't exactly how she had intended to proceed, but that was the nature of a dynamic system. Things changed rapidly. She had been the catalyst, and Jenna had accelerated things with her not too subtle attack on Paul Polanco.

Brendan was cunning but Polanco was more like a bull, confident that he could win any confrontation with brute force. Jenna had enraged him. No doubt her action was more of an instinct than a plan, but it would have the same effect. Polanco was angry, and angry people made stupid mistakes.

He was the one who had shot her parents. She was sure of that, although she didn't have proof. Polanco didn't decide to murder John and Eve Tarrant on a whim. He had been a serving police officer at the time, but shortly after the killings he suddenly left the police and started his investigation and security company. According to her digging, Brendan Connor was his first official customer. There was simply no way that the two events weren't linked. Connor was the kind of man who would see two killings as a reasonable price to protect his own legacy and fortune, the cost of doing business. He was too gutless to do the job, that much she knew. Besides, the man who had pulled her out from under the bed was large and physically powerful. Brendan was neither of those things. Even taking into account the fact that all adults seemed large to a child, Alicia was sure that Brendan had not been the gunman.

She had always wondered why the shooter had spared her life. If things went as hoped, that one act of mercy would cost him his own.

That was where Jenna would come in. Polanco was too dangerous for Alicia to handle on her own. It was much better to create a situation where Jenna would have to act to save her own life. Jenna was a straight arrow. She wouldn't kill Polanco unless she had no other choice.

Brendan was another matter. She would deal with him herself, and it was going to be personal.

Alicia breathed deeply, then slowly exhaled, imagining that she was like a baby floating in the warmth and protection of the womb. She was soon to be thrust into a world crueller than any she had ever known, but she was ready.

Thirty-one

I turned restlessly in bed, trying to drive myself deeper into sleep. I was in that in-between state, where I was conscious enough to know that I wasn't fully asleep but still asleep enough to keep coming back to the same dream. I saw Jenna in a river, a big one with a current so strong that the surface roiled like boiling water and spray hung in the air. Jenna was trying to stay afloat but struggling, reaching out one arm to me, desperate for help. I ran along the shore, trying to find some way to help her, a rope, even a long stick she could try to swim toward and grasp. The more conscious part of my brain wondered why there would be a rope left handy on the pebbly beach I ran along. Then I knew what I had to do. I had to jump in and try to save her. It was a long shot, but better to die together than stand by helplessly.

I was just about to leap into the water when I awoke with a start and sat upright, my thin nightgown wet with perspiration. My foggy brain registered the dampness and for just a second I thought I had jumped into the river. Then I felt the relief that follows when you realize a bad dream isn't real. I was in my own bedroom, safe in bed.

I looked at the alarm clock on the bedside table. It was 1:45. I knew if I got up now, I'd never get back to sleep, so I lay on my back, took some deep breaths and tried to relax. It wasn't hard to sort out the origin of my dream. The Ottawa River was still overflowing its banks in a record flood and Jenna was in trouble, or at least I was worried that she was. She was entangled with a woman bent on revenge, probably at any cost, and up against Brendan Connor and Paul Polanco, one of whom was desperate and ruthless, the other violent.

I told myself that Jenna knew how to handle herself. She had police training and experience, but it didn't make me any less worried. Knowing that your long-lost daughter would probably be able to handle herself in a shootout was far from reassuring.

I tried to think of something else. Darcy was the first thing that came to mind. He had promised to return by Friday night. If he came early enough, maybe we would go out to dinner somewhere. I knew Darcy had to work out of town, but I missed him every minute he was gone. I hadn't felt this way about a man since my ill-fated relationship with a young police officer called L.T. Hill, down in the Adirondacks. The difference was that I knew from the start that L.T. and I had no future together. We were too far apart in age and on paths that were bound to diverge. The situation with Darcy was different in a way that was both scary and good. We had a future together, or we could. To get there, I had to trust him, give myself to him in every way, mentally and physically.

Some ways were easier than others. My mind drifted to the sex we had been having and I found that I was becoming slightly aroused. This really wasn't going to help me go back to sleep. I went back to deep breathing and started counting sheep, a trick my mother had taught me when I was very little. It seemed stupid, but maybe it was a way to switch my mind to another channel. The last thing I remembered was the thirtieth sheep. Then I sunk deep into blackness.

The next thing I knew, I was awake, my heart racing and every nerve tingling. I felt goose bumps run up my arms. I jerked upright, all my primal alarm systems going off at once. I looked wildly across the room, but saw only the familiar shapes of the bedroom chair, the dresser and the closet door, all illuminated by the street-light glow that seeped through my heavy bedroom curtains. The clock showed that it was 3:30.

I didn't remember dreaming and felt like I had been deeply unconscious. What had triggered this reaction?

Then I heard it.

A floorboard in the living room creaked, then silence.

Maybe I was just imagining things.

I heard it again. A series of creaks, but this time the sound was coming from the hall and getting closer to my bedroom.

Someone was in the apartment and I was alone.

I tamped down my fear with a heavy layer of indignation. Who the hell was this person and why did he think he could come into my private space?

I rolled quietly out of bed and reached for the baseball bat that I kept under it. Then I stood as quietly as I could, my head cocked listening for the next footstep. I tried to calm my breathing and wondered if the intruder knew I was aware of him. If he did, would he run away, or attack?

I stepped quietly across the bedroom floor, my feet cold against the boards. Then I took up a position behind the door, not close enough to be hit if it swung open, but still in a place that would leave me behind the intruder if he came through the door. I had been in a few fights and I knew that the surest way to win one was with a quick, stunning blow. I was thinking the head, but what if he saw it coming and ducked? The kidneys then, a target that would cause excruciating pain. That would be ideal.

The footsteps in the hall had stopped. I thought I could hear breathing, but maybe that was just my imagination.

Then the footsteps started again. I tensed, ready to defend myself.

The footsteps became fainter, heading toward the kitchen. Then I heard the kitchen tap come on. What the hell?

Part of my brain said head down the hall, find out who this person is, then confront him. The smarter part said no, stay put in a good defensive position. Who knew how big this intruder was or whether he was armed? What did he want, I wondered, then realized that it didn't matter right now. The goal was to come out of this safely.

My heart was still racing and I was sure I was pumped full of adrenalin. Good. Maybe I was going to need it. Why had he turned on the kitchen tap? Was it to cover the sound of coming back down the hall?

I tensed and waited, then I heard the distinctive screech of the apartment door's hinges and louder footsteps heading down the stairs. He was leaving, and in a hurry.

I felt a flood of relief that was quickly replaced by anger. Who was this bastard? I raced to the bedroom window and pulled back the curtain, just in time to see a dark figure come down the front steps and start to race up the street. From the size, definitely a man but I could only see the back of him. His running was awkward, stiff. Not young then.

I turned on the bedroom lights, then advanced cautiously down the hall. I entered the living room and turned on both lamps. At first, everything looked normal, then I noticed that a picture of Jenna and me that I kept on the mantelpiece had been turned to face the wall.

I went into the kitchen and saw water flooding over the countertop. The stupid asshole had put the sink plug in. I dropped the bat and rushed across the room to turn off the tap, nearly slipping in the cold water that had already flowed onto the floor. I plunged my hand into the sink and pulled out the plug, then grabbed both of the dish towels and threw them onto the counter. That would have to do for now.

I picked the bat up again and walked cautiously toward the door of my apartment. I knew he was gone, but my body was still infused with fear and caution. The door hadn't been forced open. I rarely locked it. It seemed redundant with the main door to the house locked. Now I saw how stupid that was.

I went down the stairs to the main floor and saw the primary purpose of the break-in. Jenna's office door, which she always locked, had been forced open, the jam splintered and broken near the handle. I quickly went inside and surveyed the damage. Every drawer of her desk had been taken out and emptied on the floor, the same for all the drawers of the steel filing cabinet. I had to have been deeply asleep to have missed that.

Someone wanted to know what Jenna knew about a case and it didn't take much imagination to figure out who that would be.

I stepped out of the office in time to see the front door blow open, letting in cool night air. It had the kind of lock you could open with a credit card and I was sure someone had. Why had he come upstairs, though? Did he think no one was home, or was he just trying to scare me?

If so, it had worked.

I thought about calling 911 but that would set off a time-consuming chain of events that was unlikely to produce a result. I was sure there wasn't so much as a fingerprint left behind.

No, I would call Jenna and Darcy when morning came. It was time to show Brendan and Polanco that they had picked the wrong people to fuck with.

 # Thirty-two

Jenna surveyed the damage to her office and shook her head. "Does he think that I have a bunch of secrets locked up here? He should have at least stolen my computer."

"I think he's just sending us a message," I said.

Jenna had arrived by 7 a.m., looking like she hadn't slept and wearing the same jeans and T-shirt she had on the day before. Darcy was on his way. I had already cleaned up the mess in the kitchen and taken a shower. It didn't wash off the stink of the fear from last night. It had been the first time I had faced a physical confrontation since being shot last November. I liked to think that I would have stepped up and whacked the guy with the baseball bat, if he had come into my room. I was far from sure. I used to be fearless, able to face down a man with a gun. Then the man fired the gun, and my life changed.

"Some message," Jenna said. "Does Polanco really think that trashing my office and trying to scare you will get us to back off?"

"We don't know for sure it was him. I didn't get a look at his face."

"No, it was him. Who else would it be? This is retribution for the nut squeeze I gave him yesterday. Big tough guy, on his knees, tears in his eyes. I'm sure it was humiliating. The fact that his comeback is so gutless tells me something about him."

"Maybe he's trying to goad us into some stupid move,"

"Don't give him too much credit, Kris. I don't think that Polanco is all that bright."

"He doesn't need to be bright to be a menace."

"True," she conceded. "You didn't call the police, did you?"

"I think it would waste the better part of a day, they would write it off as a minor unsolvable crime and we'd be no farther ahead of the game."

"That sounds about right."

"What's happening with Alicia?"

"Still holed up at the hotel, waiting for someone to figure out that her car is at the airport."

"Ah, fooling them into thinking that she's made a run for it with the money."

"That's right."

"Kind of like catching a flaming torch isn't it?"

"I'm not convinced that's her real plan, or at least, not her whole plan. Alicia still hasn't levelled with me."

"You see your role, right?"

"Which is?"

"They will come after Alicia and you will protect her, killing Polanco and Brendan. Isn't that why she gave you the gun?"

"Maybe, but I hope not. It's a revolver that belonged to her father. She says the ammunition is 25 years old."

Maybe it was worse than I had thought. Was Alicia's plan to sacrifice Jenna, to create a crime that Brendan and Polanco could be prosecuted for? "What if her goal is to have them kill you, then go down for that?" I said.

"That gets a little complicated and it would suppose that I can't take care of myself. No, I think whatever Alicia has planned for Brendan, it's something she wants to do herself. What you told me about her parents certainly gives her motive, if it's true."

"I'm just worried about you."

"Of course you are. I'm worried about me, too. It doesn't mean we have to bail."

"No, but it might mean that bailing would be a smart move. Look, why not discuss this over breakfast? Let's walk down to that place you like on Elgin."

"The diner?"

"Yeah."

"You OK with leaving the house open?"

"We can still lock the main door. He didn't destroy that."

"All right. Let's go, I'm starving."

I thought I might settle for a coffee, maybe a piece of toast. My stomach was upset from some combination of nerves, anticipation and lack of sleep. The main thing I wanted was to get away from the house. It had been my place of refuge, but now I felt vulnerable there.

I hoped that the day would buoy me. It was sunny, fresh and cloud-free. As we walked up Frank, I admired the small flower beds that my neighbours had planted, the tulips just starting to fade. It was a reminder that life carried on as normal, or perhaps that nature just didn't care about human troubles.

We grabbed a booth at the diner, a warm neighbourhood spot that hadn't changed in decades. Inside it was the 1980s, maybe earlier. I ordered coffee and rye toast, Jenna a full bacon and eggs breakfast.

I was surprised that there were hardly any other customers in the place. Then the door swung open and an unusually tall man entered, looking around like he was meeting someone. He was dressed in a pair of jeans ripped at one knee, a baggy red T-shirt and a sweat-stained red ball cap. He wore sunglasses and had about a week's growth of white beard. It was a coin toss whether he was hip or homeless.

Apparently not finding the person he sought, he settled down at a table adjacent to ours and ordered a coffee. He kept glancing at us in a way that made me uncomfortable. After the fourth or fifth time, I said, "You got a problem, buddy?"

"As a matter of fact, I do," he said. His voice was cultured and his smile displayed even, white teeth. Then he took off the sunglasses and said, "I think you've been looking for me. I'm Simon Cousens."

Thirty-three

I tried to keep my mouth from dropping open in surprise, but I wasn't successful. Simon Cousens, alive and well. That blew up a few theories.

Simon reached across and shook my hand, his own hand exceptionally large and his grip firm. "You must be Kris," he said. "Pleasure to meet you. And Jenna, I remember you from the wedding. The rented maid of honour. Sorry to pop up like this. I know it must be a bit of a shock."

Jenna and I exchanged looks that said "a bit?"

"Do you mind if I join you?" Simon asked. "We have quite a lot to discuss."

I slid across the booth to create a spot for him and said, "Yes, we certainly do."

Thoughts were racing through my mind. Where had Simon been and how did he know to contact us? Had he been working with Alicia all along or did he have some separate plan of his own? I felt like everything I thought I knew about Simon and Alicia's situation was tilting and moving unpredictably in a new direction. The question was, which one?

"I'm sure you have a lot of questions," Simon said, "so let me clarify a few things and we will take it from there."

Jenna shook her head and said, "Look, Alicia is paying me to protect her life. Is she in danger or not?"

"Almost certainly. If you hear me out, I will explain why."

"I need to know if she's in danger right now," Jenna said. "If so I should be with her."

"I shouldn't think so. Does Brendan know where she is?"

"Not that I know of, but she intends to make herself visible, to spur him to take some kind of action. I'm not sure exactly what."

Simon nodded and ran his fingers across his raspy beard. "Alicia always has a plan. That doesn't mean that it's a good one. She's not going to pop up without you by her side, though, is she?"

"I hope not, but she's unpredictable."

"She is, and she doesn't know Brendan as well as I do. That's why I have set certain wheels of my own in motion."

"So you're her white knight are you?" I said.

"Hardly. More of a filthy shade of grey, really. Little about my life is black and white. I'm sure your research has shown you that."

"What it has shown us is more black than white," I said. "You've been missing for more than a week, leaving Alicia to fend for herself. Why should we believe that you're here to help her now?"

"I have been keeping a careful eye on her situation and I always put her interests first. She's my wife."

"That didn't seem to help the first four," I said.

Simon gave me a small smile that might have been either rueful or amused. It was hard to say.

"Well, affairs of the heart are extremely complex, wouldn't you say? One thing I have learned is that when the bloom has gone off the rose, it's time to move on."

That was just a fancy way of saying he'd been dumping women when it suited him his whole life. I could see why women were attracted to him, even with him looking as grubby as he did now. There was something there, an intelligence blended with confidence. It was what I had liked about my long-time lover Colin, another man who had more than his share of marriages.

"Apparently the bloom goes off the rose quite regularly," I said.

"Unfortunately, it does. One changes as time goes on and one's partner does not always keep in synch with those changes. It doesn't mean that I have ill feelings towards my former wives. Quite the contrary. I was staying with Margaret that day when you dropped around. I heard the whole conversation from upstairs."

"Margaret?" I blurted out before I could stop myself.

He smiled again, genuinely amused this time. "Yes, I realize Margaret doesn't seem the sort of person one would turn to in a crisis, but she has surprising depths of feeling. We were each other's first loves. That still means something to us both."

So a touch of the romantic as well, then. I was beginning to get a fuller picture of Simon's legendary charm. "She certainly did a good job of lying on your behalf."

"Didn't she? I was impressed. She did feel badly about it, but she has a loyalty to me. None to you, I'm afraid."

I looked at my watch, as if I were getting tired of him already. In reality, I couldn't wait to hear the story he would tell, but I didn't want to give him that impression.

"Speaking of loyalty," Jenna said, "the consensus seems to be that your strongest loyalty is to Brendan, your best friend. Why should we believe that you are putting Alicia first?"

"A good question. If you could stop quizzing me, I will be happy to tell you."

"All right. Let's hear it," I said.

Simon signalled the server for a refill of his coffee and Jenna and I took top ups, too. Then she brought our breakfasts.

"Go ahead and eat," Simon said.

Jenna dug in but I picked up a piece of toast and gave Simon a skeptical look. I didn't want him to think that I was falling for his act, not even for a minute.

"Where would you like me to start?" he asked.

"I've always found the beginning to be a good choice."

"Very well, then. I first noticed Alicia last year. She was a new player at the incubator I run out in Kanata. I assume you are familiar with the way they work?"

I nodded. I was sure my grasp of the concept was simplistic, but equally sure that it wouldn't be critical to understanding his story.

"I make a point of meeting all the new people when they come on board. I want to get a sense of their creativity and just as important, how hard they are willing to work to make their ideas a reality. Alicia was top drawer in both regards. This idea she has for an improved smokestack scrubbing technology is really quite clever. Like most innovations, it isn't something that has never been done before, but rather a better way of doing something that is being done now.

"As for her drive, I'm not sure I have ever seen its equal. Alicia has a passion to succeed that goes beyond financial reward or the satisfaction of meeting an intellectual challenge. I like that. When I was her age, I was the same way. I still am, on my better days."

"Do you think that was all that was motivating her when she sought out your company?" I asked.

"I did at the time. I learned fairly quickly that Alicia is a layered, complex person. Those are other qualities I like. I knew there had to be a strong motivation behind her exceptional drive and I was curious to find out what it was."

"Did you suspect she wanted your money?" Jenna asked.

"Of course. She asked me to take her to dinner and my first thought was that she was offering a crude exchange of sex and relative youth for all the benefits of being Mrs. Simon Cousens."

"A little presumptuous wasn't it?" Jenna asked. "You hadn't even been out on a date yet."

Simon laughed at that. I found it interesting how relaxed he seemed, given everything.

"I suppose it was, but she wouldn't have been the first one to go down that path. It's hardly a secret that getting married is one of my favourite things. It's the hope it offers, I think, and the chance to change oneself and be supported by an appropriate partner."

"Wasn't she a little young for you?" Jenna said.

"Arguably, but despite the cliché of older men being lechers who lust after young women, I have always preferred someone my own age. The mind is the greatest sexual organ, you see, and young people simply aren't fully developed in that way. Alicia was 35, a point that I have long believed is the perfect balance of youth and experience."

I looked at Jenna and she rolled her eyes. By Simon's standards she was hopelessly immature and I was past my best-before date.

"I was old enough to be her father, but I thought what harm could come from a pleasant evening with a young woman? There was something else, too. Alicia seemed curiously familiar, as if I had known her sometime in the past, but that clearly wasn't the case. I was surprised when the evening consisted of a stimulating conversation that ranged from green technology to jazz to mystery novels. There was no sexual advance from her at all, not even a goodnight kiss when I dropped her off at her apartment."

It told me something about Simon's sex life if he thought not scoring on the first date was something exceptional. Not that I was a paragon of chastity and virtue myself.

"I won't bore you with the details, but suffice to say the relationship blossomed rather quickly. I thought I had found someone who shared my deep intellectual curiosity, understood the business I am in and had a real desire to make the environment cleaner. It's not only where the money will be over the next decade, it's important for the planet. I'm afraid that I'm at the legacy stage of my life. Alicia understands that."

I wasn't sure if it would be telling tales out of school, but I felt I had to raise the unhappiness Alicia had described to us. I hesitated for a minute, but I was reasonably sure I wouldn't be telling Simon something he didn't know. "Alicia left us with the distinct impression that she wasn't happy," I said. "She mentioned your tendency for frequent unexplained absences and I got a sense of general neglect."

"Me too," Jenna said. "Alicia and I have had some detailed conversations. What she told me doesn't seem to jibe with what you are telling us."

"No contradiction at all," Simon said. "Alicia's state of mind today is somewhat different than when I married her. Quite a bit has happened since then and I know considerably more about what really motivates her. I will remind you that she employed you to find me. That's not the act of an unloving wife."

"It's not nearly that simple, though, is it?" Jenna asked.

"No. Very little in any marriage is. Trust me. I've a lifetime of experience. It's what I have found out more recently that has brought us to where we are today. I'm afraid that's not a story that I want to share in a diner. Can we adjourn to someplace more private? Your office, perhaps?"

"We could," Jenna said, "but there's been a bit of a disruption there overnight."

"What happened?"

"A break-in."

Simon nodded, as if this didn't surprise him at all. Naturally, I was curious as to why. Was he behind it?

 # Thirty-four

Alicia watched her laptop with satisfaction. She had figured that Paul Polanco wouldn't be the kind of guy who kept up with technology and she had been right. As he circled her Lexus, peering into the windows, her dual-camera dash cam was transmitting images to the cloud. Thanks to her decision to park on the roof of the airport parking garage, the quality was excellent.

She watched as Polanco shielded his eyes from the sun, trying to see if she might have left some vital piece of information in plain view, a travel itinerary, say. The great detective. His smug grin certainly told her that he was pretty pleased with himself for having found the vehicle. What he didn't know was that she was watching his every move.

Polanco looked around cautiously, to make sure no one was in sight. He reached into his pocket and pulled out an odd-looking key that he held up and admired. Then his arm dropped down and disappeared from the camera's view. He was forcing the door with an auto jiggler, a kind of fancy lock pick for cars. Things were going just as she had hoped.

Polanco's grin grew even wider when he popped the lock. Now the best part was coming. Alicia had left something for him on the driver's seat. Polanco reached in, looking like he couldn't believe his good luck. He folded open the note she had left for him. His smile disappeared when he read, "You lost me Paul. Don't worry. I'll find you soon. A."

Polanco crumpled the note and threw it on the ground, then looked frantically around as if expecting that she would be close by, watching. He was only half right.

She could have let him think he was hot on her trail, have him spend a day trying to find out what flight she had been on. But what was the fun in that? No, her point had been to piss Polanco off and remind him that she was smarter than he was. Mission accomplished.

Now it was time for the serious work to begin. She had packed her things and was ready to make her next move, but where the hell was Jenna Martin? Alicia tried Jenna's cell and got voicemail, then sent her a text. The message was clear, "The game has started. I need you here ASAP."

Alicia's plan depended on Jenna, more than she would like to admit. It wasn't ideal, but she needed a partner and she didn't have Simon. That was a worry. He had been gone far longer than she had anticipated. What was he up to? He obviously had a plan of his own. The question was, would Simon be working for her, or against her?

Thirty-five

Simon surveyed the jumbled mess of Jenna's office and shook his head. All the filing cabinet drawers had been opened and dumped on the floor, the chairs had been turned on their sides and her framed diplomas and sports pictures had been taken down and tossed in a heap.

I watched his response carefully. It certainly looked like it was the first time he had seen the destruction. Maybe I had been paranoid in thinking he had been involved. Certainly not his style, based on my short acquaintance with the tech entrepreneur.

"What asshole did this?" he asked.

"Probably Paul Polanco," I said.

"About what I'd expect from him. His intellectual development stopped around age 13. Did he take anything?"

"There was nothing to take," Jenna said. "Kris and I think he was just trying to put a scare into us."

"Did he succeed?"

"Hardly," Jenna said. "I was a cop for five years. I'm used to their boyish pranks."

"Polanco has fallen a long way since his police days. I never liked nor trusted him. Brendan relies on him, though. You are assuming that Brendan is behind this?"

"Wouldn't you?" I said.

"I would. Now, can I help you clean this up?"

"No need," I said, pushing file drawers to one side and turning the chairs back upright. "Have a seat and carry on with your story."

Simon settled into the office chair and said, "As it turns out, there was a great deal about Alicia that I did not know before I married her. I saw only what was apparent on the surface, and it was quite bright and shiny. Underneath, there is something far darker."

"The murder of her parents and her desire for revenge?" I asked.

Simon turned towards me, clearly surprised that Jenna and I knew this.

"Well, you have done your research," he said. "Yes, the sad story of Alicia's parents is what shapes and propels her, as it would any of us."

I could certainly understand that. My own sister and my father had both been murdered. I thought of it as the long hurt, the pain that would never really end. My quest for justice, or perhaps it was revenge, had compelled me to cross lines that I would never have imagined. So yes, I understood what drove Alicia, and I understood it viscerally. No need to share that with Simon.

"And when did you learn that?" I asked.

"Far later than I should have. On our wedding night, actually."

I hadn't pegged Alicia as the romantic type, but who would bring up the murder of her parents on her wedding night?

"Strange timing."

"That was certainly my first reaction. It made sense, though. I can explain why, but it means digging deep into Alicia's secrets, things I am sure she has *not* told you. First, I need to know where you stand in regard to Alicia. I am going to help her and I could certainly use your assistance, but I need to know that you are fully committed, that this isn't just a case, or worse, a newspaper story."

"I'm all in," Jenna said. "Alicia has promised to pay me well for my time, but that's not why I am helping her. She's in danger and I loathe the people who are threatening her. She has asked me to protect her and I will, whether you do or not."

"I agree with that," I said. I thought it better not to make a direct commitment about writing a story about the intriguing Simon-Alicia-Brendan triangle. That was a discussion for later, once we had figured out what the hell was really going on.

"Very well then. I had not slept with Alicia prior to our wedding night. I found her reluctance odd, but charmingly old-fashioned. I had no illusions that she was a virgin saving herself for marriage, I was sure that she would explain herself in due course. It's not like I was an 18-year-old eager for his first intercourse.

"What she told me that night shocked me and changed the nature of our relationship. It wasn't just the murder of her parents, it was who they were. John and Eve Tarrant had worked for the company that Brendan and I ran. Of course, I remembered their killings vividly. So senseless, and the culprit was never found. The murders hit me very hard.

"Alicia was convinced that Brendan and I knew what had really happened. I didn't, but I had always wanted to. She made it clear that her joining my company, seeking me out, even marrying me, were all steps in her plan to discover her parents' killers."

Simon ran his hand over his short beard. His eyes had that distant look of someone re-examining his past.

"I was devastated. I thought that I had seen all the surprises that marriage had to offer, but I never imagined that I would marry a woman who was conducting a private murder investigation, with me as the suspect.

"We were in bed at the time. I thought we were about to begin our sexual life together. Instead I found out that new my wife thought I might be a killer. I jumped out of bed and got dressed with the intention of leaving and starting immediate divorce proceedings. It was hardly a moment for humour, but I found myself imagining the look on Miranda's face when I gave her this news.

"Then Alicia told me to stop. She told me that she knew me well enough now to share the truth of her past, and that what she had discovered convinced her that I was neither a killer nor the kind of man who would cover up such a crime. I felt hope flood back, then she told me something far more troubling. She thought I might be her father.

"I was dumbfounded, but then I understood why. There was a good reason why Alicia had seemed familiar. I had had a rather passionate affair with her mother Eve. Alicia bears a remarkable resemblance to her mother. I hadn't made the connection, but she had. Her uncle had told her about the affair and the dates of our relationship overlapped with the time of Alicia's conception. Naturally, she wondered if the father might be me. Or as she put it, 'I'm not about to have sex with my own father.'"

That was a twist that neither Jenna nor I had seen coming. When people said that Simon's life was complex, they didn't know the half of it.

"Are you?" I said.

"Thankfully not, and I was in no suspense about the matter. When Eve became pregnant, she broke off our affair, saying that she wanted to raise her child with its real father. At the time, I thought there was an excellent chance that I was the father and that she was taking the easy way out. After Alicia's birth, I asked for a paternity test. It confirmed what Eve had told me.

"I no longer have the document and I didn't expect Alicia to take my word for it. She had asked for DNA testing to be done. It produced the conclusion I expected, but our relationship was never the same after that night. Ultimately, we did become lovers, but I was never sure whether her feelings were genuine or whether she just wanted to keep me on side.

"That's what explains my frequent absences. I was trying to come to grips with my situation and I needed time to think, time away from Alicia. The complication, as I am sure you have already surmised, is that Alicia had directed her suspicions to Brendan, my long-time partner and best friend.

"I accept that. Brendan isn't perfect, far from it. He can be nasty when challenged and likes to issue threats, but I think it's more to do with his insecurity than any real malice. It's critical to Brendan that he be considered an inventor as well as an entrepreneur, a thinker, not just a salesman. The reality is that I was always the creative force in our company and Brendan's skill was in attracting investors and marketing the products. I'm not belittling that at all. I'm no good at either, and if it wasn't for Brendan, neither of us would have succeeded.

"Still, Alicia was asking me to believe that a man I thought I knew better than any in the world was, in fact, either a killer or someone who would order murder and cover it up, keeping the truth even from me. It was unthinkable, at least for a time.

"Gradually I came to accept her analysis. John Tarrant had informed us that one of our early telephony idea, the only one for which Brendan claimed sole credit, had actually been John's own work. John said he was willing to challenge the patent and go public, if it came to that.

"Brendan was livid, in a rage like I had never seen. At the time, I found that understandable. Credit for scientific advances is always a bit murky, but it generally goes to the top dog. John was an employee. I suspected that he wanted to enhance his own credibility and start a spinoff company. For Brendan and me, a patent challenge would have been devastating. It would have seriously damaged the credibility of our company at a critical time, scaring off investors and permanently harming our prospects.

"For me, the situation was complicated by the fact that I had that affair with John's wife. I was hardly an objective observer. Naturally, I wondered if he had discovered the affair and was using the patent issue as a way to get back at us. I decided not to share that with Brendan. Afterwards, I wished that I had, but there is no saying that it would have stayed his hand. Instead, I told Brendan that I would let him resolve the matter using his best judgment but without explaining why I was recusing myself.

"Alicia is convinced that Brendan had Polanco kill the two of them. It's credible. Polanco is a greedy man with no moral compass. Right after the killings, he took early retirement from the police and started his own investigation agency. Brendan has had him on retainer for decades. None of that means Polanco was the killer, but it is grounds for suspicion."

"That's a lot to take in," I said, in what was a considerable understatement.

"It's also a lot more than Alicia has told us," Jenna said. "How do we know it's true? Based on what you've said, you had as much motive to kill the Tarrants as Brendan Connor did."

"Fair point," Simon said, "but Alicia wouldn't be working with me if she thought that was true."

It was a plausible statement, but given the murky layers of Alicia's mind, it was possible that she was playing Simon as a way to get them both.

From the look on Jenna's face, I could see she shared my thinking. I was about to suggest that he give us a few minutes to confer when Simon said, "I know you aren't convinced. Let me tell you about Alicia's plan and why we have to change it. Then you can make up your minds."

 # Thirty-six

Paul Polanco gave a cursory knock on the big door that led to Brendan Connor's office and then walked in, just like he had been doing for years. Brendan looked up as if Polanco represented a sudden and unwelcome intrusion, even though he had been the one who scheduled the meeting.

The little prick was in his customary position, sitting forward on one of his custom-made grey couches, a pair of half-lens reading glasses hanging on the end of his nose as he examined yet another report about some element of his business empire. Brendan held up his hand, signalling for Polanco to wait, as if whatever column of numbers he was looking at was more important than anything Polanco could have to say.

The private investigator had grown used to it over the years. Next, Brendan would tell him to come, then order him to sit, like he was a dog. Polanco could do come and sit all day for the money Brendan paid him. The thing he was wondering now, was it time to add roll-over to his repertoire of animal tricks? If he did, it would be Brendan he would be rolling over on. If this whole Alicia situation didn't work out, he was going down, but he wouldn't be going alone.

Just as predicted, Brendan said "Come" and Polanco approached and slumped into the couch across from him.

"What have you got to report?" Brendan asked, his tone brusque.

"Mixed news. I did find her vehicle. It's parked in the long-term stay building at the airport."

"So she's left town, then?"

"I don't think so. I had my contact at the airport check departures, but there's nothing under her name. I think we were meant to find the vehicle, to make us think she's gone."

"Based on?"

"She left a note saying 'You lost me Paul. Don't worry. I'll find you soon. A.'"

"So she's taunting you then?"

"It seems likely."

"Fuck, Paul. People don't just disappear."

"I realize that, but it's a city of one million people. There are lots of places where she could be."

"Friends?"

"No sign that she has any."

"That doesn't surprise me. Family, then?"

"Aunt and uncle in Kanata. You probably remember them. The uncle raised quite a ruckus when his sister was killed."

"Keep an eye on them, then."

"Already done. No sign of any contact. But get this. Kris Redner paid them a visit."

"Shit, that's not good. The more people who are involved, the harder all of this is going to be to contain. I assume you've checked hotels."

"Yes, again nothing under her name but she could be using an alias and paying cash. If so, she will be like a needle in a haystack."

"Alicia's got something in common with a needle, Paul. She's sharp. I'm starting to wonder if you are."

Polanco usually let Brendan's predictable insults roll off. The guy wasn't happy unless he was pissing on someone, but there was a point where enough was enough.

"OK, let's say I'm just a plodding ex-cop. What do you have to suggest?"

Brendan shook his head and emitted a sigh that was half impatience, half frustration. "Paul, fixing this is your job. I pay you a lot of money to take care of problems, and there is no problem more important than this.

"Now, what about Simon? Anything there?"

"Not a sign. It's like he's vanished."

"Yes, it's exactly like he's vanished. I need to know where he's vanished to, and most important, if he's still alive. What about this Redner and the young one, Martin? I'll bet they know."

Polanco wondered if maybe he should have mentioned last

night's break-in first. It was action. Brendan liked action. The problem was, he'd come up dry.

"I'm working that angle. I broke into their house last night, went through everything in Martin's office. I couldn't find a thing on this case."

Brendan waved his little hands in the air, his frustration taking physical form now. "What the hell did you expect to find?" he asked. "Did you think she'd have a file labelled Simon's Location?"

"Of course not, but most investigators take detailed case notes. It doesn't surprise me that this one doesn't. It's her first rodeo."

"And she's riding you like a bucking bronco, isn't she? In fact, to switch metaphors, I'd say that she's made you her bitch."

Polanco wasn't sure what a metaphor was, exactly, but he knew what it meant to be made into a bitch. He didn't like that thought at all.

"Don't be ridiculous," Polanco said, lowering his voice to its most menacing, rumbling tone. "I can handle her with ease."

"Can you? The security cameras in the outer lobby told me that it was her handling you in a very painful and unpleasant way."

Fuck. Polanco had hoped that Brendan wasn't aware of that. It was embarrassing and a day later, he was still walking funny. Jenna Martin had taken the first round, OK, the first two rounds, but that just meant he'd take her down that much harder when the time was right.

"Yeah, the little bitch made a move there, but she'll be sorry in the end. Now, boss, I can see you aren't happy with how this is going. Neither am I. We've both got a lot at stake. I think it's time for me to defer to your wisdom, let you plot out the next steps."

Polanco could tell from the look on Brendan's face that he knew he was fucking with him, but he couldn't very well say he wasn't smart enough to know what to do next.

"Yes, I'm afraid I will have to step in. This problem needs to be terminated immediately."

"Can you be just a little bit more specific? It was terminating an earlier problem that got us to where we are today."

"You think I've forgotten that? We need to cut out the cancer here, Paul. That means radical surgery. We need to remove Alicia and the two snoops."

Polanco shook his head. Did the guy think he was running a street gang that specialized in bumping people off? Even if he had been, it would be a tall order to get away with a triple homicide.

"I agree," Polanco said, "but I don't see a way to do it."

"Start with the desired outcome and work backwards, Paul. It would be ideal to get them all in the same place at the same time, somewhere remote, a place where it would be easy to dispose of the bodies."

"Yes, but how do we do that?"

"It's simple. We get Alicia there and the other two will follow. Martin is no doubt sticking to her like a shadow, to offer the illusion of protection. She and Redner are mother and daughter, right? If Martin is going somewhere, Redner will too. Maternal instinct."

Brendan sat back and clapped his hands, looking as pleased as could be with his solution. Polanco liked the concept but pulling it off wouldn't be easy. "How do we make it happen?" he asked.

"Leave that to me. I've got an idea."

In fact, it was an idea he'd had for a while, an idea that would solve all of his problems, including Paul Polanco.

 # Thirty-seven

"All right, I'll bite," Jenna said. "What is Alicia's plan exactly? I haven't been able to work it out."

"It's actually quite simple," Simon said. "She wants to use me as bait to lure Brendan and Polanco to a location of her choice. She will tell Brendan that she has been keeping me captive, but she will release me to their custody if Brendan lets her keep the $10 million. She plans to play to his suspicion that she has been in this for the money from the start.

"That's not all, of course. This is Alicia. When they show up, she intends to kill them both, exacting revenge for her parents. According to the plan, she and I keep the $10 million and get on with our lives."

The sun was slanting in the window of Jenna's office, leaving a curtain of light between us and Simon. I couldn't see his face clearly so I was unable to read his expression but his manner was relaxed, one leg crossed over the other and his right arm resting on the top of Jenna's desk. Either he was telling the truth or he was an exceptionally skilful liar.

"But you were unwilling to play along," I said.

"Yes, for a number of reasons, the primary one being that Alicia would never survive. Polanco and Brendan would say they would come alone, but I'm sure Polanco would bring help. Their goal would be to eliminate Alicia, the only person trying to hold them accountable for their crimes. The odds would certainly favour them. Alicia is intelligent and resourceful, but she'd be no match for five or six armed men. I would try to help her, of course, but there would be an excellent chance that I'd die trying.

"Alicia's analysis is partly correct. Brendan will want to get me back and he can certainly afford to lose $10 million. What he can't do is leave Alicia alive. As long as she is, she will be a threat. On the surface, Alicia's plan looks like a simple kidnap and ransom, but Brendan's concern will be that it's really blackmail. He can pay her and get me back, but her knowledge would still give her power over him. He won't risk that. Besides, he won't find it plausible that the $10 million will satisfy her desire for revenge. One can't put a price on the murder of one's parents, the theft of one's childhood. Brendan will see all that and act accordingly. He's already proven himself capable of it. Polanco will go along because his neck is on the line, too."

"So you had technical concerns about her plan, then," I said.

"Not just that. Brendan's actions are despicable and he has been lying to me for decades, but I couldn't endorse a scheme to murder him. That would make Alicia and me no better than Brendan. Alicia should have her justice, but that means putting Brendan and Polanco behind bars, not in coffins."

"I see a major problem with your line of thinking," Jenna said. "There is not one real piece of evidence of Brendan's guilt. It's just supposition. Whatever physical evidence there might have been proved nothing at the time, there were no witnesses except Alicia, and she was a child back then. No court is going to buy that she has some kind of recovered memory decades later, not when she is accusing one of the most prominent businessmen in Ottawa and a retired police officer.

"If you were to describe the dispute between Brendan and the Tarrants, it could point to motive, but that's where the case would end. Just as bad, people could say you had as much motive as Brendan. You'd had an affair with Eve Tarrant. You're a noted womanizer. Maybe the two of you were still carrying and you wanted to get the husband out of the way. Maybe she tried to stop you and you killed her, too."

"Except none of that is true," Simon said.

"It doesn't matter what's true. It's what can be proven that counts," Jenna said.

"I think we're getting off track," Simon said. "Alicia's plan is moot at this point. I am not going to go along with it."

"Well, she has a new plan," Jenna said. "She's made that much clear. She's going to try to kill the two of them, with or without you."

Simon shook his head and brushed Jenna's point away with his hand, like he was shooing away a fly. "We simply can't let that happen. If Alicia were to end up in jail, after all she has been through, that would make the injustice even more profound."

"Agreed," I said. "Let's skip to the part where you tell us about your own plan, the one that's going to save everyone's ass. And when I say everyone, I want to know how you think this turns out for Jenna and me. Even though we don't know much, we know more than Brendan Connor wants. If he intends to kill Alicia, he plans to kill us, too. Right now, I'm thinking our best plan is to take the whole thing to the police. Convince me I'm wrong."

"That will be up to you," Simon said. "I'm not going to stop you. I'm not Brendan Connor. Consider this, though. If you do take that course, then Brendan and Polanco will never face justice for the very reasons Jenna outlined. Brendan will bring in a team of top lawyers, deny everything and that's where it will end. Are you content with that?"

"Give us a minute," I said, then motioned for Jenna to join me in the hall. We left Simon in the ruined office and Jenna said, "Let's go out on the verandah."

We stepped out into the fresh, sunny spring day and saw normal life all around us, people walking their dogs, men playing pickup basketball in the park across the street, moms with babies in strollers. It was as if we'd resurfaced from a great depth.

"What do you think?' I asked.

"I've been torn about bringing Stillwell in on this from the start, but it's going to take more than we've got to get an old cold case like this revived. At the same time, you have any real doubt that Polanco and Brendan are behind those two killings? They're acting like men with something big to hide."

"Maybe Brendan just wants his $10 million back."

"I'm sure he does, but it's not that. He's loaded. It could be that his real concern is getting his buddy Simon back, but my take on Brendan is that when it comes down to it, his only priority is himself."

"I'm with you there, but where does it leave us? This isn't really our problem."

"It is now, Kris. I've had two physical confrontations with Polanco and I'm sure he's the one who broke into the house. We're on their radar. They need to contain the problem, and we're part of the problem."

"Bringing in the police would widen the knowledge, though. They can't eliminate everyone."

"That would be true if we had something incriminating to give them. All we've got is a wild-assed accusation. After Brendan's lawyers spike it, he can deal with us at his leisure."

I didn't like her analysis, but I couldn't argue with it. "So how do you want to play it, then?"

"We listen to his plan, see if it sounds workable and what he expects us to do. If it's no good, we come up with our own plan."

When we returned to Jenna's office, Simon greeted us with an expectant smile, like he knew all along what we were going to decide. That irked me. We weren't in his net yet.

"All right, let's hear your plan," I said. "It had better be good."

"It's really a variant on Alicia's original idea, but with a crucial difference. Rather than using me as bait to trap Brendan, I intend to use Alicia."

"I thought you were on her side?" Jenna said.

"I am. Bear with me for a moment. Alicia is right to think that Brendan wants me kept safe, but that doesn't negate his need to eliminate the threat Alicia poses. I will offer him both. It will be easy to convince him that Alicia is a threat to me as well as to him, that she wants to eliminate us both. I will assure Brendan that Alicia thinks she can trust me, so I can lure her to an appropriate location, then let Polanco take care of the rest."

"And what about Brendan?" I asked.

"He will come along, too. He wouldn't miss Alicia's demise for the world. Brendan is quite brave, as long as he has a large man with a gun accompanying him."

"So you lure Brendan and Polanco to this 'appropriate location,' then what happens?" I asked. "How do you get them to incriminate themselves?"

Simon flashed another of those self-confident smiles. "It should be easy. They won't be able to resist the opportunity to boast and gloat."

"Alicia has already launched her own plan," Jenna said. "Why would she agree with yours? She's the type who likes to be in charge and control every detail, wouldn't you agree?"

"She is indeed. She is also supremely logical. Alicia will see the sense of what I am proposing. After all, she has been expecting me to ride to her rescue."

"The dirty grey knight."

"Something like that."

"And what role do you see Jenna and me playing in this plan?"

Simon leaned forward and made eye contact with each of us separately. We had obviously come to the sticky part.

"I'm sure you would agree that Brendan won't consider this matter resolved until all knowledge of what he and Polanco did is extinguished. I would be the exception. He trusts me. That means I will have to offer him you and Jenna as a package with Alicia."

"A package?"

"Sorry, perhaps not the best choice of words, but let me be blunt. He will want to eliminate all three of you. The opportunity to do it in one place will be irresistible to him. I know how his mind works."

"How do you see all of this playing out?"

"Well, I will need video of him confessing and I will require both of you as witnesses. That means you will have to be with Alicia and be restrained like she will be, to give the scene credibility."

"You're asking an awful lot," Jenna said.

"I'm aware of that. I think this plan is our best chance of seeing appropriate punishment for Brendan and Polanco, and still have everyone else meet their goals and walk away unharmed."

"And what's your risk?" she asked.

"I'm turning in my best friend with the knowledge that he will die in prison. The entire plan turns on him not imagining that I'd do such a thing. If I have misjudged, he'll kill me."

"'You plan to meet with him directly?" I asked.

"I have to. It's the only way he will believe that I am not acting under duress."

"And this restraint," Jenna said, "is that just for a video or do you think he will expect to see it with his own eyes?"

"If we are to get him to confess, we will need to make it convincing. When he walks through the door, everything will have to look real."

"So it looks real, they confess, but what's to stop them from shooting all three of us? Tell me it's something more than just you."

"Leave the logistics to me. I have it worked out."

"That's not quite good enough," I said. "If you expect us to sit there tied to a chair facing two men who want to kill us, we're going to need to know every detail of how you are going to pull this off and have a veto over the final plan."

"Done. We will work on the denouement together."

I looked and Jenna and nodded. She returned the gesture. "All right, you have a deal."

Simon reached to shake our hands, but just then we were all distracted by the sound of the front door opening and a man's voice saying, "Hello, anyone home?"

We all turned to see Darcy fill the doorway of Jenna's office. He hadn't shaved in a couple of days and he looked rumpled, the buttons of his red and blue plaid shirt misaligned so that his collar stood up on the left side.

"Who's this?" he asked.

"Simon Cousens, the missing man. He's here to sell us on a plan to put our lives in danger."

Thirty-eight

After Simon left, Darcy surveyed the chaos of Jenna's office and said, "Jesus, this is really disturbing."

"No real harm done," Jenna said.

"Not this time. It just shows how vulnerable you and Kris are here. Maybe you should relocate, just for now."

"No way," I said. "I'm not letting these assholes drive me out of my own home. Besides, they came here for a purpose and they failed to find anything useful. They're done here."

Darcy shook his head, unconvinced. "They might be through rifling through your stuff, but they're not through with you. I have a feeling this is just getting started."

"Closer to the end than the beginning," I said. "Simon has a plan."

"The mystery millionaire? He looks like a hobo. He's been missing the whole time that his wife was in trouble, now he pops up with a plan? Let me guess, it involves both of you."

I nodded.

"How can you trust this guy?"

"Who says we do?"

"You'd better tell me about this plan."

Part of me liked it when Darcy took charge, especially in bed, but I wasn't totally comfortable with it yet. I had been making my own decisions for a long time, for better or worse. I knew his motives were good, though.

"Come on upstairs. I'll make some coffee and we'll lay it out for you."

The three of us trudged up the stairs to my apartment, Darcy in the lead. When we walked into the kitchen, he saw the mess from the sink overflowing onto the floor and asked "What happened here?"

"Whoever it was came into the apartment. I don't usually lock the door. He messed around a bit, then plugged the sink and turned on the water. Just trying to spook me," I said, and succeeding, I thought.

"Kris, you didn't tell me that. The guy was right in the apartment when you were sleeping? That's serious."

"Don't worry, I heard him and got up. I had the baseball bat at the ready. When he heard me, he ran away. Good thing, too. I'd have broken his kneecaps."

Darcy's mouth tightened into a taut line. It was the look he got when he wanted to say something but knew he shouldn't. Clearly, he wasn't impressed by my bravado.

"Just to be safe, I'm going to be with you 24/7 until this is over."

I had no quarrel with that, none at all. I nodded my agreement.

"And Jenna, what's happening with you right now?"

"I'm supposed to be providing personal protection for Alicia, but when I heard what happened here, I rushed right over. Actually, I need to get back. We have to keep an eye on Alicia, know what she's up to. In fact, I'm going to do that now. Kris, why don't you run over our conversation with Simon?"

"Sure," I said.

Then Jenna was gone, clattering down the stairs and out the front door.

I laid out Simon's plan, what little we knew of it. Darcy maintained eye contact the whole time, like he was trying to look inside my head, see what I really thought. When I got to the part about Jenna and I joining Alicia as bait in Simon's trap, he held up his hands and said, "Whoa, that's not happening."

"You in charge now?" I snapped, sounding angrier than I wanted to.

Darcy didn't blink. He said, "Look Kris, we all went through a lot up at Madawaska Mills last year. We stuck together. If we hadn't, we wouldn't all have made it out. We need to do that again."

I couldn't argue with that. The ordeal of last winter was still seared into my mind. I had taken a big risk and ended up staring down the barrel of a shotgun. Without Darcy and Jenna, that cold, snowy day deep in the forest could have been my last.

"Sorry, I'm a little tense. You're right, the break-in was serious. I woke up and realized you weren't here, then for a minute I thought it was all a dream. When I heard the definite sound of the floor creaking, I felt a shot of adrenalin with a chaser of fear."

"Nothing to be ashamed of. Doesn't matter how many fights you've been in, each one feels the same at the start. I'm not trying to be pushy here, but I'm coming into all of this late. Why don't you tell me why it's essential for you and Jenna to be tied up as part of a show for this Brendan Connor?"

"I don't like it either, but we're pretty certain that Brendan thinks we know what he did. That means he can't take a chance of leaving us alive to act on that knowledge. The only solution, from his perspective, is to eliminate us along with Alicia."

"That was a shocker about her parents. I couldn't believe it when you told me. It explains a lot about her determination."

"Yes, and I completely understand. When I found out who was behind the murder of my sister, there wasn't much I wouldn't do to square it up. I didn't worry about the consequences, what would happen as a result of my revenge. I think Alicia is in that same zone, but while I acted on passion, she had been planning all this meticulously for years."

"I can't help but think that you and Jenna are just pawns in that plan."

"More like the queen, able to move quickly and strike from any direction."

"OK, but even the queen needs protection. I'm not going to leave everything in Simon Cousens's hands and hope it all works out. Wherever this goes down, I'm going to be close by with some of my people."

I smiled and said, "You've got people?"

"I know some guys."

"You know we're not looking for some kind of shootout here? This isn't Madawaska Mills all over again."

"I was thinking more of brute force."

"All right. I've always had a weakness for forceful brutes."

"I feel like I'm being typecast, but I guess there are worse roles. Seriously Kris, we can't trust Simon Cousens. You said he has been Brendan Connor's best friend for decades. How can we trust that Simon's going to turn on him now, for a woman he barely knows?"

"We can't, so we play along and keep our eyes open."

Thirty-nine

Simon Cousens pulled his white 1969 Mercedes 280 SL convertible onto a broad gravel shoulder off a quiet rural road that overlooked Kanata and shut off the engine. This was his favourite place to come for uninterrupted contemplation and even though that wasn't the order of the day, it was where he wanted to make what could be the most fateful phone call of his life.

The sky was almost clear, with just a few white scudding clouds moving quickly across the Gatineau Hills. What he really enjoyed was looking down on Kanata, the suburban city he had done so much to create. He could see his own building, BrightFuture, as well as Brendan's Conn-Tech tower. So much of his life had taken place there, his creativity, his hopes, his triumphs, his failures. More than 30 years had gone by since he and Brendan had started out, green, energetic and brimming with confidence. How had it come down to this?

He wanted to make the call from the Mercedes because he always felt his most confident when behind the wheel. He loved its clean lines, its crispness only slightly marred by the silly little vertical rubber bumpers added as a concession to the notion that sporty automobiles should be safe. He ran his hand over the well-worn red leather seat beside him. The used Mercedes had been the first exotic car he had owned, and it was till his favourite. There had been many more since and the SEL was certainly no Porsche, but it held many memories. All of his wives had sat in that seat at one time or another, always at a good moment in the relationship.

He flipped through the images in his mind, like looking at a series of faded colour photographs. Margaret, her hair long then, both of them young and getting a first taste of the good things that life had to offer. Then Marie-France, his bohemian artist wife, so full of vitality. They liked to take picnics in the Gatineau Park, Marie-France always bringing a bottle of wine. Then he saw Paula, ball cap pulled down low, wearing her usual low-cut top. She loved to pull down some quiet lane and have sex in nature. Who had he been to argue? He hadn't imagined Miranda as the vintage sports car type, but she had surprised him in that, as in so many things.

Finally, there was Alicia. She had wanted to drive, of course. Like most young people, she didn't know how to work a standard shift and he had winced as she ground her way through the gears. He had indulged her, as he indulged her in everything.

It had been the shock of his life when she had finally explained who she was and why she had married him. After taking her time to really get to know him, her due diligence as she had actually called it, she laid out her belief that he or Brendan were behind her parents' death. How could she have thought he would do such a thing?

He had vehemently denied it, but was faced with the problem of proving that one had not done something. Fortunately, she had concluded on her own that a double slaying simply wasn't something he was capable of. The deciding factor was his relationship with her mother. Alicia had floored him with that knowledge, and with her suspicions that he might have been her father.

She had probed him about Brendan, but she had no proof of his complicity in the deaths. Simon had found her suspicions superficially logical but extremely difficult to accept. Brendan could be a hothead, but killing two people over a business dispute? It didn't seem likely, even with a great deal at stake.

Over time, he had come to accept that Alicia's suspicion was almost certainly true. The patent dispute would have crushed their company, and they had discussed the problem.

Brendan had acted strangely around the time of the killings, too. Simon could never forget a meeting they had after the shocking news of the two deaths. "Sorry about Eve," Brendan had said, "but big picture, this is good news for both of us."

Simon hadn't thought, simply reacted. He had hit Brendan a solid punch in the jaw, knocking him on his ass. It was the only fight they had ever had in all their years together. If one could even call it a fight. Brendan had not retaliated, but got groggily to his knees, then pulled himself to his feet and retreated behind his desk. The next day, it was as if nothing had ever happened and they simply carried on.

When Alicia had first presented her plan, he had found it out-landish. She intended to lure Brendan into putting a big chunk of money on the table, take the money, then take Simon, too. In her mind, it would force Brendan to confess to his crimes, to get the money and Simon back.

That's the story she told, anyway. Simon feared from the outset that her real goal was to kill Brendan and his thug Polanco. Would she stop there, or would she kill him as well? There was no way to be sure, not even now.

Simon shook his head and cursed himself for his vanity, think-ing a woman almost half his age would be attracted to him. He should have known that her love was insincere, but when it came to women, he saw what he wanted to see.

Now, he had a difficult decision to make. Would he betray Bren-dan or Alicia? There was no one in the world closer to him than Brendan, but if everything Alicia told him was true, she was the third victim of that terrible summer day so many years ago, and what's more, she was Eve's child. Alicia had a right to justice, but not to be Brendan's prosecutor, judge and executioner.

He had agreed to participate in Alicia's scheme to buy time, try to figure out what he should do. He had thought of little else in the 10 days since he had gotten into the Mercedes and driven away from his house in the country. The right course of action still wasn't clear in his mind, despite what he'd told Kris and Jenna. That had been another delaying tactic, to keep them at bay for the moment.

Everything would come down to the call he was about to make. How would Brendan explain the deaths of the Tarrants, and would it be convincing, or at least, more convincing than Alicia's version?

Then he realized that this wasn't a matter that could be settled with a phone call, although it felt infinitely safer. He had to look Brendan in the eyes, read his soul. He started the Mercedes and headed down the hill to Kanata.

 # Forty

Jenna knocked, then used her key card to enter Alicia's room. She saw a black duffel bag sitting on the bed, zipped up and ready to go. Alicia was wearing tight black jeans, a long-sleeved black T-shirt and heavy combat-style boots, like she was ready for some kind of commando operation.

"Where the hell have you been all morning?" Alicia asked. "I've sent you text after text. I called your phone, but you didn't pick up."

"I had it off."

"Off? I'm paying you to provide personal security and I can't even reach you."

"Sorry, something big came up. Have you heard from Simon?"

Alicia's anger turned immediately to shock. "Simon? No, I haven't heard a thing. Have you?"

Jenna felt like she finally had one up on Alicia. "Yes, in fact I just spent the morning with him."

"What! And you didn't call me, ask me to join you? Where did you meet him? How did you find him?" she said, her words tripping over each other.

Jenna walked over to the suite's coffee bar and plugged a pod into the machine. Let Alicia stew for a minute. She was tired of being treated like a dog on a leash.

Once the coffee was ready and she had added a creamer, Jenna said, "He just popped up when Kris and I were having breakfast at a diner around the corner from our house. Apparently he's been keeping tabs on us."

"On *you*?"

"Only because we are working with you. We're just cogs in his plan."

"Oh, he has a plan now, does he? Care to share?"

Jenna could see that Alicia was simmering but trying to keep it under control. It was understandable. Her husband takes off, not a word for 10 days, and now he turns up sharing a plan with someone else. She'd have felt the same way.

"Absolutely, but first there's something else you need to know. There was a break-in at my place in the early hours of the morning. Someone forced the front door, then trashed the office, looking for something. After that, the person went upstairs and screwed with things in Kris's apartment."

"That's disturbing. Another escalation. Polanco?"

"Presumably. Kris didn't get a good look at him but from the stiff way he ran down the street, it was an older guy."

"Tell me there wasn't anything in your office that was useful to them."

"Of course not. Don't worry about it."

"Fine, I won't. Now, tell me about Simon. Everything. Don't leave a word out."

Jenna settled on the couch and Alicia took the flowered armchair across from it. Jenna decided to run through the main points Simon had made, leaving out what he had to say about the quality of his own judgment when he agreed to marry Alicia.

Jenna said, "His main point is that he thinks your plan won't work. He believes his is better."

"Really? What is his plan?"

"He uses you, me and Kris as bait to lure Brendan and Polanco to some place he has in mind in the country. Brendan is supposed to think that if he shows up, he will get his money back and a chance to eliminate all three of us."

"Eliminate?"

"Yes, but Simon won't let that happen and neither will I. Details to follow on location and timing of his plan, but don't worry, I will have a contingency in place."

"You say that with great confidence, considering that you have only a rudimentary outline of the plan."

"Kris and I have dealt with more complicated problems in the past. Plus, we have the help of Darcy. You haven't met him. He's my Dad. Very capable guy."

"Kris's husband, then?"

"Not exactly."

"Well, Darcy is going to have to be incredibly capable if he's to overcome Polanco and whatever help he brings to this confrontation. Where will you be, exactly?"

"Tied up, just like you and Kris."

Alicia shook her head, as if this was the stupidest thing she'd ever heard. Maybe she was right, Jenna thought.

"Am I understanding this properly? Simon is going to present the three of us to Brendan and Polanco what, tied to chairs or something?"

"Like that, yeah. He will send Brendan a video of the setup and it has to look authentic when he gets there."

"What am I missing? Once he gets there, we deal with him, right?"

"Simon's idea of dealing with him is to get Brendan to admit what he and Polanco did, then take it all to the police."

Alicia slammed the flat of her hand on the coffee table in front of her, causing a stack of tourist magazines to fall onto the floor. "What is this, a Boy Scout rally? I know what Brendan and Polanco did. Now it's time for them to pay."

"You can't just kill them, Alicia."

"Isn't that what I have you for?"

"Have you lost your mind? I'm a private investigator and former police officer. I'm not a hit woman."

Alicia gave a sigh of exasperation. "All right, let me put it another way. What would you do if they attacked us?"

"I'd defend myself, and you too, but I wouldn't use lethal force unless our lives were at risk."

"Maybe that's the way it should play, then."

"We're talking premeditation now. That's first-degree murder. You want to spend the next 25 years in prison? I know I don't. Either come to your senses or I'm out."

"Fine, fine then," Alicia said, her tone suggesting the exact opposite.

"There is one more wrinkle in Simon's plan that you should know about."

"What, is he going to knock us out, too?"

"No, but he's going to tell Brendan that he's on his side. That eliminating all evidence of your parents' deaths will leave them both in the clear."

Alicia sat back in the chair and thought about that. "All right, that makes sense. He couldn't sell it to Brendan any other way. Brendan has to trust Simon *not* to do exactly what's he planning to do."

"I just have one question. Can we trust Simon?"

All at once, Alicia looked sad and tired. "I don't know," she said. "I just don't know."

Forty-one

Simon got off the elevator and strode confidently across the reception area toward the office door. Ekaterina, Brendan's executive assistant, looked up in shock at the sudden intrusion, apparently not recognizing him with his beard and grubby clothes. She had blond hair, blue eyes and a flat, Slavic face. Her sleeveless green dress showed lean, powerful arms. Brendan had been rather vague about her background, but Simon had always felt it was something to do with athletics. Ekaterina got to her feet, came out from behind the desk and looked like she was ready to tackle him, if it came to that.

"It's Simon Cousens, Ekaterina. Please excuse my appearance. I've been taking a bit of time off."

"Oh, Mr. Cousens," she said, relaxing. "I didn't recognize you. It has been a while and as you say, you do look a bit different."

"I need to see Brendan immediately."

"Of course, sir. I'll tell him that you're here."

As Ekaterina hurried to the office door, Simon noticed her powerful legs. Weightlifting?

Simon heard Ekaterina's muffled voice, then a loud "My God!" from Brendan. Simon stepped into the office and Brendan rushed to him, giving him a hug. As there was more than a foot of difference in their heights, Simon found himself staring down at the wispy baldness of Brenda's comb forward.

Brendan relaxed his grip, then said, "Simon, so relieved to see you safe. You had me worried."

"We need to talk."

"Of course, absolutely. Ekaterina, excuse us please and hold all my calls."

They both watched Ekaterina leave the room, then pull the door closed behind her.

Brendan looked Simon up and down, as if drinking in the sight of his old friend. Then he said, "Simon, where have you been? You look like hell."

"Just taking a bit of time, trying to work out what to do about our mutual problem."

"Ah, so you know what Alicia has been up to?"

"I do. In fact, she tried to involve me in her scheme. That's why I had to take off, get out of her clutches."

"Don't worry. I can protect you."

Simon smiled at that. Brendan couldn't deter even the weakest assailant. He had people for that, of course.

Seeing the look on Simon's face, Brendan said, "You know what I mean. Polanco is on the job."

"Ah yes, Polanco. It seems he has a rather central role in this little drama."

"Oh?"

"This wouldn't be the time to bullshit me, Brendan. I know far more than I did about what happened all those years ago, but I want to hear it from you. The truth this time, the whole truth."

Brendan turned toward a glass and steel credenza beside his desk and said, "Drink?"

"Yes, whisky, no water."

"I know what you drink."

Brendan poured them each a double, handed Simon one of the glasses and gestured toward the pair of couches that dominated the area in front of the fireplace. Simon faced the window and the view of the Kanata tech park that spread out beneath them. The sunlight pouring into the office from behind Brendan cast his face in shadows, making his expression more difficult to read. Simon was sure that was deliberate, like most things Brendan did.

Simon decided to cut right to it. "June 10, 1995. What happened?"

"You know what happened. John and Eve Tarrant were murdered. I felt terrible about it. John was a pain in the ass but I knew how much Eve meant to you."

"But that didn't stop you from killing her."

"I've never killed anyone in my life, Simon. God's truth."

"No, you had Polanco do it for you, didn't you?"

Brendan leaned forward, hands on knees and head bowed. Then he sighed and said, "It was all a terrible mistake. I told Polanco to take care of the problem. I thought he'd just put a scare into them. You remember that patent suit Tarrant threatened. It would have been crippling, for both of us. Polanco was a serving police officer at the time. I never for a minute thought that he'd go so far over the line."

"Well he did, didn't he?"

"Yes. I was shocked, horrified by what he had done, but I couldn't bring them back. I had to consider the best course to protect all of us. My first priority was to keep you out of it, Simon. I couldn't let you be dragged down by something that wasn't your fault and I realized that your connection with Eve could cast suspicion on you. So, I kept the information close. Only Polanco and I know what happened.

"We've had a kind of mutually assured destruction pact ever since. I helped Polanco get his investigation business started and I provide him with a significant annual retainer."

"Protection money."

"Protection for everyone."

Simon struggled to suppress his fury. Two innocent people killed, including a woman he had loved. And now Brendan had the gall to say that he covered it up to protect Simon. It was partly true, no doubt, but Brendan was protecting Brendan. Even now, he wouldn't admit that.

"Why didn't you tell me at the time?"

"I didn't want to implicate you. I wasn't sure how thoroughly Polanco had covered his tracks. If someone was going to go down, it would have been me, not you."

"How could you work with me every day, keeping this secret?"

"It wasn't easy, but what choice did I have? Once the decision was made, there was no reason to go back."

"No reason? How about the fact that our friendship has been based on a lie for more than 25 years?"

Brendan raised his hands in a placating gesture, then said, "Let's not allow this to define us, Simon. We've had so many good years together."

Simon shook his head in disgust.

"You've always been more than a friend to me, Simon. Remember Cambridge, the times we had together?"

"Don't you dare bring that up now. That was youthful experimentation on my part. I'm not homosexual Brendan and I've never loved you in that way. We've discussed this."

"It was real at the time and I've never stopped loving you."

Simon had hoped that Brendan wouldn't play that card. As a young man, he wanted to explore every aspect of his sexuality, no boundaries. Then Margaret came along. It hadn't taken him long to decide which team he was on.

"I understand your feelings, but let's get to the point. What are we going to do about the mess you've gotten us into?"

Brendan's eyes brightened when Simon used the word "we."

"So you've come to help?"

"Certainly." He just wasn't prepared yet to specify who he would be helping or in what way.

"As I analyse it, there are three dimensions to the problem," Brendan said, back in charge now. "First, Alicia. She knows far too much and has to be dealt with. Out of curiosity, did you know who she was when you married her?"

"Absolutely not. I was shocked, taken completely by surprise when she finally revealed her identity. And get this, she thought I might be her father."

"Good lord. You're not, I assume."

"No, but she demanded a DNA test done to prove it."

"She's devious, like a snake that's trying to slither between us."

"And the rest of the problem?"

"Polanco. His own jeopardy has always kept him in check, but if there is any chance that all of this is going to unravel, then I worry about him saving his own skin at the expense of ours. I think it's time to eliminate that possibility."

"Agreed."

"Finally, there is the issue of my money. I hesitate to even mention it, given everything, but what has become of it?"

"She cashed it out," Simon lied.

"Cashed it out? What gave her the right to do that?"

"The documents we both signed when the corporation was established, the ones you probably didn't read, gave her the title of chief financial officer with the authority to sign off on any transaction."

"Fuck! That's a shitload of money," Brendan said, as Simon

wondered yet again how his value compared to that of the lost money. If Brendan bought into his scheme, it wouldn't matter. He'd think he could have both.

"More than 200 pounds of money, when taken in hundreds. Don't worry. I know where she has it."

"Excellent," Brendan said, grinning. "You're free and you can retrieve the money. That takes away her leverage."

"Not quite. I said I knew where it was, not that I could get it. She's rented a storage locker in one of those Dymon buildings. Security cameras all around and I don't have the keys."

Brendan nodded, then said, "If she were deceased, that problem would be solved."

"I suppose it would, but that brings us back to the most difficult part of the equation. It's even more challenging than you might think."

"How so?"

"I have made myself friendly with Kris Redner and her daughter the investigator, Jenna Martin. They know far, far too much about what went on. If we eliminate only Alicia and Polanco, they will point straight to us. We need to take care of all four of them."

"That doesn't surprise me, and I have to agree with your conclusion. When this is over, only you and I can know what happened. What does surprise me, Simon, is that you are willing to do this. Always more the lover than the fighter, I would have thought."

"Yes, but what choice do I have now? Alicia and the others constitute an existential threat. We have to eliminate that threat, for our mutual survival."

"I hope you're going to tell me that you have a plan to do just that."

"I do, and I think you're going to like it."

Brendan sat back in the couch, relaxing for the first time since Simon had come through the door. "Those are the magic words," he said. "I'm looking forward to this Simon. It's going to be just like old times."

 # Forty-two

When Simon called suggesting they meet, Alicia had been deliberately cool, no wifely relief at his reappearance. He would expect her to be royally pissed and she was. It was no act. Her revenge on Brendan and Polanco had been meticulously planned, a complex scheme that took years to organize and execute. Sure, there had been some surprises and she had to adapt, but that was to be expected. When she had explained it all to Simon, an enormous act of trust, he had rewarded her by taking off to think his deep thoughts, then he came back with his own way of doing it. She hadn't taken him for a typical man, but perhaps she had been wrong. Clearly, he wasn't going to be content unless he organized and directed everything.

He had been contrite and apologetic in his late afternoon call, but she wasn't buying it. She could hear the excitement in his voice. He was never happier than when he was the man in charge, whether it was in the bedroom or the boardroom.

Well, let him think he was the boss, then. She could work with it. As long as Polanco and Brendan ended up dead, her own plan would be a success.

Alicia had suggested that they meet at their house. The familiar surroundings would put Simon at ease. Besides, she needed to check in on Rex. Jill Collins, the retired architect who lived next door, had been coming in to feed and walk him. She'd have to remember to send her a bottle of wine as a thank you, a good red. Since her husband Aaron died, Jill had been consuming wine at an impressive pace. Maybe she should make it a case.

Alicia settled back in her favourite armchair, the recliner with a pattern of grey and gold pussy willows on a white background. She reached down to scratch Rex's ears and the big Bernese sighed contentedly. Dogs were easy to please. Maybe they were the ones who had life all figured out.

Looking up at the soaring, two-storey ceiling of what Simon called the great room, Alicia thought again about how eager she was to get out of this place, once this was all over. The house was so large and had so many rooms that served only a vague purpose that it always felt more like a public space than a real home. She'd be looking for something much smaller, maybe on top of a hill where you had a chance of seeing trouble coming before it got there.

She looked at her watch, a Patek Philippe that had been a gift from Simon. She had told him to come for six, so that they could have a drink before dinner. She'd ordered delivery from their favourite Indian place in Kanata.

He'd better not be late. She could use a drink right now, something a lot stiffer than the sweetish Viognier she would serve with the Indian. She didn't want to be drinking before he got there, though. That would make it look like she needed to drink, that she was nervous. It was true, but she needed to appear completely confident and under control.

Then she heard the sound of a car in the driveway. Rex got up, ran to the window and barked. She could see the white Mercedes, top down and Simon in the driver's seat wearing one of his scruffy old ball caps. Despite herself, Alicia felt a little surge of relief at seeing him again. Developing real feelings for him had never been part of her plan, but it had happened anyway. She brushed the thought quickly from her mind. This was a business meeting, not a lovers' reunion.

Simon came in the front door and Rex ran eagerly to him, jumping up and delivering a dog's version of a hug. Simon looked freshly showered and wore khakis and a navy golf shirt. She was surprised to see his short white beard. She liked a beard on a man, but only if it wasn't long enough to make him look like a hillbilly.

"Good boy, Rex. So glad to see you again," Simon said, bending down and stroking the dog's fur and rubbing his ears. "You missed me, eh?"

Alicia wondered who Simon had missed the most, her or the dog. She suspected she knew the answer, but it didn't matter now. She got out of her chair and walked into the foyer wearing a thin smile and a short, red summer dress that she knew Simon liked. It was a deliberately mixed message. Look what you were missing, but you're not off the hook yet.

"Alicia," Simon said, smiling. He seemed uncertain whether to reach out and hug her or to shake her hand. Alicia crossed her arms across her chest in answer.

"Well, the wayward husband returns. I hear from other people that you've solved all of my problems."

"Let's have a drink, shall we?" Simon said.

"Sure," Alicia said, turning and heading back to the great room. She poured him his customary 10-year-old Ardberg. Not a scotch drinker herself, Alicia chose a generous glass of Limoncello. Before handing Simon his drink, she sipped hers, appreciating the immediate jet fuel burn of the Italian lemon liqueur.

"I've ordered from the Taj for 6:30."

"Splendid. My favourite. Very thoughtful of you."

"Don't butter me up. It won't do you any good."

"No, of course not. I know my behaviour has been inexcusable, but there's a good reason for what I've done and I think you're going to like the results."

Alicia settled back in her chair and Simon took the matching one opposite. Rex had deserted her, slumping at Simon's feet.

"So where *have* you been all this time?"

"I own a small island in the Ottawa River, just across from my cousin's place north of Arnprior. It's just a cabin, but I knew no one would disturb me there."

"An island in the river? Why didn't I know that you owned an island?"

"We all have our secrets, don't we?"

Alicia nodded, conceding the point. "With this flooding going on, that must have been challenging," she said.

"Not if you have a proper boat and know how to run it."

"So I assume no cell phone coverage, then. That must be the reason why I haven't heard from you for all this time."

"That's partly correct, and why I left my cell phone behind. The main reason I haven't communicated is because I just had to think. The plan that you described to me left me uneasy, but I didn't immediately see a better way to achieve your goal. Brendan and Polanco need to be punished, severely punished, for what they did, but killing them would make you no better than they were."

"Hah! They were killing for money and greed. I want justice."

"Not to go over old ground, but we don't live in a society that tolerates vigilante justice. You'd end up in prison."

"Maybe, but that's a risk I am willing to take. After all, Brendan and Polanco killed two people and got away with it for a long, long time. I think I can safely say that I'm smarter than either of them."

Simon allowed himself a small smile and said, "I wouldn't dispute that."

"Nevertheless, you must be smarter still, because you think you have a better solution to the problem and I understand you've already put it in motion."

"A different solution," he said, gently. "Nothing will be in motion until you agree. I only spoke to Kris and Jenna to see if I could count on their support. That's critical."

"Kris and Jenna, is it? Do you have your eye on one of them, or maybe both?"

"Come on, Alicia. Don't play the jealous wife. It doesn't suit you and it's not fair, considering that our marriage was a fraud, perpetrated by you."

Alicia had to concede that point, but it wasn't the whole story. "It was, yes, initially. I couldn't assume that you were not involved in my parents' deaths. Once I got to know you and to know Brendan, I understood what kind of man you are. That's why I trusted you with the details of my plan. I didn't have to."

"'I get that. I felt that I could achieve the retribution you wanted, but also protect you. I just needed to work out how."

"And now you have."

"Yes, but you will have to agree, of course."

Although she was already aware of the main points of the plan, thanks to Jenna, Alicia said, "Let's hear it, then, and it had better be good."

Simon had described his scheme in some detail by the time the doorbell rang. It was the delivery person. Alicia accepted the bag of food and handed the man a $20 tip. As she passed by the great room, she said, "Let's eat in the kitchen." She loathed the dining room and all its pretensions, including a table that could seat 20.

Alicia laid the food containers on the kitchen table as Simon got out plates and poured glasses of water. It was a brief moment of the sort of domesticity they might have achieved, had everything been different.

"Let's say I agree to this plan, when will it happen?"

"Tomorrow. I want to get everyone up to the island, film the video and get Brendan and Polanco there promptly. I have already wired the cabin for video and audio. We will have their confessions to give to the police."

That wasn't enough, not nearly enough, but maybe it would have to do. At the very least, it was a backup plan, but if circumstances presented an opportunity to do more, Alicia intended to take it.

"One last thing," she said. "Brendan. Does he already know about this?"

"Of course not, but he's going to like it. It solves all his problems. He will rush like a minnow into a trap."

Alicia was quite sure there would be a trap and a minnow, but maybe not exactly the ones Simon anticipated.

Forty-three

Friday had dawned cold, wet and miserable. Now at 10 a.m., rain was falling so hard that I couldn't even make out the far shore of the Ottawa River on the Quebec side. I could see several islands on the broad expanse of the river in front of Rob Cousens's place, but they were murky, indistinct humps. The river was still flooded from the record spring rains, and even though it was deep and broad here, pieces of trees torn from the banks upriver floated by at an incredible speed. Fall into that current and even the strongest swimmer wouldn't have a chance.

Jenna and I both wore yellow Eddie Bauer rain jackets and waterproof hiking boots, but our jeans were already soaked. Alicia was the only one who came properly prepared, in a full black rain suit and rubber boots, hood pulled up and tied tight. Simon wore a Tilley hat and an old denim jacket. He seemed not to notice the rain.

The four of us stood on the slippery plank dock, waiting while Rob readied the boat in the adjoining boat house, a swaybacked structure of bare wood that had slumped down into the river over the years.

"Which island is yours?" I asked Simon.

"It's the big one to the left. The view is partly blocked by a smaller island in front of it. Cousens Island, that's mine. It's half a mile long. You'll see better when we get close to it."

"Cousens Island? You named it after yourself?"

"No, it has always been called that. I bought it from a Pennsylvania couple about 20 years ago, but it was in my family for generations before the American bought it. I thought it should be again, so when it came up for sale, I picked it up."

"How long is this going to take?" Alicia asked.

"Which part?"

"Getting the bloody boat ready, for a start."

"Just a few more minutes, then it's about 10 minutes across to the island."

Alicia had seemed tense and irritable on the drive up. She had insisted that we all come in her Lexus and she had driven but she'd barely exchanged a word with Simon in the front seat and hadn't said anything at all to Jenna and me in the back.

I understood how she felt. Alicia had devoted most of her life to taking revenge on Brendan and Polanco. Now the moment was here and she was no longer in charge. Simon was. Or so it seemed. I still wasn't sure if the two of them were working together or if they each had their own agenda. Either way, Jenna and I were props in the drama Simon planned to stage once we got to the island. I wasn't happy with that, not at all. We had our own backup plan. I just hoped that it would work if we needed it.

I heard a deep rumbling, then saw a mahogany cruiser back out of the boat house. I knew a bit about these kinds of boats from hanging out with my grandfather, who had been a fishing guide in the Adirondacks. Rich people used them on the mountain lakes back in the day. Most of them were made in the '50s and '60s and were powerful, beautiful and expensive. Rain beaded on the shiny hull as Rob manoeuvred the big, automobile-type steering wheel so that the boat would point bow first into the river.

Rob let the current pin the boat against the dock, just ahead of a pontoon boat that was tarped over like it hadn't been used yet this season. Rob threw two heavy ropes up, one for each end of the boat. As Rob zipped up his camouflage raincoat, Simon took the bow rope and I took the stern, then tied it to a heavy metal ring using a slip knot.

"Beautiful boat," I said.

"It's a 1956 Grew Jolly Giant, very rare," Simon said. "Twenty-three feet long with a 225-horse Fireball V6. Do you know boats?"

"A little," I said. The boat I knew best had been my grandfather's battered 14-foot aluminum with a 6-horse Sears motor. I decided not to trade boat stories with Simon.

"I had it fully restored. It's quite a pleasant ride, very solid. Just what we need in this kind of current."

"Can we save the boat talk for later?" Alicia said. "I'd like to get out of the rain."

"Of course," Simon said, holding Alicia's hand as she stepped down into the boat. I got in, then looked back at Jenna.

"I've never been in a small boat," she said.

"Really?"

"Funny, none of my foster parents were into boating."

I felt stupid when she said it. Boats had been a regular part of my life when I was young, but that was just one of many things I hadn't passed on to Jenna.

"Nothing to worry about," Simon said. "Safe as can be."

Jenna stepped in beside me and squeezed in between me and Alicia on the broad back seat. Its green vinyl was covered with water, but my ass was already wet. Simon cast off then got into the front passenger seat beside Rob and we were off.

It might have been a nice trip on a sunny day, but the wind was gusting, making the already choppy water unpredictable. Rob seemed to know what he was doing, but a few rogue waves still came splashing over the bow. The boat's small windshield deflected them up and into our faces. We were running across the current and Rob had to continually adjust the wheel to keep us pointed at the island.

In the front, Rob and Simon exchanged no words but they exuded the relaxed familiarity of two men who had worked together for a long time and knew each other's moves. There was certainly more to their relationship than Rob had let on when Jenna and I had interviewed him on his patio. I had suspected as much at the time. While Simon's first refuge had been with Margaret, he had spent most of his unaccounted time on the island, we had since learned. It was clear that Rob was the one he trusted most. The question was, could *we* trust Rob? He seemed like a decent, straightforward guy, but he was on Simon's team, not ours.

Our team consisted of Darcy and possibly some other guys I had never met. When I had told Darcy last night what the setup would be, he had immediately thought of his friend Pierre Groulx, an old buddy from junior who had played 10 years in Detroit and used some of the money to build himself a nice cottage only a couple of miles upriver from Simon's island. Darcy had quickly packed some things he said he'd need, then headed up to Pierre's place. He assured me that he could get a couple more guys to help and they'd work out a plan, probably to land on a nearby island and keep the cottage under surveillance with binoculars.

It wasn't terrifically reassuring. I didn't know exactly where

Darcy would be and I wasn't sure I would be able to contact him. I had my phone with me, and so did he, but cell coverage was spotty and I anticipated that I'd be tied to a chair. If something went south, it would happen fast, almost certainly before Darcy could come to the rescue. And even if he got there, I was worried about him. Polanco would be armed and I was sure he wouldn't be alone. Darcy didn't say whether he would bring a gun and I didn't ask, but either way, he'd be putting his life on the line if he had to try to rescue us. I hoped it wouldn't come to that.

As we passed the small island in front of Simon's, I hoped it might be where Darcy and his friends had set up. I searched the shoreline, trying to catch sight of a boat, but the rain made visibility too poor. That was good, in a way. If I couldn't see Darcy's boat, neither could Simon and Rob, or more important, Brendan and Polanco.

I remembered that I didn't even know if Darcy's plan had come together. Jenna and I could be on our own out here. It was best to assume that we were.

Rob slowed the boat as we approached the narrow lee side of the island. The current was visibly slower here, but the dark water still frothed and churned with debris, including several dead fish. I could just make out the lights of a cabin in the woods, maybe 100 feet from the shore. So Rob had already set things up. I hadn't expected that.

Jenna leaned close to me and whispered, "Something's going to go wrong. I can sense it."

"Maybe it already has," I said.

# Forty-four

As Rob tied the boat to the dock, we all scrambled out and ran for the cabin. I wasn't sure what the urgency was, since Jenna and I were already as wet as we could be and Alicia was dry in her rain suit. I supposed getting out of the rain was an instinct that went back as far as people did.

Simon led the way, getting to the porch first, then swinging open the door. The cabin was fairly large, maybe 30 feet by 50, and everything that a real cottage should be. The walls were made of big pine logs and the ceiling was open to the rafters. The walls were covered with fish on wooden plaques and stuffed ducks meant to look like they were in flight. A buck's head was mounted over the cobblestone fireplace, but the welcome warmth came from a potbellied woodstove in the centre of the cabin that was sending off heat in waves. Jenna and I got as close as we could. The heat wouldn't dry us off any time soon, but at least it would stop the shivering.

The feeling of cosiness and familiarity was offset by the three pressed-back wooden chairs that were lined up facing a small video camera on a tripod, all arranged to create the illusion that would draw Brendan in.

"Can I get anyone coffee before we start?" Simon asked. "There's a pot already brewed."

Jenna and I accepted, but Alicia declined. We peeled off our dripping rain jackets and hung them on pegs by the front door. Alicia took a little longer to remove her rain jacket, pants and boots. Underneath, she was wearing a black button-up shirt of the outdoorsy hiking kind, and black jeans.

The coffee was dark, strong and welcome. I sipped from a white mug as Simon explained how his little drama was going to work.

"This has to look authentic to Brendan and Polanco. If there is the slightest clue that what they are seeing is fake, they will spook. I want him to buy my story that Alicia has kept me in captivity with the goal of drawing them here to the island to kill them, but thanks to Rob, I have gained the upper hand. I have the three of you under my control, and I want him and Polanco to come here and eliminate the problem for good."

I reached out and squeezed Jenna's hand. I knew she would be thinking back to being tied to a chair by another man in another cabin and how all that turned out. She looked at me and nodded, then said, "I'm solid."

"So you will need some acting from us," I said.

"Yes, you will need to look like you've been overpowered. Now you're distraught, afraid, betrayed and fearful for your lives. A few tears wouldn't be amiss."

Jenna snorted at that and said, "Not fucking likely." Then Alicia chimed in with "Not really my style, either."

"Well, do your best. Remember that this will only take a few minutes, then you will be untied and we can all relax until it's time for Brendan and Polanco to arrive. Then we need to restage the scene.

"So, if I could ask you to take your places, Alicia in the centre please."

I put down my mug of coffee and took the chair to Alicia's right. Simon's wild-assed idea had better work. I had to confess I didn't have a better way to neutralize the threat that Brendan and Polanco posed.

"Rob, would you tie them up please?"

Rob pulled three lengths of thick white rope from a black duffel bag sitting on the kitchen counter. The rope was heavy enough to restrain a horse, but I supposed it would contribute to the tied-up effect Simon was shooting for.

"Arms behind your backs ladies, please," Rob said. One by one, we complied and he wrapped several loops around me and Alicia. When he got to Jenna, he started to do the same, then patted her jacket down near her waist, reached in and pulled out a small revolver.

"That's mine," Alicia said.

"Well, I'd better hang on to it for safe keeping. Just in case Polanco frisks you," Rob said. Simon gave Alicia a surprised look, then Jenna nodded her assent and Rob roped her up. When he was done, the scene reminded me of the way women looked tied to the train tracks in those old silent movies. The only thing that was missing was a moustachioed villain in a top hat.

"All right, this looks very good," Simon said, fiddling with the camera. "Remember there is going to be sound with this video. I'm not going to script what you say. Keep it natural. Imagine that Rob and I have seized control of the situation. There has been a struggle. You've fought your hardest but we overcame you. You feel angry, betrayed."

I looked at Jenna and smiled. The odds of a couple of older guys overwhelming the three of us weren't great. Not unless there was a gun in play, and even then.

Simon saw the expressions on our faces and said, "The only problem is that you all look remarkably calm, like you've just dropped by for tea. It's not remotely convincing."

"We can glare at you, if it helps," Jenna said.

"No, I have another idea and I apologize in advance. Rob?"

Rob stepped in front of us, gave an "I'm sorry" shrug and then slapped me across the face with a hard, meaty hand. My head snapped to the left, my face stung and burned. "What the fuck?" I blurted out, just as Rob gave me the back of his hand, whipped my head in the other direction. The force of the blows brought tears to my eyes.

"Hey, this wasn't the deal," Jenna shouted. Although tied to the chair, she got awkwardly to her feet, to come to my aid. Rob put both hands on her shoulders and forced her back down, then delivered two heavy slaps to her face. "You bastard!" Jenna shouted.

Rob stepped in front of Alicia, who fixed him with a ferocious stare. "Simon, get this under control," she snapped.

"I'm afraid it is under control," he said.

Rob reached to give Alicia the same treatment Jenna and I had received, but Alicia reared back. Instead of slapping her face, his hand connected with her nose. Blood immediately flowed from her nostrils, over her mouth and down her chin. He grasped the front of her shirt and ripped it open, the buttons popping until they were stopped by the heavy rope.

"Sorry," Rob said, looking like he might even mean it. Then he stepped back and I saw the red light on the camera turn on. Simon was filming.

"You double-crossing bastard!" Alicia shouted. "I knew I should never have trusted you. You're going to kill us, aren't you?"

If it was a performance, it was heartfelt. I had the sinking feeling that it was the truth. How could we have been so stupid?

 # Forty-five

Brendan Connor eyed the surging river with alarm. He was neither a boat person nor a swimmer and this water looked like it was being shot out of a fire hose. No, a thousand fire hoses.

"Are you sure this is safe, Paul?"

"We'll be safe enough on the pontoon boat. It will be slow but stable. It would take an ocean wave to capsize it."

Brendan immediately visualized tall ocean waves tipping over the clumsy-looking boat. After having seen The Perfect Storm years ago, he had vowed never to go on the water again.

"How far is it?"

"About half-way across. You can see it from here. Big, humpy island."

Brendan stared into the driving rain. All he could see was a series of grey, menacing shapes barely visible under clouds so low they looked like you could reach up and touch them.

"And your men, they are in place?"

"Yes, they've been on the island since last night."

Polanco had gone over all of this repeatedly, but Brendan needed his hand held. Polanco would be surprised if the big talker could get through what lay ahead without pissing himself. At least Brendan wouldn't have to worry about the trip back. His was going to be a one-way journey.

He would take care of the women first. Once they were in the water, nature would take its course. After the pounding their bodies would take on the journey down the river, there would be no meaningful evidence. If he was lucky, they'd never be heard from again.

Then Straczynski and Peters would step in, finish the job. They were both former police tactical officers, the best employees he had. They had been reluctant to undertake the mission, but once he offered them six figures for the work, they'd come around.

Brendan pulled his hood down as far as it would go and watched

Polanco pull the tarp off the boat, doing whatever was necessary to get it ready. The guy seemed relaxed. Far too relaxed. He had something up his sleeve. Brendan sensed it. The fact that Polanco had men on the island worried him. Why were they necessary? The way Simon had it planned, the women would be helpless. Polanco would eliminate them, then Simon's cousin would eliminate Polanco. That was the plan: Simon had assured him the fellow was up to it.

Then the cousin would clean things up and Brendan and Simon would leave the island. They'd be free for the first time in decades. Maybe things would even go back to normal.

Brendan felt his phone vibrate in his pocket and pulled it out. It was an email from Simon. It consisted of a single word_ Ready. There was an attachment which he clicked on, then waited in frustration as it slowly downloaded. Typical poor rural connection.

Finally, a video came up and Brendan pressed play. It was short, but satisfactory. The two troublesome investigators were securely tied to chairs, their faces red like they'd been beaten. The centrepiece, the glorious centrepiece, was that bitch Alicia, shirt torn open and blood running down her face and onto her chest. Brendan's nostrils flared in anticipation of what lay ahead. His only heterosexual satisfaction came from inflicting pain on women, but he'd assumed that Simon wouldn't allow it. It looked like he had been wrong. Alicia would need to be punished, severely punished, before she went to her fate. She had caused so much grief for both of them and nearly torn them apart. That was unforgiveable.

"Is that it?" Polanco asked.

"'Yes, we're set. You want to take a look? You will enjoy this."

Brendan handed Polanco the phone and watched as the investigator viewed the short video, then watched it again. "As promised," he said. "Good work. Too bad they didn't give that bitch Jenna Martin the same treatment. I owe her one. No, make that two. You have no objection to my evening the score, I assume?"

"None at all. We're not in a particular rush."

Let him die happy, Brendan thought. Why not? Brendan knew that he could be cruel, but only when it served a purpose, either business or pleasure. If Polanco wanted to put on a show, he'd be content to watch. Just not for too long. The sooner he and Simon got off this river and back to safety, the happier he'd be.

 # Forty-six

"Let us go!" Alicia demanded, her voice a shriek of fury.

"I know that was the plan," Simon said, "but Brendan and Polanco aren't far away. We wouldn't have the time to release you and then restage the scene. I can't be sure how quickly they might get here."

"Not far away?" I said. "You mean you tipped them off as to where this was going to take place?"

"I thought it would expedite things. They're going to come here anyway. Let's get it over with. I really am sorry about the way this had to play out, but they're both cunning bastards. If they smell a trap, we lose our opportunity.

"Rob, can you get a clean cloth and some ice for Alicia's nose?"

I looked at Jenna. Her mouth was a taut line and I could see the tension in her arms. This was an eventuality for which we had not planned. Darcy and his friends should be on the nearest island, but we had no way to signal him to tell him we were in trouble.

How had I misjudged Simon so badly? I wouldn't say I had trusted him, exactly, but I didn't see him conspiring with Brendan, although it sure looked like it now. Why else tell him in advance where the action was going to go down? Then I had a worse thought. The advance notice would have given Polanco enough time to station additional men on the island. Not only did we not know just what Brendan and Simon had planned, we didn't even know how many we were up against.

Maybe, just maybe, I was jumping to conclusions. Simon seemed remarkably calm, nothing like a man who was about to contribute to a triple homicide. Rob was similarly calm, whistling as he added a bit of wood to the potbellied stove. I had taken Rob for a nice, simple Valley boy. It had been a shock when he slapped Jenna and me, then broke Alicia's nose.

Family was a lifetime bond that ran deep. I should have known that better than most. Maybe Rob's simplicity boiled down to knowing that Simon was in trouble and needed his help. Nothing else would matter if that was it.

"Look, Simon," I said, "we could use a bit of reassurance here. Things aren't going as we expected and we're sitting here helpless waiting for two guys who want to kill us. Surely you understand how that must make us feel."

"I do," he said, with apparent sincerity. "I'm afraid it can't be helped. Remember, our goal here is to get Brendan and Polanco to confess what they did all those years ago, so we can take it to the police and get justice for Alicia and her parents, at last.

"I have installed multiple cameras in the cabin. Everything those two say and do will be recorded. The five of us could overpower them, force a confession, but it wouldn't be admissible in court if it was given under duress. I want them to boast about what they've done. That will finish them with any judge or jury."

It made a certain amount of sense, I had to admit, but I still felt like bait in a trap.

"That's exactly what you'd say if you and your cousin plan to join Brendan and Polanco in killing us, end all of your problems," Jenna said.

Simon nodded thoughtfully and said, "I suppose you're right. It is what I would say. You're just going to have to trust me. Once we've got what we need, it will be Brendan and Polanco tied to those chairs, not you."

"And how are you going to accomplish that?" Alicia asked, her tone as sharp as a knife. "Two old men aren't going to take Paul Polanco. He's a ruthless killer."

Rob pulled aside the heavy plaid shirt that hung over his jeans and revealed the grip of the handgun he had taken from Alicia. "Don't worry. I've got a little surprise for him."

"Fuck, you think Polanco won't be armed and wary? For all we know, he intends to take out the lot of us, Brendan included. Brilliant play to tip them to where this was taking place, Simon. How do you know Polanco doesn't have backup on the island? They could be watching us right now."

A small shadow of worry moved across Simon's face as he looked at Rob, but then he said, "Don't waste your time on what ifs and conspiracies, Alicia. Things aren't playing out exactly as you hoped, but I know Brendan. He's going to believe what he sees because he wants to believe it. He's a coward, too. No threat to you. I'm aware that Polanco is a wild card. I'm also aware that he killed your mother, a woman I once loved. I can't say that I want Polanco dead as badly as you do, but I won't shed a tear if that's the way it turns out. Brendan is another matter. He needs to face appropriate justice."

"Hah! Appropriate justice," Alicia said. "That would be a bullet between the eyes. The same thing he ordered for my parents. The slimy little shit is behind everything that happened. He ruined my life."

"And now we'll ruin his."

Alicia looked him up and down, contempt obvious on her face. Then she expelled a projectile of spit and blood that fell on Simon's right shoe. He looked calmly down, took out a handkerchief and wiped up the mess.

"Save your fury for the right person," he said. "Your moment is coming."

Alicia's response was to scream. Then I joined her, Jenna close behind. I had only the faintest hope that Darcy would hear the screaming over the roar of the river, but it was better than no hope at all.

* * *

Brendan Connor clung to the railing of the pontoon boat, his knuckles white and head down, trying to keep the worst of the rain and spray from his face. The boat wallowed awkwardly as the current kept threatening to push it sideways. Polanco struggled to keep it heading toward the island. He had just assumed that Polanco knew what he was doing, but when had he ever been in a boat? He hoped to hell this wasn't his first time, because if so, it could be the last time for both of them.

Brendan understood why Simon had chosen the island. It was under his control, there would be no witnesses and the bodies could be disposed of easily. All well and good, but first he had to get there.

"Hold on," Polanco shouted, then he hauled the wheel to the left. Brendan looked up and saw a whole bloody tree, the current propelling it straight at them. Although Brendan had turned the wheel hard, the boat was about as responsive as a garbage scow. Brendan scrambled away from the railing and went to his knees, clinging to the base of one of the central seats.

The boat's right-hand pontoon lifted up out of the water as it rode over the trunk of the tree, scraping against its branches. For just a moment the boat hung up on the tree, losing forward momentum and starting to move down river with the tree. Then the boat broke free from the clinging branches, crashed back into the water and slowly turned its bow into the onrushing current.

"You can get up off your knees," Polanco said. "We're only 150 feet off shore now."

Brendan got to his feet, his legs wobbly. "Must have slipped," he said.

"Right. Just stay still while I guide us in."

The boat was now behind the island, which blocked the force of the current. It was still strong, but not as aggressive as it had been in the main stream of the river.

As they edged closer to the dock, Brendan saw Simon's fancy old wooden cruiser. He remembered once, it had to be 15 years ago, Simon had taken him up to this spot to show off his boat. He'd even offered Brendan a ride. Declining had been a smart move, he could see now.

Once they were 30 feet from the dock, Brendan began to feel more confident. He straightened up and remembered that he had to project the air of a man in charge. Then he heard something over the thrumming roar of the river. It was women, screaming. He felt a little jolt of adrenalin. Simon must have started without him. Brendan hoped he wasn't going to be too late for the fun. He was looking forward to seeing Alicia Jameson die.

Forty-seven

Darcy parted the branches of the blind they had created on the island next to Simon's. All he could see was wind-driven rain and the grey outline of the island 200 feet away. His directions from Kris had been frustratingly vague. He was to get as close as he could, then stay in place until he saw a boat heading toward the island. That would be Connor and his thug Polanco. Then he was to get close to the cottage as quickly as possible.

His only knowledge of the terrain came from a Google maps aerial view. He had been tempted to land on Simon Cousens's island itself, get close to the cottage, but Kris had been afraid of spooking Cousens, so instead Darcy had chosen the nearest island, an uninhabited hump of rock and scruffy trees that offered just enough cover to keep them hidden. They had pulled his 14-foot aluminum up on shore and hidden it behind some bushes. He was confident that no one on the island could see them, but he couldn't see much on the other side, either.

He and his two men had been in place since dawn and they were cold, cramped and wet. Kris said she had no idea what time it would all go down. It all depended on Connor and when he decided to show up.

Darcy didn't like anything about the situation. All he knew was that Jenna and Kris were in that cabin. He'd seen that much when they'd pulled up in Cousens's fancy boat, along with another guy and Cousens's wife Alicia. Everyone seemed calm and he didn't see any weapons or suggestion of force.

The deal was supposed to be that they would set up this fake kidnapping scenario, then send a video to Connor. When that was done, Kris had told him she'd step out onto the dock and stretch her arms in front of her as a sign that everything had gone OK. Surely enough time had gone by to shoot that video. It wasn't a feature-length film. And yet, no Kris. That was a worry that was getting larger by the minute.

Darcy was getting pretty close to saying fuck it and heading over the island when he thought he heard something, a high pitched sound muffled by the roar of the river.

He leaned close to Pierre Groulx and said, "Did you hear that? Sounds like women screaming."

Groulx cocked his head, his ear turned towards the island. The former NHL defenceman wore a camo rain jacket stretched across his massive shoulders. His curly hair pushed out from under his green cap and his thick black beard glistened with rain. Darcy and Pierre had been friends since they were teenagers. When Darcy was looking for good men for his log home company, he'd asked Groulx to come in as a partner.

Groulx hadn't hesitated when Darcy had asked for his help with today's wild-assed adventure. The guy was rock solid. He wasn't quite as sure about Kevin Lamont, one of the carpenters from his crew. He knew Kevin had been in a few bar fights, because he'd been the one who'd bailed him out. How he'd stand up today was an open question. At least Lamont had some size. He was six foot six, but wiry. It was the best Darcy could do at short notice.

"I'm not hearing it," Groulx said, "but look at that."

He pointed to a pontoon boat lurching its way upriver toward the island. A big guy in a black rain suit was at the wheel and another man was covering on his knees in the middle of the boat.

"That's the company we've been expecting. Kevin, get the boat ready. As soon as they head into the cabin, we will cut across up island, land and then approach the cabin. You guys remember what I said. We're here to resolve this problem with a show of strength, not kill anyone."

Darcy could have brought a shotgun or a rifle and now he was wishing he had. Instead, he and Lamont were to be one anyway, and he'd be the guy without a gun in his hand.

Groulx picked up the big axe he had brought and grinned. "Don't worry," he said, "when these guys see an ugly fucker like me swinging an axe, they're going to shit their pants."

Yeah, Darcy thought, unless the other guys had guns and it seemed almost certain that they would. Kris had been adamant that she didn't want to risk a shootout. Now, Darcy feared that there was going to be one anyway and he'd be the guy without a gun in his hand.

He listened again for what he had taken to be screaming, but heard only the sound of the whistling between the two islands.

* * *

Brendan Connor stepped onto the dock. The wet grey planks were slippery from the rain but they felt like heaven after slopping around on that ungainly boat. He didn't want to think about the trip back He made an effort to keep his gait steady, confident. He needed to reassert his dominance over Polanco, to recoup from the poor decision of cowering on his knees in that bloody boat.

"How do you want to play it when we get in there?" Polanco asked.

"Let's make the most of the opportunity. I have a score to settle with Alicia and I'm sure you want to square things with Jenna Martin," mentioning it to remind Polanco that he wasn't so tough, having been taken twice by a woman.

Polanco gave him the stink eye, but said, "Fine. What about the other one, the newspaper writer?"

"She can watch her cub die. That's what will make her day special. Unfortunately, she won't have a lot of time to dwell on it."

As they stepped up the mossy path, Brendan spotted Simon's cabin, a wood-sided structure set up a slight rise. Warm light glowed from within, but he was sure the three women weren't finding it cosy.

Brendan let Polanco swing open the door and enter first, just in case there was any kind of surprise. Seeing no trouble, he followed. The scene in front of him was exceptionally pleasing. The nosy reporter was tied to a chair, her face red like she'd been slapped around good. Or maybe it was fury. She'd stumbled into trouble she wasn't going to get out of. The daughter was firmly roped up, just like the rest. That was good. Of the three, she was the only potential threat. Then there was the centrepiece, Alicia Jameson, nose puffy, blood running down her face. It was a start, but he had far more planned for her. The gall of this woman, who thought she could interject herself into his life, then destroy it. Best of all, each of them had a broad piece of duct tape across their mouths. Alicia, shut up at last.

Simon and his cousin stood to one side by the wood stove. Brendan gave the three women his most pleasant smile, then turned to his old friend. "Simon, my god it's good to see you."

Simon stepped forward and said, "Likewise."

I had a sinking feeling as I watched the two old bastards hug. My sense that they had cooked this whole thing up together was overwhelming now. The last vestige of hope had disappeared when Simon duct taped our mouths shut. In his usual calming way, he had assured us it was only to make sure that we didn't interfere with his questioning of Brendan and Polanco, like he was the director, the man in charge.

And of course he was. Jenna, Alicia and I were only bit players at this point, but that didn't mean we had to just sit there and take it. I started to make all the noise I could muster with a strip of duct tape across my mouth.

"What's that? I can't hear you," Brendan said, a grin on his smug little face. "Don't worry. I'll take the tape off later, when I give you a chance to beg for your life."

I reminded myself that I had been up against people a lot tougher than Brendan Connor and come out on top, but no reasonable person would have liked the odds I faced right now. Where the hell was Darcy? I hadn't been able to go out and give him the signal that we had arranged, but surely he would have gotten into the game once he saw Polanco and Brendan approaching in the boat.

I had told him about Simon's plan to get the two of them to confess on tape. Maybe he was allowing time to let that play out. Right now, I'd place the odds of Simon being sincere at about 20 to 1. I knew he was a smooth-talking charmer and yet I'd let him charm me anyway. Stupid.

About the only positive thing I saw was that the camera Simon had set up in the ceiling was running. I could see its red light. Maybe that meant he was going to get the goods on Brendan, but even so, it might only be to hold it over him later or, worse, so they could both look back at this moment and share a good laugh.

"Brendan, why don't you tell Alicia the whole story," Simon said. "I'm sure she's figured out most of it for herself, but given the price she's going to pay, I think she's earned the truth."

"What's the harm?" Brendan replied. "Alicia, maybe you don't remember your father John. You were so young when I had him killed. He was quite a stickler for the rules, John was. One of my first employees, very clever engineer. I won't bore you with the details, but John had an insight into how to improve telephone switching systems quite early on. Simon and I saw the value in it and ran with the idea. Only later did we discover that John had begun the process of patenting his work. It was outrageous, of course. As his employers, we owned everything he did. John was stubborn, though. Claimed he'd had the idea before he came to work for us, even had a pile of paperwork to back up his contention.

"We could have gone to court, but it would be a messy, prolonged process that would have tanked our company just as we were about to launch an IPO. Once you get into court, anything can happen. Maybe John would have won.

"In any case, it was a business risk I couldn't afford. The only practical solution was to eliminate the problem. I asked Mr. Polanco here to take care of the problem. He was a police officer at the time, but a very flexible man with a good eye for an opportunity."

Brendan paced back and forth in front of us, like a TV lawyer summing up his case. The only difference was that he was describing his own guilt.

"It was unfortunate that we had to kill your mother, too. Eve was a lovely woman, and to make things more complicated, Simon had had a fling with her. I knew I couldn't bring him into the decision because he might let emotion cloud his judgment. So I took it all on myself. I've had to bear the burden of that all these years."

I looked at Alicia. Her body was taut as she strained against the ropes. Her eyes burned with some combination of anger, fear and hatred. This bastard had ordered her parents killed and now he was complaining that making the decision was a "burden."

"I did tell him to spare you. It seemed a safe decision, since you were only a child. Little did I know what a mistake it would turn out to be. You've created quite the challenge with what I'm sure you think is a quest for justice.

"Perhaps you've figured this out now, but there is very little justice in the world. It's survival of the fittest, and I'm afraid that you aren't the fittest, my dear. Paul, anything to add?"

Polanco turned to Jenna and said, "Thought you were pretty smart didn't you? Figured you could get one up on me because I had to play within the rules. That was your basic mistake. Too bad you had to drag your mother into this. I'm going to make you both very sorry that you didn't mind your own business, then you're going to go for a nice swim."

Jenna and I both stared straight ahead, trying to remain expressionless. So, the plan was to beat us, maybe torture us, then dump us in the river. Given the strength of the current, it probably wouldn't matter much if we were dead or alive at that point.

Polanco was looking for satisfaction, a make-good on the humiliation Jenna had given him. I was sure she was determined to deny him that, to the extent she could. I would follow suit.

Once again, I thought of Darcy. Where was he? What had happened? He only had a small boat. What if it had capsized?

"Simon, anything to add?" Brendan says.

"I think you've covered it all Brendan. I wish you'd come to me back then, but I'm glad I had the chance to help fix it now."

That was bad, very bad. Not at all what he should have been saying if he was playing straight with us. He had gotten what he needed to put Brendan and Polanco away. What was he doing?

"Why don't we take the tape off their mouths, let them each have a final say?" Simon said.

"I don't see any harm in that."

"Rob, remove the tape will you?"

Rob walked toward us and I tried to read his face. It was expressionless, like his mind was elsewhere. The man had to be fantastically loyal to Simon to get involved in this. He pulled the tape from my mouth, none too gently, then did the same to Alicia and Jenna.

"Simon, you lying bastard!" Alicia shouted. "You've been working with Brendan all along, haven't you?"

"You're right, Alicia. I am a lying bastard, but I haven't been lying to you."

Alicia's look said she didn't believe a word of that, but then Simon gestured toward Rob and said, "I think it's time we ended this little drama."

Then I heard two loud bangs, followed in quick succession by three more. Gunshots. Darcy, I thought, then remembered that I had told him not to bring a gun. Polanco must have men on the island. Darcy was dead. I knew it.

I struggled to my feet, the chair still holding my arms behind me, and rushed at Polanco as hard and fast as I could, screaming like a banshee.

 # Forty-eight

Darcy, Pierre and Kevin hit the ground, pressing themselves flat into the soft, wet, pine-needled surface of the forest floor. The shots had come from ahead of them in the direction of the cabin, but they couldn't see a thing, not even a faint hint of the shooters.

"Fuck, I wasn't bargaining on this," Kevin whispered.

"Don't worry, they weren't trying to shoot us," Darcy said. "The bullets went way over our heads. They just want to scare us off."

"They're doing a pretty good job."

"If it's too hairy for you, kid, head back to the boat and wait for us," Pierre said, then added, "What's the plan, Darcy?"

"I've got an idea," Darcy said. "Kevin, you flank them to the left, Pierre to the right. They can't be far in front of us. Give them a wide berth, then try to get up behind them. I'll give you a couple of minutes then draw fire so you can locate them."

Kevin looked reluctant, but then nodded his acceptance. He and Pierre swung wide and slowly advanced through the underbrush, moving cautiously. Kevin gave Darcy a final, uncertain look back before he disappeared in the misty gloom.

Once he thought they must be close, Darcy shouted "Hey, assholes. We're fishermen with motor trouble. Why the hell are you shooting at us?"

There was no response, only the rushing of the river and the sound of the wind whipping through the trees overhead.

"We're going to walk up to that cabin now, see if we can get some help," Darcy said, his voice booming through the forest.

Straczynski and Peters looked at each other. In their black tuques and black combat pants and jackets they looked almost like twins. They each held Colt C8 carbines. Except for the grey hair and slight paunches, they looked just like they did back in their police tactical squad days. The only difference, and it was a big one, was that they were operating way outside the law.

"This isn't good," Peters said.

"Think about the $100K," Straczynski said.

"It's a lot of money but it's not worth going to jail over. We were supposed to be backup for Polanco, not players in a fire fight."

"These guys didn't shoot back. They must be unarmed."

"That just makes it worse. What if they are stranded fishermen? There's only so much of Polanco's shit that I'm willing to sweep under the rug."

"What if we fire a few more rounds, lower this time, then retreat toward the cabin, see if Polanco has things under control?"

"If these guys follow, we'd be cutting ourselves off from our boat."

"Polanco has a boat."

"You want to rely on him?"

Straczynski sighed. Peters was no pussy and he had a point. Polanco was a prick to work for and he wouldn't trust him as far as he'd like to throw him. He was ruthless, too. If Polanco committed crimes on this island, he and Peters could be inconvenient witnesses. Turn their backs on him and he'd be likely to shoot them. Still, Straczynski was pissed off. He was going to take that off-the-books hundred grand and buy himself a cabin cruiser. He'd already found one he liked on line.

"Come on Strac," Peters said. "I say we bag it and haul ass. This isn't our fight."

"This all works out the way Polanco wants it, he'll have our asses when we get back to the city."

"Fuck him. He's not the only show in town."

"All right, I'm with you Peters. Let's take that path by the shore, but when we get to the boat, cast it off quietly and let it drift out past the island. At least buy Polanco some time."

Having said that, Straczynski raised his Colt and let loose a volley in the general direction of the so-called fishermen, keeping it high enough not to hurt anybody, but low enough to keep the average guy glued into place.

With the semi-automatic fire ringing in their ears, Peters and Straczysnski hadn't heard the two men come up behind them. Peters was jolted by a rib-cracking blow in the back. He pitched forward and hit his head on a rock. Straczynski heard him grunt, then started to spin around to see what had happened. He saw the massive torso of a black-bearded lumberjack holding an axe in both hands. Even in the dull light, he could see the axe head shine. The worst part was the grin on the guy's face, like he was hoping to use that axe. To the big guy's left was another super-tall freak, this one thinner and carrying a baseball bat.

Straczynski still had his rifle in his hands, but he knew that by the time he could bring it into play, he might not have hands. He laid the gun carefully on the ground and said, "Look, we don't want any trouble."

Then he turned back at the sound of another voice, this one now in front of him. This guy wasn't as big as the other two, but looked just as mean, and somehow familiar.

"Could have fooled me," the guy said, this one the leader, the one who had shouted out.

"We're licensed private investigators," Straczynski said, seeing if maybe he could find some way to talk himself out of this.

"Really?" the guy in front said. "I know a little about that line of work. You're not legally allowed to carry guns, much less shoot them at innocent civilians."

Straczynski couldn't argue with that. "What do you want?" he asked.

"I want you to lie down and kiss the dirt while my friends make sure you aren't going to cause any more trouble. Do it now, arms beyond your backs."

Straczynski didn't like to put himself in that kind of vulnerable position, but it seemed like the least bad option. "Peters, you OK?" he asked.

Peters, already on the ground, grunted in reply, then Straczynski felt a big knee in the middle of his back as the axe man pulled his hands behind his back and secured them with zip ties. Then he pushed Straczynski down and did the same with his feet. The ties were tight, but he wasn't going to moan about it. He'd have done the same thing.

"You have a good day now," the leader said. "You might want to spend some time figuring out how you're going to get off this island. Personally, I just can't see a solution.

"Grab their guns boys. They might come in handy."

Darcy and his men set off toward the cabin, going slowly in case there were any more surprises. He figured it was about half a mile to their destination.

Forty-nine

Polanco reared back in surprise when he saw me charging at him, chair tied to my back. His confusion was only momentary. Just as I reached him, he sidestepped and pulled a gun from a holster on his belt.

Then he pointed it at me, dead centre. I was only six feet from him. If he fired, I would be dead. "This isn't going to work," I said, trying to keep the desperation from my voice.

Behind him, I could see Jenna get to her feet. I was about to shout a warning not to move, but then I saw her plan. She ran backwards as fast as she could. The chair she was tied to smashed into kindling when she hit the cabin's wooden wall.

Polanco took his eyes off me and turned to see what the noise was.

Jenna gasped at the force of the contact, but quickly shrugged the remnants of the chair from her back. The ropes that had tied her to the chair were now loose and she pulled them down and stepped out of them.

Polanco turned back to me, then to Jenna, unsure what to do.

"Shoot them!" Brendan shouted.

Polanco raised his handgun and aimed it at Jenna. I drove desperately at him, trying to hit him low. In my awkward position, all I could do was hit him in the hip, but it was enough to throw him off balance. His shot was deafeningly loud in the cabin, but all it did was blow one of the stuffed ducks off the wall, feathers floating through the air.

Polanco stumbled back and reset himself, but Jenna hadn't wasted the few seconds I had bought her. She rushed at Polanco, then darted left, got behind him and tried to sweep his legs out from under him with a strong sideways motion of her own powerful leg.

Polanco stumbled, but didn't go down. Jenna got in tight behind him and grabbed his left wrist, twisting his arm up behind his back. His gun hand was still free.

"Bitch!" Polanco shouted. He was in agony, but he knew he was in a fight for his life. He spun around, trying to dislodge Jenna from his back, firing wildly again, this time hitting the ceiling.

I looked at Simon, Rob and Brendan, all standing there watching the action unfold. Clinging to my last shred of hope that Simon was on our side, I yelled, "Simon, do something!"

He turned towards me and shook his head sideways, as if trying to clear his mind. Then he said, "Rob, put a stop to this."

Rob Cousens reached behind his back and pulled Alicia's old Smith and Wesson from his waistband. Rob pointed the gun, looking for a target, but Polanco and Jenna were intertwined. There was no safe shot. Polanco stumbled towards the centre of the cabin, Jenna riding on his back, hauling on his left arm and kneeing him in the back and upper thighs.

Polanco didn't go down and now I could see his plan. He was headed toward the woodstove, glowing hot from the fire within. If he got close enough to turn and smash Jenna into the stove, the force of the blow and the burns would take her out.

"Jenna, the stove!" I screamed.

She reacted instantly. Dismounting from Polanco's back, she kept her grip on his left arm, then grabbed the right. Digging in, she propelled him forward with all her force. The stove was only three feet away and when he was almost there, she slipped her leg between his, tripping him forward into the stove. With both of his hands restrained, Polanco was unable to stop himself. He crashed into the stove, then bellowed in pain and tried to rear back from the hot metal.

Jenna kept a grip on his gun hand but released his left arm, then used her own to force his face onto the surface of the stove. Polanco screamed in agony as the extreme heat seared the left side of his face, filling the room with the smell of burning meat.

"Fry, you fucker!" Jenna said.

Polanco waved his right arm frantically in a vain attempt to escape Jenna's grip. He dropped his gun and it skittered across the floor, stopping just in front of Brendan Connor. To my surprise, he bent and picked it up, then pointed the gun at Jenna and said, "Release him," his voice a cold, authoritative bark.

I watched as my daughter looked at Brendan, then back at Polanco. I could see her weighing the odds. Would the gutless little weasel pull the trigger?

"Don't take the chance, Jenna," Alicia said, her voice loud but plaintive. "He'll do it. He's a rat in a corner."

All of us swung our attention to Alicia, momentarily forgotten in the struggle between Jenna and Polanco. She was still securely tied to the chair, having failed to follow Jenna's lead in smashing it into the wall.

Jenna let Polanco loose and he collapsed to his knees in front of the woodstove. The left side of his face looked like it had melted, a liquid mess of red and black. Polanco lifted one hand gingerly towards his face, then recoiled from the pain of the contact.

"Shoot the bitch, Brendan. Shoot them all," he said, his voice slurred.

Brendan looked quickly around the room, now not liking the situation. There were five of us and Rob Cousens was holding a gun. Even an expert killer would have a hard time shooting us all before Rob got him. I doubted that Brendan had ever held a gun before.

"Put the gun down, Brendan. You can still get out of here with your life," Alicia said.

"I can," he said, "but not if the three of you do, too. You've heard me confess what I did."

"It doesn't matter. We couldn't prove anything. We've never been able to prove anything. It would be your word against ours, but it won't come to that. Let us go. I've found out the truth. That's all I ever wanted."

I was sure that was untrue, but it wasn't a bad pitch, under the circumstances.

Brendan turned to Simon and said, "What do you think? Can we get out of one more scrape?"

Simon shook his head, a look of great sadness on his face. "I'm afraid not, Brendan. You're responsible for two people's deaths and you lied to me about it for years. You need to take responsibility."

Brendan's expression was a combination of shock and incredulity. "What are you saying? Are you on their side?"

"I'm afraid so. What you've done is monstrous Brendan. I can't let you walk away, not this time."

"Then why did you capture the three women and confine them here? You've set the stage for us to come out on top, Simon. Don't throw it away now."

"That was all for your benefit Brendan, a little show to give you an opportunity to confess. In fact, I've recorded the whole thing. I'm still recording it now.

"Put the gun down, Brendan, before anyone else gets hurt. I don't want to see you die, but you need to be held accountable."

"You don't want to see me die? Is that the best you can do after all I've done for you? You'd have been nothing without me Simon, just another obscure techie with an idea or two. I'm the one who built our empire."

"You're a deal maker, Brendan. It's true. Now you need to make one more deal. Put it down and let's finish this thing."

"You're asking me to accept 25 years in prison. I'd die in there."

"Quite possibly, but you committed the crime. You've told us all that."

"You bastard!" Brendan shouted, his voice cut with venom. He raised the gun and pointed it at Simon.

Before he could fire, Rob pulled the trigger of Alicia's revolver. The click of the hammer striking a dud round lasted for just a second before Brendan fired Polanco's gun, hitting Rob in the right shoulder and spinning him around. Rob fell to his knees and his gun slid under the woodstove.

The rest of us froze in shock as we realized that Brendan was desperate enough to kill us all.

"Do it," Polanco groaned. "Kill them, kill them now."

Brendan pointed his gun at Jenna, the one most likely to pose a real problem.

"I'm sorry to have to do this," he said.

Then the back door of the cabin slammed open and Darcy charged in carrying some kind of automatic rifle, followed by two other exceptionally tall men, one with a rifle and another with an axe.

Brendan whirled towards the new threat and squeezed off two shots both wild and high.

Darcy let a shot go, close enough to Brandan's head that he flinched as the bullet whizzed by.

"Drop it you little fucker, and get on your knees," Darcy commanded in a firm, deep voice. He advanced across the cabin, the two others flanking him.

My eye caught a flicker of motion in front of the wood stove. It was Polanco, pulling up his right pant leg and pulling a small gun from an ankle holster. Just as he started to struggle to his knees, I yelled, "Darcy, gun."

The huge, bearded guy with Darcy was the first to see the threat. Polanco had the gun about half way up but the giant had reached him in two long strides. He swung the axe through the air in a scything motion, striking Polanco in the wrist.

Polanco let out a single scream, then stared in disbelief at the sight of his hand hanging from his wrist by sinews and tendons. Blood shot up like a fountain from a severed artery. Polanco collapsed face forward onto the floor.

While we all watched the end of Paul Polanco, Brendan Connor took advantage of the moment. He raced out the front door of the cabin and I could see through the window that he was sprinting toward the dock.

 # Fifty

"Don't let him escape. Someone go after him!" Alicia screamed.

Darcy took charge. "Kevin, free the women," he said. "Pierre, come with me."

As Darcy ran toward the door, Simon said, "Brendan doesn't know how to run a boat. He can't go anywhere." Then, "Don't hurt him."

Darcy glanced back at Simon but headed out the door, the bearded giant close behind. Then Simon followed.

"Hurry up," I said to the young guy who was untying the ropes that still held my hands behind me. He fumbled with the ropes for a minute, then I was free.

I rushed out into the pelting, ferocious rain and was immediately soaked to the skin. I raced for the dock, slipping and sliding on the wet, mossy trail, head down as I tried to see the treacherous rocks at my feet. When I looked up, I saw the scene on the dock. Brendan had backed half way up the dock and was looking desperately left and right, trying to see a way to escape. He looked like a wet, cornered rat.

Darcy and Simon had stopped just where the docks began. Even with the rain and the rush of the river, Simon's voice was loud and clear when he said, "Brendan, don't. It's over."

I stopped on the small rise above the dock and watched with a little satisfaction at the desperate situation of the man who was going to let his thug torture us, then throw both of us in the river. He didn't look so sure of himself now, a little man with wet, stringy hair and eyes bulging out of his head. Behind him, the river stormed around the island with an almost unnatural intensity. White frothing water swept by. I saw the carcass of a deer, then it was gone, swept into a foaming vortex.

Simon started to advance slowly down the dock, Darcy hanging back. "Come with me now, Brendan. I'll take care of it. You'll be OK."

"Sorry, Simon," Brendan said, his voice high-pitched, desperate. "I don't believe you."

Then he turned and ran toward Simon's boat. Brendan hadn't taken more than three steps when his city shoes slipped on the wet planks of the dock and he lost his balance. He pirouetted, arms flailing as he tried to save himself. Then his left leg came down onto thin air and Brendan pitched over the edge of the dock.

He disappeared from sight beneath the murky grey waters. Simon ran to the place where Brendan had gone in, peering into the water and calling Brendan's name. Then his friend bobbed to the surface, furiously treading water.

"Thank God," Simon said, kneeling and reaching to grip his hand, pull him out. Brendan struggled to keep his head above water while trying to grab Simon's hand. Although the current was weaker behind the island than it was in the main stream, it was still strong enough to push Brendan back and away from the dock.

Simon leaned even farther out over the water and yelled, "Swim, Brendan, swim this way. Get up to the dock."

Brendan tried a few strokes, but he was still losing ground.

Simon turned to Darcy and said, "Save him. Can you save him?"

I rushed to Darcy's side, grabbed his sleeve and said, "Don't do anything stupid." Then I turned to Simon and said, "Let him go, Simon. You know he deserves it."

"I can't," he shouted, his voice desperate, his habitual control gone.

Brendan had been pushed back beyond the end of the dock now. He waved one arm in the air and said, "Save me, Simon."

Simon jumped in and swam towards Brendan with strong confident strokes. Then he hit the current and was carried rapidly away from the dock.

"Oh for fuck's sake," Darcy said. I heard a sound behind me and saw that Jenna had come running down from the cottage. "You two start the boat, get close to them," Darcy said. "I'll try to keep their heads above water."

Then he jumped in.

I gasped, my heart pounding. It was like the dream I had had, but it wasn't Jenna in the water, it was the man I loved. I realized as I thought it that I'd never said the words. I prayed it wasn't too late.

"Go, go!" I shouted to Jenna.

"You know how to run this thing?"

"Sure," I said, knowing that I was going to have to figure it out in a hurry.

I jumped into the boat as Jenna began to untie it from the dock. Fortunately, Simon had left the key in the boat and I turned it, then heard the engine rumble to life. The controls looked simple enough. Reverse, neutral and forward, all controlled by a long stick shift like something from an old truck.

Jenna clambered in after me and I let the current push the boat away from the dock, then eased it into gear and began to turn the bow into the river.

"Where's Darcy? Do you see him?" I asked.

"Yes, he's doing OK, but he's nowhere near the other two."

I looked through the spray-streaked windshield and tried to plot a course to cut Darcy off. My priorities were clear. It would be too bad if Simon died, but I didn't give a shit about Brendan and I wasn't about to lose Darcy.

"Darcy!" Jenna shouted, straining to be heard over the rushing water. "Swim to the boat."

Either he didn't hear us or he was just determined to do what he could for the other two. I was pretty sure I knew which.

The boat was difficult to manoeuvre in the swirls and cross-currents. I was used to small tiller boats, not something 23 feet long controlled by a steering wheel. Then I hit the main current and the boat was suddenly driven by the thrust of the river, not its own engine.

"Hang on," I said, as I fought with the wheel. Water lapped in over the stern. I knew I should be bow first into this current, but I was afraid that if I tried to turn the boat it would capsize.

"Which way is he?" I asked.

"About 100 feet to our right."

"What about the other two?"

"No sign of them."

Then I saw Darcy, being propelled rapidly by the current. Jenna got to her feet and yelled, "To the right, to the right," gesturing with her arms. She was trying to direct him back into the slower water behind the island.

I was going to have to get as close to him as I could. I didn't think he'd last long in these conditions, the damned, brave fool.

"There's a life ring in the middle of the boat," I said. "Secure it and get ready to toss it when we get within range."

Then I heard a shout to my left, only 50 feet away and saw a long arm waving at me. It was Simon. He and Brendan had come up against a big tree, maybe 75 feet long, that had snagged on something under the water. Simon clung to its bare branches, pulled part way up out of the water, one hand clutching Brendan by the hood of his coat, keeping his head above water, but just.

"They're all right," I said. "Let's get Darcy."

I glanced to the right and saw Darcy trying to swim towards the boat, but making no real headway. Like the logs and bits of timber that were being carried down the river, he wasn't in control of his destiny. I steered the boat in his direction while I quickly calculated how to handle the problem. If I got out in front of him and then swung the boat, it created the risk of him being carried under the boat, plus I wasn't sure how stable the old mahogany cruiser was. It had a broad beam, but it rode high on the water. If we went over, we were all done.

I goosed the motor and started to feel that I had some control. I could see now what had to be done. I would get ahead of Darcy, bring the boat around facing the current, then try to hold steady as he was carried back to us. Jenna would toss him the life ring and haul him in.

I pushed the boat as hard as I could, but it was bouncing and weaving, buffeted by the current flowing around the island. I tried not to think about rocks or underwater logs.

We were close to Darcy now, and Jenna picked up the ring and said, "Let's give it a shot."

"No, we're not close enough. I want to get within 10 feet. Tossing the ring will be like throwing a Frisbee in a wind storm."

"I can do it," Jenna said, then propelled the ring out over the heaving water. It flew true for a few feet, but then the wind caught it and directed it downstream, well out of Darcy's reach.

"Shit," she said. "This isn't going to work. We need to get a lot closer."

"Working on it. Keep your ass down, I don't want you in the

water, too."

I powered the boat 150 feet down the river, then tried to turn the bow back into the current. The boat got half way around, then wallowed and turned back downstream. I could see it was going to take more power than I was comfortable with to make the turn.

"Hold on," I shouted, pushed the throttle, then cranked hard on the wheel. This time we made it. I could just make out Darcy's head above the water, arms working rhythmically as he tried to get closer to us. Darcy was now about 75 feet behind us and with the boat nearly stationary in the water, he was closing fast.

"All right, this is it," I said. "Try to get the ring ahead of him, let him come to it."

All my attention was on Darcy as I fought the current and tried to edge the boat closer to him. I didn't see the log until it was too late.

It hit the boat on the right side with a tremendous thud, causing the boat to stagger and turn sideways, pointing toward Darcy. I hauled on the wheel to straighten the boat out, then heard a wrenching sound as the log let go. I looked down and saw that a heavy branch had punctured the boat's wooden hull and we were taking on water fast.

Jenna had fallen to her knees when I swung the boat, but she was back on her feet now, life ring in hand.

"Darcy, here it comes," she shouted, then hurled the ring in his direction as hard as she could. It landed five feet from him and was swept downstream in an instant.

"I can't get it that far," she shouted, straining to be heard over the wind and current.

I took a deep breath, trying to suppress my panic. I needed to slow down, just for a few seconds, and think. I stole a glance back, trying to see if there was anything else in the boat we could use. Then I saw it. A long boat hook secured to the side of the boat with clips.

"There's a boat hook to your right," I said. "Grab it and get ready. When he's in reach, hook him."

I swung the boat around again. I could already feel that it was getting heavier, harder to handle. Water was gushing through the puncture in its side. This could be our last shot at saving Darcy. I knew I couldn't let the boat sink and lose Jenna, too.

I quickly caught up to Darcy, the boat running parallel to him about 20 feet away. I tried to edge closer but it was like steering a car with flat tires. The water we had taken on and the buffeting of the current made the boat almost impossible to handle. I knew I was now down to luck, not skill.

Then a side current hit us, pushing the boat rapidly toward Darcy.

"Now! This is it!" I shouted.

Jenna leaned as far forward as she could and reached out with the eight-foot pole. Darcy was just in range. The hook snagged in the hood of his coat and she began to pull, working the pole back through her hands. Darcy was starting to come our way when the hook let loose, sending Jenna tumbling backwards. Almost before I could register the problem, she was on her feet again, pole extended. Darcy was six feet away. Jenna pushed the pole forward. Darcy grasped it with one strong arm, then reached around to take it with the other.

""Got him," Jenna said, again hauling back on the pole. Within seconds, she had Darcy up to the side of the boat. He reached up and grabbed the gunwale, but was too exhausted from his ordeal to pull himself over. Jenna hooked her hands under his arms and hauled. It was enough to get his upper body out of the water, allowing him to grab one of the seats and pull himself into the boat.

"Bitch of a day for a swim," he said.

"You stupid ass," I yelled. "None of these people are worth your life."

"No, but I didn't want to let two old men drown. Are they gone?"

"I don't know. Last we saw, they were clinging to a tree half-way back to the island."

Then Darcy saw the hole in the side of the boat. "Shit," he said. "We haven't got much time."

Darcy grabbed a life jacket that was floating in the bottom of the boat. He handed it to Jenna and said, "Stuff this in that hole and keep it there." Then he headed to the back of the boat, looked down and said, "Bilge pump is running but it won't keep up with that. We need to get back to the island as fast as we can. If the water gets high enough it could kill the engine."

"What about Brendan and Simon?" Jenna asked.

"I'll take it near the tree. If they are still there, we'll attempt a rescue. If not, there's nothing more we can do."

We weren't more than 500 feet from the island but the sluggish boat made slow progress against the current. It felt like we were crawling. Every minute felt like 10. Finally, we were in sight of the tree where Brendan and Simon had been snagged.

Simon saw the boat and waved an arm. I could hear his shouts for help even over the noise of the river. I knew I'd be hearing them for the rest of my life if I didn't do something.

"I'm going to try to get them," I said.

Darcy looked down at the water sloshing in the boat and said, "We'll only have one shot. If it doesn't work, we've got to save ourselves."

I didn't reply. There was no need. I plotted a course toward the snagged tree, but it required constant correction as the current pushed the bow of the boat back. Finally, we were within 15 feet of the two men. Simon looked all right, considering, but Brendan was swaying in the current. Simon was keeping Brendan's head above water, but I couldn't tell if he was dead or alive.

"I'm going to bring the boat right up against you," I yelled to Simon. "We'll try to pull you in."

"Take Brendan first. He's in bad shape."

I let the boat drift toward Simon until it was held in place by the current. Jenna and Darcy knelt and reached down into the water, each of them taking one of Brendan's arms. They heaved him up into the boat and Brendan promptly vomited river water, then dragged himself partly upright, leaning on one of the seats. My first thought was to be sorry that he was still alive, but then I remembered that we were keeping him alive so he could spend the rest of his years in prison.

Darcy and Jenna helped Simon into the boat, too. The first thing he noticed was the water flowing in through the puncture. The life preserver that Jenna had shoved into the hole had been pushed free when she rescued the Brendan and Simon

"Thank you. Thank you," Simon said. "That was heroic. Now let's get out of here. This boat is going down."

Fifty-one

I pushed the boat up to full power, the big engine roaring. The boat, overloaded with people and sloshing with water, barely made headway. I glanced at the engine, which was housed in a bulky structure in the centre of the boat. Water was lapping around its base. Surely it wasn't waterproof. Darcy's comment about the water killing the engine was foremost in my mind as I tried to calculate how long it might keep running compared to the time it would take us to reach the dock.

Quickly realizing that I didn't have a clue, I maintained my white-knuckled grip on the wheel and hoped for the best. I couldn't see any alternative. If the engine flooded out, we'd all be swimming for it and having seen what the current had done to Darcy, I didn't think we'd have a chance.

Finally, we closed on the dock; only another 50 feet now. The engine began to splutter and cough. Come on, come on.

With one final surge of the throttle, I ran the boat up against the big white fenders attached to the dock. Jenna scrambled out and I tossed her the ropes to tie the boat up.

Darcy was slumped in the bottom of the boat, exhausted. Simon leaned against the side of the boat, the lower part of his body in the water that was filling the boat. He looked bedraggled and a decade older than he had at the start of the day. Brendan was collapsed against Simon's side, eyes closed. I assumed he was still alive, but I couldn't tell for sure.

"Let's get them out," I said to Jenna. I helped Darcy to his feet and Jenna reached out a hand to steady him.

"It's all right. I've got it," Darcy said, stepping up onto the dock. "Let's get the other two out."

Simon struggled to his feet and lifted the much smaller Brendan up. We each took an arm, then Darcy and Jenna leaned forward and pulled Brendan onto the dock as well. Then Simon accepted a hand up and I clambered out of the boat behind him.

"Your boat is going to sink," I said.

"Yes, but it doesn't matter now. It did its job."

The five of us began to move slowly up the slight hill towards the cottage. Simon was leaning on Darcy for support, and I propped up Brendan, who was mumbling and groaning. "Shut up, you little prick," I said. "You're the reason we are all in this mess."

Brendan didn't reply, but at least he stopped talking. There wasn't much left of the man who had so recently boasted about the unpleasant deaths he had in store for us.

As we got closer to the cabin, the two men that Darcy had brought opened the door and rushed out to help us. I realized that I didn't even know their names. As I handed Brendan over to the big one with the dark beard, I said, "Hi. I'm Kris."

"Pierre. Darcy and I go way back. This other fella is Kevin."

The string bean nodded. He looked young, scared and worried about what he had gotten himself into. I couldn't say that I blamed him.

"What the hell happened out there?" Pierre asked.

"Some of us went for a swim," Darcy said.

Pierre nodded, realizing that the less he knew about this whole situation, the better.

We entered the cottage and there was Paul Polanco, lying dead on the floor. His sightless eyes stared up from his grotesquely burned face and his right arm was stretched out beside him, the hand dangling from the wrist.

"We didn't know what you wanted to do with this guy, Darcy," Pierre said.

Darcy looked at me and said, "What do you think?"

Before I could answer, Simon said, "The river. It's where he would have put us. The current and the rocks will rip up what's left of him. It's the best solution. Does that work for you Alicia?"

I had momentarily forgotten about Alicia, the other reason we were all on this island. She stood back to the wall, arms crossed, surveying all of us with a look of distaste.

"Yes," she said, her voice as cold as the roaring river. "He's the one who killed my parents. Dispose of him and Brendan, too."

"Not Brendan," Simon said. "That wasn't the plan."

"Not your plan, but it was mine."

"Well, that plan has been superseded. We have a recording of Brendan's full confession. His gloating and the fact that three of you were tied up will certainly prevent him from claiming that he was coerced. He's going to jail for what he did, as he ought to."

"I still can't believe you're siding with her over me, Simon," Brendan said.

Simon shook his head in dismay, then turned to Brendan and said, "You still don't get it, do you? You caused the deaths of two people, Brendan, one of them quite dear to me. You ruined Alicia's life. There have to be consequences for that."

"Certainly, I agree. Don't think I haven't felt remorse, regret, guilt, all of those."

Alicia gave a contemptuous snort, then said, "You never regretted any of it for a minute, you lying shit."

I watched the three of them go at each other as Pierre and Kevin looked on in amazement. I assumed that Darcy had not filled them in on the whole sordid story.

Finally, Darcy said, "All right. That's enough of this. Save it for the judge, Brendan. Let's get this done. Boys, we need to drag what's left of this guy down to the river and take care of business."

"I don't know if I want to get any more involved in this," Kevin said, backing away from the rest of us.

"Oh for fuck's sake," Pierre said. "It's done now, lad, but we'll spare you the rest. Darcy, would you grab his feet? I'll take his arms and we'll get this over with."

Before they lifted Polanco, Darcy went over to Kevin and said, "You did well today. I'm proud of you. My advice, forget everything you saw today. Just remember, if this blows up, you're as deep in shit as the rest of us."

Kevin nodded meekly, then said, "I understand, Darcy. I was never here. I didn't see a thing."

"That's the boy," Darcy said. Then he and Pierre struggled to hoist Polanco's body up. I held the cabin door open so they could take him to the river. It wasn't an ideal solution, but it would have to do. I wondered if anyone would miss Polanco. I knew Jenna and I wouldn't.

Then Brendan piped up, thinking he'd found an angle. "I'll have you all charged for his murder," he said.

Simon slapped Brendan across the face hard and said, "Shut up or I'll drag you to the river myself."

Seeing that he didn't have a hope or a friend left, Brendan slumped into a kitchen chair to await his fate.

It didn't take Darcy and Pierre long to deal with Polanco. As they came back into the cottage, dripping wet, Darcy said, "Kris, we ran into a couple of Polanco's people up the island. That's what the gunshots were. They weren't trying to kill us, just doing a job they shouldn't have taken. I'm inclined to let them go, then head back to shore with Pierre and Kevin. If we leave the guys there, they'll die of exposure. Can you and Jenna take it from here?"

I looked at Simon, apparently on our side, the demoralized Brendan and the mercurial Alicia. Each one was a challenge in his or her own way, but yes, Jenna and I could handle them.

"Sure," I said. Jenna knelt down and reached under the wood stove to retrieve the handgun that Rob had tried to use earlier. She said "Just in case there is any trouble," and tucked the gun into her belt.

Rob Cousens had remained silent throughout all of this. His plaid shirt was open and I could see a large patch of gauze where one of the others had dressed his wound. It was still seeping blood.

"Do I get a vote here?" he asked. "I say let's get the fuck off this island now."

No one argued with that, not even Brendan.

"I can run us to the shore in the pontoon boat," Simon said. "It's a bit of a scow, but it will get us there."

"Let's go, then," I said. I gave Darcy a quick hug, then he and his two men left the cottage and headed into the woods.

*　*　*

The pontoon boat bucked and heaved as we headed toward the shore, but even the mighty current of the Ottawa River wasn't going to capsize the broad, stable boat. The rain had finally stopped, but the wind-whipped spray replaced it.

We weren't in danger, though. I began to decompress a bit. In a few minutes, we'd finally be safe.

Simon was at the wheel and Brendan and Alicia were in the

two seats behind him. Cousin Rob was up at the front of the boat, huddled in a tarp. I was keeping an eye on Alicia, to make sure she didn't chuck Brendan overboard, but both were slumped forward, heads down, either to keep the spray out of their faces or, more likely, in their own versions of defeat. Brendan would die in jail, but Alicia hadn't gotten the satisfaction of ending his life. I was happy about that, not because I gave a rat's ass about Brendan, but because killing him would either have destroyed her life or made us all complicit in the crime.

I thought of how far outside the law I had gone in an attempt to avenge the murder of my sister. I couldn't help but empathize with Alicia. She was the victim in this story, even though she was an unpleasant and scheming individual. Still, I would have turned her in if I had to. I wasn't going to be her accomplice and I couldn't let her taint Jenna.

As we plowed slowly toward the shore, I began to wonder what I was going to do with this story. It had developed rather quickly from an intriguing tale about a tech legend who had disappeared and a missing $10 million to a story of murder and revenge decades in the making. Brendan would have to be the centre of any story, but I would need to think about what to do about Simon and I would definitely need to leave out the roles I, Jenna and Darcy had played. It wasn't entirely satisfactory but no story ever told the whole truth. I did know that I would feel compelled to tell as much of it as I could.

The shore was now no more than 30 feet away. I turned to Jenna and said, "You OK?"

She gave a small nod in response. I knew only too well how traumatic the kind of experience we just had could be. Jenna hadn't killed Polanco, but she'd done quite a number on him. I imagined she'd be seeing his hideously burned face in her dreams for a while. It was something we'd need to talk about, but in a warm room with a good bottle of wine.

Simon took the boat upstream of the dock, then reduced power and let the current carry us in. I could see that he was going to take us right into the boat house. He gave the boat just enough throttle to keep us moving forward, bumping along the dock as we went.

Finally, we were in the boathouse and out of the wind, waves and spray. Even though the day was gloomy, the boathouse was dark by comparison. I was momentarily disoriented, but then my eyes began to adjust.

There was a grinding sound as the front of the pontoons hit the back of the boat house, then Simon slumped against the wheel, the relief visible on his tired, haggard face. His plan had worked but I was sure it hadn't gone as smoothly as he would have wanted. Who could have foreseen Brendan falling into the river?

"All right," Simon said, "it's finally over."

"Not quite yet," said a voice from the dark end of the boathouse.

Then I saw the outline of a short, stocky man, and as he stepped toward us I noticed that he had a thick grey beard and was wearing a Tilley hat. The most important detail, though, was the rifle he had pointed at us.

Alicia jumped to her feet, suddenly rejuvenated, and said, "Uncle Alex!"

"Just as promised. Where's the other one?"

"Dead."

"Glad to hear it."

I heard Jenna say, "Shit," in a low tone.

So Alicia had come up with a fail-safe, in case Brendan and Polanco didn't die on the island. Then it hit me. This had been her plan all along. Alex would take out whoever survived the ordeal on the island, then he and Alicia would walk away, probably with Brendan's $10 million. I had totally misread Alex Jameson. He hadn't registered as a threat at all when I met him in Kanata.

The question was, would he have the guts to carry it out? Not everyone could shoot five people in cold blood, but Brendan was behind the killing of Jameson's beloved sister, not to mention the ten million other reasons he might have.

Simon held up his hand like he was stopping traffic, then calmly said, "Alex Jameson. I remember you from the wedding. I wasn't expecting to see you here today."

"I'll bet you weren't," Jameson said, his voice gruff and aggressive. "Don't think you can talk your way out of your own role in all of this. You seduced my sister, threatened her marriage then dropped her when someone else caught your fancy. You are a swine, sir."

Simon nodded and shrugged apologetically. "It's true Alex, I can be a swine, but I had nothing to do with Eve's death. Brendan Connor was behind the whole thing. I've recorded his complete confession. I'd be happy to show it to you."

Alex turned his gaze briefly to Alicia and said, "Is that true?"

"No. The two of them have cooked up that story together. They had me tied to a chair. I was lucky to escape with my life. This so-called confession is never going to see the light of day, and even if it does, Brendan will have the best lawyers money can buy.

"If we want justice, Uncle Alex, now's the time. This is our moment, the one we've been waiting for."

Then Alicia jumped nimbly from the boat to the floor of the boathouse. To clear Alex's field of fire, I realized.

"Wait a minute," I said. "I understand why you want revenge. I would, too, but Jenna Martin and I aren't part of this Brendan and Simon thing. We're only here because we are trying to help Alicia."

"It's true," Alicia said, "you both proved to be very useful, but I'm afraid our arrangement is over. Brendan and Simon are going to die, and so is Cousin Rob. I'd like to spare you two, I would, but I can't ask Alex to kill three people and leave two witnesses alive. It's simply not logical. Sometimes, life's just a bitch."

I couldn't argue with that so I took a different tack. "It's about the money, isn't it Alicia? It always has been. You've got the $10 million and with everyone dead, it's free and clear. Admit it."

"No, you're wrong. It's about avenging my parents' deaths. The money is simply a bonus, a little compensation for the money these two made on the idea they stole from my father."

I saw Simon edging forward toward his cousin, trying to create space between Alex's targets, to give one of us time to react. Unfortunately, Alex saw it, too.

"Stay right there, Simon. None of your tricks."

"My cousin is wounded, shot trying to stop Polanco. He saved Alicia. He will bleed to death if we don't get him medical help."

"That's too bad," Alex said. "I have nothing against your cousin, but he's in the wrong place at the wrong time."

"Enough talking," Alicia snapped. "Do it, Alex. Shoot them all. Now!"

Alex swung his weapon around and pointed it at Brendan, who

raised his hands in front of him in a pathetic attempt to protect himself. "Look, it was me, all me. Let the rest of them go."

"Too late," Alicia said. "You can add their deaths to your total."

The interchange between Brendan and Alex had given Jenna just enough time and distraction to reach behind her back and pull out Alicia's revolver.

"Drop the gun," she barked in her commanding police voice. "Do it now or I'll shoot."

Alicia's face contorted in fury at this one last attempt to thwart her plan. "Don't listen to her, Alex. The gun doesn't work. It was Dad's. The ammunition is old. It's misfired once already."

Alex hesitated, not sure what to do. I knew Jenna would like to fire a shot into the air, to make her point, but what if the gun really didn't work?

"She's right," Jenna said. "The gun has misfired once. I've got five more cartridges in the cylinder. You want to bet your life that they're all duds?"

From the look on Alex's face, I could see that he was doing a quick calculation, but the odds were unknowable.

"Maybe this isn't the best approach Alicia," he said. "Why don't we just leave, take the money and start a new life, like you said?"

"What about your sister, my mother? Are you going to leave her murder unavenged? Be a man, Alex."

Then Alex decided to be a man, a smart man. He began to lower the gun. When it was around his waist, Alicia reached out and grabbed it.

Jenna was already on the move, out of the boat in two strides, then on Alicia who swung the rifle in an attempt to stop her. Jenna ducked, locked both hands on the gun and drove the butt into Alicia's forehead. Stunned, Alicia collapsed to her knees. Alex Jameson quickly followed, cowering on his knees with his hands behind his head.

Alicia looked up at Jenna and screamed in wordless frustration. Jenna looked down and said, "Hey Alicia, like you said. Sometimes life's just a bitch."

 # Fifty-two

I leaned back against Darcy and watched our campfire flicker. It was almost dusk on a small, nameless lake just outside Algonquin Park. The outlines of hemlock and yellow birch trees were like black fingers against the faint red glow of the departed sun. The day had been hot, but the mid-September evening was cool.

Once everything was done, including my book about what happened in Madawaska Mills, we had come north, portaging into this little lake that Darcy said he had been coming to for years. We'd been in camp a week, maybe we'd stay another week but I wasn't counting the days. We had shut out the world, turned it off and focused on ourselves. In the morning, we would make love, then fish for trout that I cooked on the open fire. In the afternoon, we'd start to drink, sharing wine right from the bottle. Then it was skinny dipping and more sex.

Slowly, I had felt myself decompress and drift into a simple state of being that I had always imagined possible, but had never attained.

"What do you want to do tomorrow?" I asked.

"Same as today," Darcy replied. "In fact, let's just go with the same plan every day until it gets so cold that we have to stop."

I nodded in agreement, knowing that we'd be leaving his little paradise long before that. My book writing leave was up and I had a job to return to at the paper, assuming I wanted to return. I wasn't sure that I did.

Collaborating with Jenna on the Simon and Alicia case had been far more rewarding than my usual routine of working the courts and police for three columns a week. I was good at it, but I'd done it most of my adult life. Maybe it was time for a new challenge.

"Do you find yourself thinking about it?" I asked. "I mean all the stuff we went through with Alicia, Simon and Brendan."

"Sometimes, but I'm good at putting the past behind me, where it belongs."

That wasn't one of my gifts. I divided my time almost equally between the past and the future. This stay on the lake was the exception. I was living in the moment and I could see the clarity of that approach. Intellectually, I knew that I couldn't control the future or change the past, but old habits die hard.

I thought of Alicia and how the past had destroyed her future. After Jenna had disarmed Alex Jameson at the boathouse, Alicia still had a chance to walk away. She hadn't committed any crimes, or at least not any that she was likely to be charged for. It looked like she was going to do it, too, until Brendan made his play.

Looking back now, I wondered why I had ever thought Brendan would meekly accept his guilt after a lifetime of denying it. I should have been skeptical but not even the biggest skeptic would have foreseen how slippery Brendan would prove to be.

He had caught, or more likely created, a major break. Simon had gone to the police with the video recording as promised and an investigation had begun. Although I wasn't officially back at work I got an exclusive hit on that story, but only a few weeks later, the police announced that the memory stick holding the video recording had become damaged while in their possession. The video of Brendan admitting his guilt was destroyed. I wondered how much that convenient development had cost him.

It was enough for Brendan's lawyer, the redoubtable Ben Bernstein, to start disassembling the Crown's case before it even got to court. The centrepiece of the plan was to offer an alternative narrative. The facts would show, Bernstein said, that Paul Polanco had acted alone when he killed John and Eve Tarrant all those years ago. The story was supported by a suicide note that had been discovered at Polanco's office by one of his colleagues, one I was sure was hoping to succeed him as Brendan's go-to fixer. It was an eloquent story of remorse, certainly not something Polanco could have written, but without a body, the suicide sounded plausible, and no one who had witnessed Polanco's death was in a hurry to come forward.

I knew that the story wasn't true, but in court it didn't matter what was true. What you could prove decides a case. Brendan

Connor was likely to escape conviction, despite his guilt. Then, Brendan decided to push it too far. He held a media availability in front of the courthouse to defend what he liked to call his good name.

Thinking ahead to my next true crime book, I was there for the performance, hoping that he would see me and my knowledge of the truth would deter him, but it didn't in the slightest. His statement was carefully scripted, theatrical and even credible, if you didn't know anything about the man.

Brendan's face had the smirk of a poker player who has just won a big pot with a pair of deuces, but the look didn't last long. He was the first to notice Alicia coming up behind the media throng. He faltered in mid-sentence and we all turned to see what had disturbed him. It was Alicia, looking just like she had when I had first met her with her black power suit, heels and long red hair flowing free. The only thing different was the gun she carried in her right hand. It wasn't the old revolver that belonged to her father. Jenna had taken care of that. This new gun was a Glock, dark, menacing and effective.

The reporters and I all backed away from her, leaving no barrier between Brendan and Alicia.

"You had my parents murdered, you lying shit. Admit it," she said, her voice cracking with anger.

Cameras swung Alicia's way and other journalists pulled out their cell phones and started recording. No one ran to get help.

"I certainly did not," Brendan said. "This woman is a con artist who tried to defraud me of $10 million in a blackmail scheme. The whole thing is a figment of her deranged mind."

I had been impressed by his bravado. I would have expected him to drop to his knees and beg. Maybe Brendan had started to believe his own bullshit.

Alicia did look deranged, her beautiful face transformed into an angry mask. That didn't stop her from raising the Glock and firing three shots into Brendan's chest. The first two staggered him, the third knocked him flat.

Some of the reporters were screaming now and a police constable came racing out the doors of the courthouse, weapon drawn. Alicia knew her time was running out. She stepped forward and pointed her gun at the prone Brendan, who had just enough strength left to raise his arms in a feeble attempt at self-defence.

"Burn in hell you bastard!" she said, then shot him between the eyes.

By this time the constable had reached the scene and he pointed his weapon, shouting "Drop the gun! Do it now!"

Alicia gently lowered the gun to the ground, then laid face down on the concrete sidewalk. She'd probably seen people do that on TV. The constable kicked the gun away, then cuffed her hands behind her back just as three more cops came rushing up.

Alicia's trial was still pending. Simon was covering the costs of her defence. It was a slam-dunk first-degree conviction unless she could prove diminished mental capacity. I thought it was going to be an uphill fight. The likeliest outcome for Alicia was 25 years in prison. She'd be about 60 when she got out.

There was going to be a hell of a book in all of this, once her trial was complete. I was still weighing whether I could write it, given the direct role Jenna and I had played.

"You're lost in thought," Darcy said. "What's up?"

"Just thinking about Alicia and the day she killed Brendan."

"Come on, Kris. Why are you thinking about that stuff? We came up here to get away from all of that."

"I know, sorry. It's just the injustice of everything that happened to her."

"I thought you didn't even like her."

"I don't, but I understand revenge. It can make good people do crazy things."

I still hadn't told Darcy the whole story of my quest to avenge my sister Kathy's death. I felt he'd understand it, but I was still worried that it would make him see me differently.

"Do you think she was crazy or was she standing up for her parents?"

"Oh, I know she's not crazy. Her whole life was dedicated to creating a situation where she could finally avenge their deaths. She didn't plan for it to end like it did, but all her cleverness was for nothing once Simon got involved."

"What do you think about him, in the end?"

"He's a complicated man. He's a chameleon who has reinvented himself so many times that there is no way to know who the real person is. I'm not sure even he knows."

"He tried to do the right thing in the end, though."

"I think so. Hey, did I tell you about his latest romance?"

Darcy laughed. "Jesus, another? He's had like five wives, four divorced him and the latest one is going to prison. Now he's back at it?"

"Yes he is, and I have to say I'm surprised. He's taken up again with Margaret Radmore, his first wife. Apparently they reconnected when he was hiding out at her house. Now, she *is* his first love and the mother of his children, so it probably makes more sense than anything he's done since leaving her, but still, I wouldn't have predicted it."

"OK, maybe I can see it for him, but what about her? Money?"

"No, Margaret is well set. She's a full professor at Carleton and she'll retire soon on a nice pension, I'm sure. Besides, it's unclear just how much money Simon still has. Alicia told us that he was so short of cash that he couldn't come up with his $10 million share of that project she was pushing."

"Imagine being that broke."

"Yeah, I know, it's all relative. He must have some money, though, because Alicia's defence will be high six figures or more."

"Speaking of money, was that missing $10 million ever found?"

"No, but either Simon or Alicia has it. I'm betting it's Simon. I'm good with it either way. It's not like Brendan is going to need it."

"What an unmitigated little shit that guy was. Cruel, cowardly and egocentric."

"But most important, dead."

"I'm sure he won't be missed."

"No. I'll never forget what happened at his funeral."

"The former wife, Paula, right?"

"Yes, now that one is crazy. As you know, I went to the funeral, thinking of it as a scene for the book. I was surprised to see Paula there because she hated Brendan, but as the ex-wife she was able to persuade the funeral director to let her throw some dirt on the coffin. Instead, she reached into the big purse she was carrying and pulled out a bag of dog shit, which she dumped right onto the coffin. It created quite a scene. No one knew what to do, but it quickly became obvious that there were no volunteers to climb into the grave and clean it up, so they went ahead with the rest of the dirt. Brendan will spend eternity under a pile of dogshit."

"Seems about right."

Darcy got up and picked up a couple of pieces of wood that he fed into the campfire. Then he came back and settled in beside me again. "What about Jenna?" he asked. "She went through a lot again in this case, so soon after what happened up in Madawaska Mills. You think she's OK?"

"It's hard to tell. I wouldn't say that Jenna is ready to share her innermost thoughts with me, not yet anyway. Are you doing any better with her?"

"No, worse if anything. She treats me like an uncle she doesn't know that well. She's friendly, but I wouldn't say that I really know who she is."

"She didn't treat you like an uncle when she fished you out of that river. She'd do anything for you, Darcy."

He nodded, then said, "Maybe we just need to give her more time. After all, we've been missing in action almost her entire life. She doesn't know us yet, not fully."

"Do you ever know another person totally?"

Darcy thought about that one for a minute, then said, "No, I think we know some combination of what the other person wants us to see and what we want to see in them."

"And what do you want to see in me?"

Darcy turned to me and grinned at the straight line. "Surely you must know by now."

"Maybe you'll have to show me."

Darcy stood up, took my hand and led me toward the tent. I followed him willingly and felt like I'd follow wherever he led for a long time to come. In that moment, I saw with perfect clarity that I'd attained something I never thought I would have. I'd had affairs, infatuations and fond relationships, but I'd never had real love with a man who I knew in my heart was the one. Now I did.

ABOUT THE AUTHOR

RANDALL DENLEY is the author of four Kris Redner mysteries, including *Payback*, which was nominated for the Crime Writers of Canada Award for best crime novel set in Canada. He lives in Ottawa and is a political columnist for the *Ottawa Citizen* and the *National Post*. Find out more at randalldenley.com.